Praise fo[r]

D0355940

"One of America's best writ[ers]... [News]

"Besides a fine spinner of tales, Mike Blakely is a poet and a musician at heart, which makes his narrative sing and his unusual characters dance their way through the epic story of the changing West."
> —Elmer Kelton, seven-time Spur Award and three-time Western Heritage Award winner

"Painstakingly researched and carefully written, the novel is an obvious labor of love that merits comparison with such established classics as *Bury My Heart at Wounded Knee, Little Big Man,* and *Hanta Yo.*" —*Booklist* on *Comanche Dawn*

"A well-made novel can sometimes inform a reader far better than documents of history. *Comanche Dawn* is such a novel."
> —Dee Brown, author of *Bury My Heart at Wounded Knee*

"Funny, suspenseful, and affecting."
> —*Publishers Weekly* on *Come Sundown*

"*Come Sundown* is a marvelous book, full of action, color, and meaning. . . . Read it for its insight—*and* for its gripping story."
> —David Nevin, author of *Dream West*

"*Come Sundown* is great fun, witty, and highly believable. . . . Blakely is deservedly among the top Western authors working today." —*True West*

Forge Books by Mike Blakely

The Last Chance
Shortgrass Song
Too Long at the Dance
Spanish Blood
Dead Reckoning
The Snowy Range Gang
Comanche Dawn
Come Sundown
Forever Texas
Moon Medicine

SUMMER
OF PEARLS

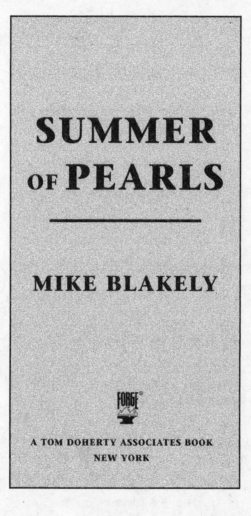

MIKE BLAKELY

A TOM DOHERTY ASSOCIATES BOOK
NEW YORK

SUMMER OF PEARLS

Copyright © 2000 by Mike Blakely

A Forge Book
Published by Tom Doherty Associates, LLC
175 Fifth Avenue
New York, NY 10010

www.tor-forge.com

Forge® is a registered trademark of Tom Doherty Associates, LLC.

Library of Congress Cataloging-in-Publication Data

Blakely, Mike.
    Summer of pearls / Mike Blakely.
        p. cm.
    "A Tom Doherty Associates book."
    ISBN-13: 978-0-7653-2257-9
    ISBN-10: 0-7653-2257-9
    1. Texas—Fiction. I. Title.

PS3552.L3533 S86 2000
813'.54—dc21

                                                    00-034722

First Hardcover Edition: September 2000
First Trade Paperback Edition: December 2008

Printed in the United States of America

0 9 8 7 6 5 4 3 2 1

Dedicated to the memory of my
grandfather, Jim B. Blakely,
1906–2000

AUTHOR'S NOTE

Between 1850 and 1910, a series of "pearl rushes" occurred from New Jersey to Texas and from Florida to Wisconsin. In some isolated areas, for mysterious reasons, freshwater mussels produced unusually high numbers of pearls. These local discoveries led to small-scale economic booms for some rural communities as working families enjoyed the treasure-hunting aspects of opening mussels in search of pearls. Most pearl rushes lasted for a year or two at best, as local mussel populations were depleted.

One of the last pearl rushes occurred in 1910 at Caddo Lake, on the Texas-Louisiana border. For this novel, however, I have created a fictitious pearl boom set in 1874 in the dying riverboat town of Port Caddo, Texas, on Caddo Lake. Port Caddo, now a ghost town, was a viable community until railroads preempted the riverboat trade in East Texas.

The Great Caddo Lake Pearl Rush did not occur in 1874, as this novel suggests. All characters in this story are fictitious, and none is based on any particular historical figure. I have, however, attempted historical accuracy in all else, including the riverboat trade, the freshwater pearl industry, life in Port Caddo, and the clearing of the Great Raft by government snag boats. If the Caddo Lake pearl boom had started in 1874 instead of 1910, it might have happened this way. . . .

SUMMER
of PEARLS

PROLOGUE

Goose Prairie Cove
Caddo Lake, Texas
1944

To understand the summer of pearls, you must hold the tears of angels in your hand, and know what made those angels cry. You must realize that for every ten thousand moons, only one reveals itself through a rainbow.

I talk crazy when folks ask me about that summer, but if you'll listen long enough, it'll all make sense. It's like the murky floodwaters of this lake, or the morning shade of a cypress brake up some twisted bayou. It's dark and confusing until you stay with it long enough; then it comes clear.

It has taken me a lifetime to absorb everything that happened here in the summer of 1874. I was a youngster of fourteen then. I am a youngster of eighty-four now. You've probably heard there was a lot of killing that summer—the summer of pearls. But there was a lot of living, too. The boilers blew on the *Glory of Caddo Lake*. Gold and silver and pearls circulated like schooling fish. A Pinkerton man shot two outlaws aboard the *Slough Hopper*, and I kissed my first girl.

Some folks say I killed Judd Kelso that year. They say I stabbed him in the chest with a butcher knife. I let folks believe what they will. I am the only one who knows the truth anymore. All the others are dead and gone.

At the time, nobody really cared who killed Kelso anyway. By the end of that summer, just about everybody in Port Caddo *wanted* him dead. Nobody cared to find the killer, except maybe to give him a medal, or a key to the city or something. Of course, a key to the city wouldn't have been worth much, seeing as how Port Caddo barely rated as a village, much less as a city, and would soon be nothing more than a ghost town.

Port Caddo was a riverboat town at the dawn of the age of iron horses. Marshall, the county seat, already had a rail line that went to Louisiana. The Texas & Pacific had plans to build on to that road and make Marshall a major eastern terminal. Railroads could move stuff faster and cheaper than riverboats could, and Port Caddo was not situated well for a railroad, perched as it was at the edge of Big Cypress Bayou, just above Caddo Lake. The railroads were going to be the death of her, and everybody in town knew it.

My pop pretended not to know. That was his job. As editor of the *Port Caddo Steam Whistle*, he was the town's most active booster. In his editorials he kept coming up with schemes designed to keep Port Caddo alive after the railroads took away the riverboat trade.

"We must hold a county bond election to fund a narrow-gauge line from Port Caddo to Marshall," I heard him say one day in the barbershop. "It will link us with the main rail lines."

But few county residents cared to pay to keep our town alive.

Pop also suggested Port Caddo promote itself as a resort town, with duck-hunting clubs, fishing camps, and steamboat excursions on Caddo Lake. "Just think of the folks coming here to line our pockets with money from as far away as Memphis and Little Rock," he told the butcher once in church.

But not many folks had money to burn at resorts that soon after the fall of the Old South and the ruination of the plantation economy. Oh, Pop came up with a lot of wild ideas for the town, and people humored him for doing his job, but we all knew the town was doomed.

I was a boy then, and couldn't stand to think of Port Caddo dying. I still remember the sounds of the steamboat whistles and all those valves and engines hissing hot vapor. I could hear them from the Caddo Academy where I took my lessons. Our teacher, Mr. Diehl, would have fits trying to hold us boys in class when a boat was calling at our stretch of bayou.

Port Caddo was heaven on earth for boys. The steamers would whistle at us when we were out on the lake fishing or fixing up our duck blinds. In summer, all the boys in town turned amphibious and could swim like alligators. On the farms and timber lots, which started just outside of town, we could hunt squirrels, rabbits, hogs, and deer in any patch of woods without even having to ask the owners. All the land was private, but the woodlands were treated as free range then and people just let hogs and boys run wild in them. I knew a thousand secret places in the uplands, and about a million more out in the cypress brakes of Caddo Lake.

Looking back on it after all these years, I forget about the mosquitoes, the water moccasins, the odor of dead fish, and the suffocating summer heat. I can only remember the aroma of pines on the hills, the flat-bottomed hull of my bateau bumping against the cypress knees, and the cool waters of Caddo Lake always at my feet.

Just because the place was heaven for us boys, it doesn't mean it was exactly hell for anybody else, either. Even womenfolk liked it. It was tolerably civilized. A stretch of the main street leading up from the wharf was paved with bricks. We had churches for Methodists, Baptists, Episcopalians, and Presbyterians. Old Jim Snyder ran a store, well-stocked, and Widow Humphry kept a first-rate inn for a town as small as ours. We didn't have a doctor, but as my pop used to say, "We have the healthiest climate in the world. Why the devil would we need a doctor?" We numbered about four hundred souls and everybody knew everybody else's business. Ours was just a podunk backwater bayou town, but we could get anything in the world. The riverboats linked us to New Orleans.

I couldn't tell you how many steamers plied Caddo Lake back then.

I never took the time to count them. They came up the Mississippi from New Orleans, entered the mouth of the Red River and steamed past Alexandria to Shreveport.

There they had to find a channel around the Great Raft—the huge logjam that held back the waters of the bayous. The government snag boats worked for years trying to clear the Raft, but every time they carved a channel through the tangle of driftwood, a flood would come along and plug the channel again with trees washed down from upstream.

"Those snag boats are a sin and a waste of taxpayers' money!" my father would rail. "God put the Great Raft there, and when He wants it gone, He'll wash it away. The government has no business playing God!"

To get around the Raft, some steamer pilots came up Cross Bayou, through Cross Lake. Others took the Twelve Mile Bayou route. It depended on where they could find the deepest water. The channels shifted constantly.

Once around the Great Raft and across Albany Flats, the riverboats entered that ancient enigma called Caddo Lake. I have lived by her waters my whole life, and she still hasn't let me in on all of her secrets. She hides things in her muddy waters. Her murky bed swallows all kinds of property. Boats sink and leave no trace. People disappear in her mossy cypress brakes and never come back. Snakes and alligators populate her bayous and sloughs, but they represent little danger. The real killer is the lake herself. You must respect her and suspicion her every little ripple and undercurrent. The moment you trust her, she'll rise up and suck you under like a twig.

Caddo Lake sprawls across the Texas–Louisiana border, like a crazy ink blot, and backs up into a thousand sluggish bayous and still-water coves. She has a lot of open water in her middle, but thickets fringe her shores, islands, and shallow swamps. Huge cypress trees, taller than Roman columns of stone, stand in the water and grip the lake bed. Their roots come up as if for air, bulbous nodules called cypress knees. The branches overhead intertwine and grow bundles of Spanish moss like beards and mustaches. They shut out the sun, channel the wind, and lead the innocent explorers astray with a dark and mesmerizing beauty.

If you want to come home from the cypress brakes, you have to use the wind, the water currents, and the sun. You have to know which sides of the trees the moss grows on in each thicket. You have to know which way the birds fly to feed, and where the snapping turtles go to sun. If you know all that, you might still get lost. If you don't know any of it, the lake owns your corpse as soon as you stray from open water.

But the old steamboats stuck to the open channels, and the pilots knew them well. The water ran shallow in some places, and during the driest months of late summer, the steamers couldn't get into Caddo Lake at all. The trade usually lasted eight months out of the year. From July until some time in October, we didn't see many steamers at Port Caddo. But when the fall rains came and the lake rose again, our little town emerged out of the dog days like a blooming rain lily.

"Spruce up!" my pop would write in his editorial. "The steamers are coming! Pull the weeds and paint the privy!"

Our steamers were small, shallow-draft workhorses for the most part. We didn't have the huge floating palaces like those that plied the Mississippi. Most of ours were stern-wheelers built to handle freight. Side-wheelers were built for wide waters. Our bayous and channels were narrow. Our stern-wheelers carried out a lot of cotton and corn, burned plenty of pinewood, and brought back boxes and barrels of all sorts of things from New Orleans. They also took passengers, of course. We were just two weeks from New Orleans by steamer.

Port Caddo had a favorite riverboat, and her name was the *Glory of Caddo Lake*. Captain Arnold Gentry—as big a local hero as ever walked the streets of Port Caddo—was her owner, builder, captain, and pilot. I can still call his long, spare frame and his gangling gait to mind. He grew pointed mustaches and had a narrow strip of beard on his chin.

Captain Gentry had designed the *Glory* specifically for the Caddo Lake trade. She was the fastest, cleanest, fanciest boat that ever moored in Big Cypress Bayou. She measured a hundred feet and was in the hundred-and-fifty-ton class.

Whenever she steamed into Port Caddo, the *Glory* reminded me of a four-tiered wedding cake, frosted with white paint and trimmed with so much gingerbread work that her carpenters must have worn out a hundred jigsaw blades putting her together. She drew only eighteen inches light, and could get out of the lake, fully loaded, in less than four feet of water. Her five-note steam whistle used to shiver me from the backbone out, and pump adrenaline through my legs like steam through a boiler pipe as I ran to the docks to meet her.

Captain Gentry maintained the *Glory* as a smaller version of the finest Mississippi packets ever to run between New Orleans and St. Louis. The tops of her tall black chimneys were notched and splayed to resemble huge crowns. The smokestacks had hinges. They could fold down to rest along the hurricane deck so the boat could get up under the cypress boughs in the tight places. Captain Gentry could call at almost any plantation or wood camp on the lake.

For a figurehead, the *Glory* used a beer keg, tapped with a silver spigot extending over the bow. "She draws so light," I once heard Captain Gentry boast in his classic Southern riverboat drawl, "that I can get over the driest sandbar by opening that beer spout and floating on the suds!"

I remember like it was yesterday the last call the *Glory of Caddo Lake* made to our little bayou town. It was the day her boilers blew. The day Captain Gentry died. The same day the stranger, Billy Treat, became our new town hero. That was in June of 1874, and all anybody could talk about were the railroads and the sure fate of Port Caddo. Then Billy Treat came and gave us one last stab at splendor before the town died.

That was the fabulous summer of pearls—a time of great wonder, joy, and hope; of deep tragedy and ruin. When it was all over, Captain Gentry and Judd Kelso weren't the only ones dead. I will tell you about it. The parts I lived I will tell from my own experience. The other parts, the pieces I have put together over the decades, I will tell to you as a story. I have studied over it and thought about it—and even dreamed of that summer—for a lifetime. Even the parts I didn't witness with my own eyes, I can tell with true conviction, for I know what happened.

I guess the mystery over who killed Kelso that night in 1874 will live on forever with some folks, regardless of the truths I am about to unfold. As I said, I'm the only one who knows the truth for sure. I'm the only soul left around here who even remembers the summer of pearls, seventy years ago. I know what happened. I remember it well.

Port Caddo, Texas
1874

JUDD KELSO FELT AS IF HE HAD JUNE BUGS IN HIS STOMACH. HE STOOD AT the stern of the *Glory of Caddo Lake*, staring into the muddy waters.

The bayou lay dark and flat as ink in a well. Strange silhouettes of moss and cypress towered around its fringes, raking the dying stars. A pale yellow light reached into the sky from the east, defining the dark, angular shapes of Port Caddo squatting among the pines.

Kelso set his jaw, his facial muscles writhing like animals under his beard stubble. He listened to the sounds of men throwing wood into the furnace, the boat creaking under her load of cotton bales, the cook clanging his skillet down onto his wood-burning stove. He smelled bacon and coffee he knew no one would have a chance to eat or drink. The June bugs crawled in his stomach, and he turned around to study the riverboat.

The *Glory of Caddo Lake* sat low in the water, her first two decks encased in bales of cotton. A buyer in Jefferson had held the cotton in a warehouse for almost a year, waiting for prices to climb at the cotton exchange in New Orleans. Each bale was worth a few pennies more now, and was on its way to market. Captain Arnold Gentry had taken on as much as the *Glory* could handle, careful not to swamp her. She was drawing four feet, but the lake was high and the *Glory* would skim the shoals and plow through the sandbars that lay between her and deep water.

The rousters had stacked bales all the way to the ceiling on the main deck, leaving labyrinth-like passages to the engine room. Then they had stacked more bales on the boiler deck. Cotton completely filled the promenade around the staterooms, blocking the doorways, shutting out the light. The passengers could only enter their rooms now from the doors inside the passenger cabin.

Up the bayou, in Jefferson, Kelso had mused over all the work the rousters put into loading and stacking those bales—bales he knew would never reach New Orleans. He had felt a dark power. Now all he felt were the legs of bugs crawling in his guts.

As the first light of dawn struck the high tops of the cypress trees, the whistle blew. Four notes stepped off harmony as they climbed the scale, then a fifth shook windows as it struck an octave below. Roosters croaked feeble replies. Twin columns of smoke boiled from the chimneys and merged high in the morning air. Cords of pine stood on the foredeck, in front of the furnace. Captain Gentry rang the bell, signaling the engineer to throw open the valves and set the big paddle wheel to work.

Judd Kelso felt the nervous flutter in his stomach surge as he walked forward through the narrow passages left between the cotton bales. "You heard the bell," he said to his apprentice as he reached the engine controls. "Back her into the channel."

The apprentice, seventeen-year-old Reggie Swearengen, cracked the valves and fed steam to the twin engines. The riverboat shuddered as the blades of the paddle wheel dipped into Big Cypress Bayou. The *Glory* backed slowly away from the Port Caddo wharf to the pop and hiss of exhaust valves, rippling the inky bayou.

"Listen for the bells," Kelso ordered as he left the engine room at the stern. "I'm goin' forward."

"Yes, sir," Reggie replied.

Kelso was engineer and mate on the *Glory*. As engineer, he was barely competent, and he knew it. He had little experience with steam machinery. His apprentice had a much better knack for it than he did. He knew just enough about mechanics to keep the steam engines stroking. His real value came in his capacity as mate.

At bossing rousters, Kelso knew he had few equals. The deckhands were muscled-up black men whose scowls alone might wither a timid man. It was Kelso's job to work them as long and as hard as he could without killing them. He gave them no rest when there was work to do taking on freight or fuel, stoking the furnace, or winching the boat over shoals. This was his real job, and he liked it. He thought of the men as little better than animals, and treated them as such.

Kelso stood stump-like in build, shorter than six feet, but weighing over two hundred pounds. His jaws rippled constantly with ridges of muscle as he ground his teeth smooth. The rousters said he had gator eyes—mean little beads set at a slant under the ledges of his bony brow. No one on board liked him, but Captain Gentry knew his worth as a driver of men.

Kelso's father had worked as overseer at a big Caddo Lake plantation before the war. Judd had grown up learning where to poke a man to hurt him without ruining him. He remembered watching his father taunt black slaves with a whip. He remembered that same whip stinging him at times. It had made him tough. That's what he told himself. He took pride in meanness, considered it a strength. When rousters fought on his boat, he thought nothing of splitting their scalps with four-foot-long wedges of cordwood. He was worse than his old man in that respect. In his father's time, black men had held value as property. As far as Judd Kelso knew, they were worthless now.

He grabbed the iron capstan bar as he left the engine room and walked forward along the dark corridors formed by the bales of cotton. The majestic old boat creaked and moaned as she backed slowly into the bayou under him. In spite of the June bugs that continued to crawl, Kelso wore a smile on his face. He was going to have a little fun with the stokers.

He found the firemen standing back from the furnace, four-foot lengths of pinewood in their hands.

"Give me fire, damn it! Don't just stand there!"

The black men looked at each other. "She's hot, Mister Judd," one of them said.

"Oh, she is?" Kelso waited until the man turned his face away, then jabbed him hard with the capstan bar, between his rib cage and hip. The black man buckled, and the others reluctantly threw their billets of wood into the furnace.

"Get up, boy!" Kelso said to the injured man. "Stoke the fire! Damn you to tell me she's hot. You ever heard of a nigger engineer? I'm the engineer on this boat, and I want steam."

The stokers chucked in more fuel as the roar of the fire grew. Kelso knew they were hoping he would just go away.

"If you don't want to do your job, I can boot your black asses over the guards right now. I guess it wouldn't make much difference. Your jobs are all goin' to shit anyway."

The stokers glanced at each other and scowled at Kelso without looking him in the eyes. "What you mean, Mister Judd?" one of them asked.

"Haven't you boys heard about the railroads comin'? There's a new one gonna build in from Louisiana, through Marshall and Jefferson. They call it the Shreveport, Houston, and Indian Territory. The S.H. and I.T.!"

Kelso laughed like a rasp, but the stokers just looked at one another, puzzled.

"If you boys could spell," Kelso said, "you'd know S.H. and I.T. makes *shit*. Like I said, your jobs are all goin' to shit!"

"Yours too, ain't it, Mister Judd?" said the stoker who had been stuck with the capstan bar, now pulling himself back to his feet and grabbing a chunk of wood.

Kelso brandished the iron rod again, but only grinned at the man without using it. "I'm a mite smarter than you. I already got it planned to make my fortune."

"How you gonna do that?" another stoker asked.

"You'll be the first to know, boy. Now, stoke that fire good. The captain wants to show this town some speed. Good for trade."

Four hogsheads of spoiled bacon stood among the cords of firewood. The bacon had gone bad in a Jefferson warehouse. Captain Gentry had bought it cheap to use for quick heat when the *Glory* needed speed. Kelso pried a lid off one of the barrels and grabbed a hunk of bacon. "Come on, boys. Pour it on!" He threw a few pieces of bacon into the furnace, then brandished his bar at the black men. "We'll need the steam to move all this cotton. Come on, damn it, hurry up!"

The stokers plunged their powerful hands into the stench of putrid bacon. They fought the blistering heat to get near enough the furnace door to throw the fuel in. The bacon fat crackled fiercely as it hit the wood coals and flared.

"Use that whole barrel up," Kelso ordered. "I'll be back directly and it better be empty!" He waved the capstan bar at the stokers. "And sing one of them damn coonjine songs loud enough for the captain to hear. You know he likes to hear you boys sing."

The stokers scowled, but one of them lit into song, hoping Kelso would leave if they started singing. He sang low as a foghorn, and the others grudgingly joined in.

> Oh, shovel up the furnace
> Till the smoke put out the stars.
> We's gwine along the river
> Like we's bound to beat the cars. . . .

They continued singing as Kelso disappeared behind the boilers, heading aft. But he paused to listen and make sure the men continued to feed the fire. He could barely hear two of them talking over the singing and the roar of the flames.

"That fool's gonna blow us to hell," one of them said to the other.

"Just listen for them safety valves," the other replied. "They won't let out steam fast enough to keep her from blowin', but if they start talkin', you know it's time to jump."

Judd Kelso grinned, the nervous crawl in his stomach increasing. He passed quickly by the heat of the boilers, until he got aft of them. Then he stopped, the warmth still reaching his back down one of the corridors of cotton bales. He turned slowly and watched the boilers as he listened to the stokers sing. Poor bastards. They would never know what hit them.

Then he heard it. Above the shuddering of the boat, the hissing of the steam engines, the singing of the firemen, and the crackling of the pork fat, he heard the faint ticking of boiler plates. They were expanding, pulling against their rivets. He eyed the edge of the starboard boiler. Maybe it was his imagination, but he swore he could see it swelling, heaving like a living thing taking in breath. He turned quickly back toward the engine room.

Ellen Crowell rolled out of her berth in her stateroom on the boiler deck. The movement of the boat had wakened her. Feeling her way across the tiny six-by-six room to the window, she pulled the curtains back and saw only shreds of light seeping past the bales of cotton. She had forgotten in her sleep how cotton-imprisoned she was, denied escape to the outer deck in case of an emergency. Her only way out of her stateroom was by the door that led into the saloon. Boats made her nervous. She couldn't swim.

Her son could swim. That gave her some ease. Ben could shame otters. She felt her way back across the tiny room and put her hand on him as he slept in the upper berth. She was taking him to New Orleans to visit family. They had boarded in the night at Port Caddo and waited for hours as the rousters took on wood and the engineer made repairs and adjustments. Now, at last, they were under way.

Ellen knew she couldn't sleep through the vibrations of the steamboat. She put on her robe and opened the door into the saloon. She didn't understand steamboat nomenclature. She was on the boiler deck, but there was no boiler on it. The boilers were below, on the main deck. And this saloon wasn't a saloon at all, but a long, broad hallway running between the two rows of staterooms.

The saloon's piano stood right outside her room. It was a grand piano—too big for a small steamboat, but Captain Gentry did things in a big way where the *Glory* was concerned. Her door almost hit the piano bench as she opened it. She didn't know if she liked the piano being there. She could imagine drunken revelers keeping her awake with wild song, every night, all the way to New Orleans. The thin stateroom walls insulated against sound little better than mosquito bars did.

The so-called saloon was quiet, except for the rattle of pots and pans in the galley, where the cook was fixing breakfast. Ellen passed polished hardwood tables and walked a few doors down to the ladies' washroom. She found a community towel on a rack, and even a common toothbrush tied to the washstand by a string. She was glad she and Ben had brought their own towels and toothbrushes.

She tried to calm herself. She had chosen the finest steamer on the lake for their trip. Nothing bad would happen. She looked for something to ease her worries. Tin washbasins were nailed down to the wooden washstand. In them, she found fresh spring water. Now, see there. Most steamers used common bayou water. Yes, she had chosen well.

Billy Treat opened his galley door out onto the promenade and threw a bowl of eggshells over the guardrail, into the bayou. The rousters had left him a gap in the cotton bales on the boiler deck so he could throw refuse overboard. The rousters took good care of Billy Treat. He always cooked double what the passengers could eat. Rousters ate leftovers, and the deckhands of the *Glory* fed as well as any on the bayou, thanks to Billy.

He lingered at the rail. It was a beautiful morning. Summer coming on. The boat was still backing into the bayou, getting in position to steam down the channel toward Caddo Lake. He listened to the stokers sing the coonjine as his pale blue eyes swept the sky over the cypress tops.

Billy was a stranger to every man in the crew, though he had cooked for them now for a year and a half. They knew him as a courteous fellow, but one who avoided long conversation. Nobody knew where he had come from. He didn't talk about his past. And, though he didn't frown, he rarely smiled, and never laughed. He was young—

maybe thirty. He moved with strength and grace. He had more than his share of good looks. But he was suffering something powerful.

Just as he was about to go back to cooking breakfast, Billy saw the young apprentice engineer, Reggie Swearengen, climbing the guardrails and jigsaw work up to the boiler deck. He enjoyed watching the boy climb recklessly about the boat.

"Good morning, Reggie Swear-engineer," Billy said.

Reggie Swearengen grinned. "Mornin', Billy!" he shouted as he climbed around the cotton bales.

"What are you doing?"

"Kelso told me to lower the yawl."

Billy smirked. "The yawl? What for?"

"Said he wants me to tow him behind the paddle wheel when we get underway so he can look at something."

"Look at what?"

"I don't know," Reggie said, throwing one hand into the air as he clung to the hog chains with the other.

Billy shook his head. "It would be a shame if you should loose your hold on the rope when you were towing him."

Reggie laughed at the suggestion and climbed onto the hurricane deck to lower the yawl.

The *Glory* continued to back slowly up the bayou as Billy turned back into his kitchen. He tested the heat of the griddle, flicking some water onto it with his fingertips. He heard Captain Gentry ring the bell, giving the signal to stop the engines. He felt the vibrations cease, and heard the coonjine, louder now that the exhaust valves were silenced. The pulleys squeaked as Reggie lowered the yawl to the water.

Billy heard the splash of the yawl as he whipped a wooden spoon through a huge bowl of pancake batter. Now the captain would align the boat with the channel, ring the bell for full speed ahead, and blow the whistle as the *Glory of Caddo Lake* steamed down Big Cypress Bayou.

The bell rang. Billy waited for the engine-room vibrations. They didn't come. The captain repeated the bell signal. Something was wrong. Putting his pancake batter aside, Billy stepped back out onto the promenade and looked toward the engine room. He saw Reggie climbing down from the boiler deck and Judd Kelso stepping into the yawl. One of them should have been in the engine room, following the captain's signals. It was Kelso's fault. Reggie was just following orders. Kelso had no business being an engineer.

The entire boat suddenly came alive under him. It felt as if he were trying to stand on a monster gator twisting its prey to death underwater. The air shook with a sound so loud that he heard it with the marrow of his bones, and something hit him in the back with incredible force.

Now the waters of the bayou were all around him, morning-cold. He felt disoriented, couldn't find his way to the top. As he held his breath and waited, hopefully to surface, he realized that he had heard a double blast, absorbed a tremendous percussion. It seemed long ago, but his senses were coming back to him now, and he knew it had just happened. He found the morning glow of the surface above him and swam upward.

2

THE WORLD SEEMED OUT OF CONTROL. THE SKY RAINED BALES OF COTTON.
One splashed ten yards away from Billy Treat, covering him momentarily with spray. Screams and shouts accompanied a vicious hiss of steam. Something ripped into a cypress tree behind him. He treaded water with some difficulty in his long pants and waterlogged shoes. He shook his head to clear his thoughts. Pieces of wood were splashing all around him now, and clattering down on the hurricane deck of the *Glory*. His right shoulder and the back of his head were smarting from whatever it was that had struck him.

His eyes focused. The steamboat was listing severely to port, vomiting hysterical people, shooting a geyser of steam. He began to think clearly. Two of the boilers had exploded and blown bales of cotton away from the starboard side of the boat, throwing her off balance. The pilothouse was gone. There was probably a hole in the hull, because the boat was sinking steadily, tilting ever farther to port.

People floundered around him in the water. He went under and yanked his shoes off. When he came back up, he heard someone moaning. He saw a black man, face burned horribly, clinging to a splintered mass of wood. He swam to the man, helped him pull farther up on the floating lumber.

"Kelso!" he shouted. The son of a bitch was rowing the yawl toward the Port Caddo wharf! "We need the boat!" He saw the apprentice engineer treading water, dazed. "Reggie, get the yawl from the wharf! Swim, Reggie!"

The young apprentice squinted and saw the yawl. He waved at Billy and started swimming with powerful strokes. Billy knew he would make it. The lad was strong, and obviously uninjured.

A deckhand was floundering, screaming, frothing the water with his blood. He went down in a swirl. "Just hold on," Billy said to the burned man he had helped onto the floating lumber. To his surprise, the black man nodded and pushed him away.

Billy marked the spot where the rouster had gone down. He took long, steady breaths as he swam easily to the place. Filling his lungs, he jackknifed his body and plunged downward, headfirst.

The horrible sounds of the world above ended and he could barely see his own hands, outstretched, through the murky water. He descended, pinching his nose and forcing air into his ears to equalize the pressure. He felt for the drowning man with his arms and legs. An air bubble passed between his fingers. More met him in the face. He had plenty of oxygen left. He knew how to conserve it underwater. He plunged until he crashed into the thrashing body of the deckhand.

The black man grabbed him with desperate force. Lord, he was powerful! Billy used all his strength to turn the man around. He pinned one huge, muscled arm back and locked his own elbow under the man's chin. He started kicking for the surface, the drowning man clawing at him with his free hand.

When they finally broke into the air again, the black man was exhausted, holding Billy's hair in his fist, coughing water from his lungs. The man's forearm was ripped open and pumping blood. Maybe the cool water would slow the flow, Billy thought. He kicked toward the floating mass of lumber, which he now recognized as a big piece of the hurricane deck. It was just starting to really dawn on him what had happened. The boilers had blown. People were drowning.

As he fought the bleeding deckhand to reach the floating wood, he looked toward the town and saw Reggie coming with the yawl. That worthless Kelso was lying on the wharf as if he were hurt or something. He had looked healthy enough rowing away.

Above the hiss of steam, Treat heard a bell ringing in town. The Port Caddoans were coming down to the bayou, manning boats. Some of them were in their nightclothes, or in long underwear. They dragged skiffs, pirogues, bateaux, all manner of vessels into the water.

Suddenly five horsemen came galloping down the brick pavement. They plunged across the flood bank to low ground, passed the log jail-house, and leaped their barebacked mounts from the wharf. They splashed into the bayou, the horses grunting as they started to swim. The riders slipped from the backs of their mounts and held onto the manes. They would tow people to shore, one or two at a time. It would help.

The bayou writhed with screaming people. Billy saw a few sensible men and women doing good work, pulling others onto floating debris. A woman was holding calmly to a bobbing bale of cotton with one arm while she clutched two crying children with the other.

The *Glory* was tilting harder to port, sinking, still spewing steam. The main deck went under and water boiled instantly around the furnace, sending up a cloud of hot vapor.

Billy pulled the bleeding man onto the floating section of hurricane deck and told him to hold pressure on his own arm to stop the flow of blood. The man was starting to recover from the sheer percussion of the explosion, and he nodded vacantly as Billy spoke to him. The other man, the one who had been so badly scalded, was still there, unconscious but grasping the wood.

Without taking time to rest, Billy stroked back toward the throng. He was not even winded. A woman was becoming hysterical, clinging to a piece of wood too small to keep her afloat. She would go under before he reached her, but she would be easier to save than the big deckhand had been. The boats would be there soon.

One at a time, he told himself. You can't save everybody yourself. God knows, even that wouldn't set your life right, even if you could, but you can't.

Ellen Crowell woke up on the floor of the washroom. She smelled her own blood in her nostrils. She had been bending over the washbasin when, suddenly, it had risen to smash her in the face. What was happening? What had gone wrong?

The sounds came to her gradually—the screaming, the hissing of steam. She remembered only now having heard and felt the explosion. She tried to stand up, but seemed too dizzy to keep her feet under her. Then she felt herself sliding across the washroom floor and knew it was a tilt in the boat that prevented her from standing. Ben was in the stateroom, and the steamboat was sinking.

Clawing across the slanting floor, Ellen reached the door frame and pulled herself up into the saloon. The saloon floor was gone forward of the washroom. She could see water coming up in the hole. Morning light streamed in from another hole above. Now she understood what had happened. The boilers had exploded, tearing through the thin planking of the boiler deck, the hurricane deck, the texas, and even the pilothouse.

Luckily, her stateroom was aft of the gaping hole and she didn't have to cross it to rescue Ben. A few passengers were still floundering toward the end of the slanted saloon, but most had already gotten out. Ellen realized that she must have been unconscious for a minute or two. She had lost valuable seconds, but she was sure she still had time to get out with Ben. After that, she would probably drown, but that didn't concern her yet. Ben wouldn't drown. Thank God that the boy could swim.

She scrambled on all fours toward her stateroom. Why wasn't Ben coming out? Was he all right? Relax, Ellen. He can't reach the doorknob the way the floor is slanted. He's waiting for you. She heard his voice:

"Mama!" He sounded more confused than terrified.

She had almost reached the door when the boat settled suddenly to port and the grand piano slid against her stateroom door, blocking it.

She screamed.

"Mama?"

"Ben!" she cried, trying to move the piano.

"I'm all right, Mama. There's water in here."

"Help!" she yelled. "For God's sake, somebody come help me!"

A man appeared at the back end of the saloon. "Come on, lady! This way!"

"The piano!" she yelled. "My son's in there! Help me move the piano!"

"Forget about the damned piano, woman! Get out this way!" The man was gone.

She whimpered in terror. Water was coming up through the hole in the saloon floor.

"Mama! I can't reach the door!" she heard Ben say.

She clawed at the door until her fingernails were bloody. She beat against it with her fists, then kicked it, trying to break it in, but she wasn't a very large woman and the door was solid wood. "Ben?" she cried again, trying to preserve some chord of normalcy in her voice.

"Mama, it's getting deeper!" he yelled through the door.

"Swim, son!" she shouted, tears gushing down her face. "And if the room fills up, you hold your breath!"

Ben didn't answer.

"Do you hear me, Ben?"

"Yes," Ben said.

"I have to get help, son. I'll come back as quick as I can."

"Don't go, Mama!" her son's voice said.

She had to tear herself away from the door and the piano and her son. "Swim, son!" she yelled, so he would hear her going away. "Keep swimming!" She wanted to crawl back to him, but there was no time. She was thinking rationally now. She was trying to save him. But she felt as if she were deserting him, leaving him to drown alone.

•   •   •

Billy Treat had gone under six times for drowning people, bringing most of them up to Reggie, who was strong enough to pull them into the yawl. Other boats were arriving now, and he could no longer see anyone floundering in the water. The five horses had people clinging to their tails as they stroked toward the wharf. The horses had made several trips, and they were exhausted. People were settling down, helping each other. Then a woman emerged from the passenger cabin of the sinking steamboat and began screaming bloody murder.

"My son! Ben is in there! The piano!"

Billy swam to her and climbed onto the tilting boiler deck. "Where is he? Where's your son?"

The woman gripped him with hysteria, but spoke quite plainly. "The piano slid against the door, and I can't open it. Ben is in there. He can't get out!" She virtually shoved him into the flooding cabin.

Billy Treat waded to the door with the piano before it. "Hey!" he yelled. "You in there?"

"Help!" the voice said. "The water's getting deeper. I can't get out."

Billy put all the strength he had into moving the piano, but he couldn't lift it or slide it away from the door. "Can you swim?"

"Yes!"

"I'm coming right back for you! Keep swimming!"

The water was knee-deep in the saloon now, and deeper in Ben's room, which was on the sinking side of the boat. Billy waded to the aft end of the passenger cabin.

"Where's Ben?" Ellen cried when she saw Billy come out alone. "Where's my boy?" Some of the men had forced her into a boat.

"Ellen!" cried a man from another boat. "Where's Ben?"

Billy knew it had to be the boy's father. He didn't answer the mother's questions, or the father's. He just dove into the water and disappeared. He felt his way under the boiler deck, around a few bales of cotton lodged there, and to the submerged engine room on the main deck. He found the door handle and swam into the darkness. Feeling around, he soon located Judd Kelso's iron capstan bar. He knew where Kelso kept it, because he had considered many times throwing it overboard. Of course that wouldn't have solved anything. Kelso could always find something else to hit the rousters with.

He noticed, just before he broke the surface, that his lungs were aching. The swimming underwater was beginning to take its toll on him. Once he had been among the best in the world, but he hadn't done it in a long time.

The woman screamed wildly when he came up. He only waved the bar at her, taking no time to explain. The men held her in the boat. Otherwise, she would have rushed back in to try to save her son.

Billy knew the old *Glory of Caddo Lake* well. He was thinking about how she was put together as he made his way through the water in the saloon, now deep enough to swim through. The cheapest, thinnest wood was between the staterooms. The paneling that formed the walls between staterooms and saloon was pretty thick. The doors were solid. There wasn't much time. Ben's room was almost completely under water now. He decided to tear through the thin wood partitioning the rooms.

"Keep swimming, Ben," he said when he got to the piano. "I'm coming through the wall of the next room to get you!"

"I'm swimming!" the boy cried.

He admired this boy who was being brave, trapped in that dark room as the bayou squeezed his air out. He forced himself to relax for ten seconds and took long, deep breaths. Then he slid through the open door of the room next to Ben's and disappeared underwater.

It took a full minute of hard work to punch a small hole in the wall with the capstan bar, but Billy could not see wasting the seconds it would take to go up for air again. The boy might not have seconds. He didn't know how far the boat had sunk as he worked. Maybe the boy was drowning now. Billy had stayed under longer than this before. No need to go back now. Go forward! In the dark, he tore at the boards he had loosened until he had two of them broken away. There was enough room to squeeze through now.

Every little moment became an eternity. His lungs ached for air. They racked him all the way up to his eyeballs. But he had already decided to swim into Ben's room, hoping he would find an air pocket left there. It was a big gamble, but he was not going to take a chance on letting that boy drown. He couldn't take the guilt of leaving someone to die while he lived. Not again. He would rather drown with Ben, a boy he didn't even know.

He bumped his head in the very uppermost corner of the room and felt air on his face. His lungs had already started sucking. If there had been no air, he would have drowned. Then the hands of the boy pulled him under, and he thought he would drown anyway.

"Hey!" he said, coming up again, gasping. "Take it easy!"

They treaded water together, the tops of their heads jammed against the upper corner of the stateroom. They didn't speak, as Billy was gasping for air. They could hear a couple of men grunting through the wall, trying to move the piano above them.

"You holding out all right?" Billy finally asked, having caught some wind.

"Yes, sir," Ben said. "Who are you?"

"Name's Billy Treat. Here, get on my back. Now, listen to me and take long breaths. Stop swimming, just relax. I'll keep you up. Listen while you breathe deep and I'll tell you what we're going to do."

"Yes, sir."

"Shut up, I said. Just listen. Now, when the water gets to our chins, you're going to take in as much air as your chest can hold. We'll go under together. Don't swim. Let me pull you. You just relax and hold your breath. I made a hole in the wall down there. I'll help you through it, then come through after you and we'll swim out through the door of the next room. Easy."

"How long will it take?"

"Shut up, I told you. Breathe deep. Don't worry. You can hold your breath that long. Just relax and let me swim for you."

Someone was beating on the door above them, shouting, "Ben! Ben!"

"Don't answer," Billy said. "Save your breath. It's time now. Ready?" They breathed deeply together. "Go!"

• • •

Ellen was standing in the yawl, weeping, wringing her hands. Her husband and another man had gone in after the stranger with the iron bar, but no one had come out. She could tell that Ben's room was all the way under water now. She was trying to hold on to some hope, but it was growing thin. She prayed aloud, though no one understood her words, muffled by the sobs.

Then, through the blur of her tears, she saw a movement down the half-flooded saloon. A man emerged. Not her husband, and not the stranger with the iron bar. Then, there was John. John Crowell, her husband! Was he smiling or crying? He reached back into the saloon and pulled someone else into the morning light. It was the stranger, and the stranger had ahold of Ben! Merciful God!

3

I GUESS I SHOULD GET AS MUCH CREDIT AS ANYBODY FOR MAKING BILLY Treat an instant hero in Port Caddo. I was the boy he rescued from the sinking *Glory of Caddo Lake* the day her boilers blew. I'm Ben Crowell. I've told the story a thousand times since then, and people always think I'm spinning yarn when I do. But I won't water it down just to make it more believable. I've been known to branch out a little, mind you, but never when I talk about that summer.

Anyway, saving me made Billy a hero overnight, because by the next day, my father had printed a special extra-edition of the *Port Caddo Steam Whistle*. Pop was wise enough not to celebrate my rescue until the third page. The event was a catastrophe, after all, and a terrible blow to the town's spirit and economy. Seven men were killed, a lot of property destroyed, and our favorite steamboat sunk. The first two pages of the paper quite properly lamented the whole thing as a horrible tragedy.

But my pop was an unquenchable booster and knew he had to keep the spirit of the town going. On page three, he started listing acts of heroism. A woman from Jefferson had taken off her dress and stuffed it with floating pieces of firewood to make a raft for some children to float on. One of the big, strong deckhands had held up a collapsed portion of the forward passenger cabin with his back so people could crawl out under it. The people of Port Caddo, in general, had done all they could to ease the plight of the victims.

There was a big mystery concerning the five horsemen who had jumped their mounts into the bayou. Nobody in town knew who they were. They simply disappeared after the last of the passengers had been rescued. My pop didn't say so in the paper, because he didn't print rumors, but most folks believed they belonged to Christmas Nelson's outlaw gang, which was supposed to be hiding out in the woods around Caddo Lake.

The stranger, Billy Treat, got a whole column all to himself. He had gone under seven times to pull near-drowning people to the surface. Everybody in Port Caddo was talking about how long he could hold his breath. A minute, two minutes, five minutes. Who was this Billy Treat? Was he part turtle, or what?

My rescue was the most detailed account in the special edition, which only made sense, seeing as how the editor was my pop. So I figure I had as much to do as anybody in making Billy the new Port Caddo hero. He was already my own personal hero. I knew that the moment he stood me safely on the wharf.

I remember collapsing beside Judd Kelso and looking back over the bayou. The *Glory of Caddo Lake* had settled crooked on the bottom, only her texas sticking out. The pilothouse was gone. I wondered what had become of Captain Gentry. Then I saw him, hung in a fork of a cypress tree, bent backward, his head almost cut clean off. A huge section of boiler plate was in another tree near him.

Embedded in the wharf, not far from me, was a cotton bale, dry as a candlewick. The explosion had thrown it all the way there from the boat. My mother was clinging to me, sobbing. People were helping others out of boats, onto the wharf. Many were crying and all were drenched and shivering. Some people were hurt bad. I saw more blood than I had ever seen before, and I had experienced a lot of fishhooked fingers, skinned knees, and bloody noses.

That's when I really got scared, after the danger was all over for me. I might have stayed shook up for a long time if it hadn't been for Billy.

"Ben!" he said. "Get up and grab this corner!"

Billy and my pop were lifting one of the deckhands to the wharf, using a blanket as a stretcher. I stared at Billy in disbelief. I thought I was a victim and didn't have to do anything. My mother thought so too, and she held me back and probably gave Billy some kind of fierce look.

"Come on," Billy said. "You're all right. Help these hurt people."

He was right. There was nothing wrong with me. I had just been treading water for a few minutes, that's all. I had a knot on my head where the explosion had thrown me against a bedpost or something in my sleep and knocked me silly for a minute or two until the water seeped into my room and got my attention. But I wasn't really hurt.

I pulled away from my mother's arms and grabbed the corner of the blanket, which had a knot tied in it, making it easier to hold on to. The man in the blanket was the poor scalded deckhand Billy had saved. His skin looked blistered and horrible. He was unconscious, but moaning. I never learned his name, but I knew him from the *Glory*'s frequent visits to our town. He was the one who sang the low notes of the coonjines.

Billy jumped onto the wharf. "Kelso! Get up and help," he ordered.

Judd Kelso was lying there on his back with his hands over his face. "I can't," he said.

"Why not? You hurt?"

"No."

"Then what's wrong?"

"I don't know."

Billy sneered with disgust and gave me a signal with his eyes to lift my corner of the blanket. I watched his every move and followed his directions. He was helping people, and I wanted to be just like him.

I don't know how things got organized so quickly that morning, but by the time Billy and I and my pop carried the scalded deckhand past the constable's one-cell log jailhouse and up to high ground where the cobblestones started, old Jim Snyder had already turned his general store into sort of a makeshift hospital. There was a bed there where we lay the deckhand down.

Billy motioned at me to make another run with him down to the wharf and we started out, me right on his heels. Suddenly, I bumped into his back, for Billy had stopped dead in his tracks. I followed his eyes and found his stare locked on Pearl Cobb, who was wrapping a man's foot in bandages.

Some people believe in love at first sight. I think it's rare, but it happens. What I saw in Billy's face was love at first sight, only I didn't know it at the time, because just about every man alive looked at Pearl the same way, unless his wife happened to be with him. I was probably the most unabashed Pearl-gazer in Port Caddo. I had a crush on her something fierce.

Nobody appreciates the beauty of a full-grown woman more than a fourteen-year-old boy. He has no point of reference. He doesn't have enough experience with women to know how to judge one from the other. He doesn't even know what to look for. He just looks up one day and sees beauty, and it is absolute. Later, he grows up, gets particular, and starts ranking women and giving scores and silly things like that. But that first beauty a boy sees when his loins go to surprising him is flawless. All of a sudden he feels like as big an aching idiot as ever lived, and he loves it.

That was how Pearl Cobb made me feel. She was a little darker-skinned than your typical white gal, as if tanned by the sun, though I rarely saw her out in the daylight. Women envied her hair, long and dark and full. It possessed a sculpted quality, yet bounced and floated as free as clouds when she moved.

That's when Pearl got to you, when she moved. I don't think women can learn moves like that. Some things you're simply born with. I don't think she could help it. Just the way she was put together made her turn heads when she walked, and even when she just brushed her hair back from her face.

And as faces go, you can take your Mona Lisas and your moving-picture stars. Pearl had them all beat. I guess now I would have to say her features were perfectly proportionate, or something like that—her cheeks round, her lips full, her nose small and cute, her jaw straight and delicate. I might try to tell you about her eyes, how they melted you, embraced you too briefly, shamed you. But when I was fourteen, all I knew was the sheer truth of their large, shining beauty.

Don't think I didn't notice more than her eyes. Pearl had other attractions. A scribe couldn't copy her curves. They defied duplication. No mere line or graduated plane could render likeness to any part of her. You could cast her in gold and not capture the living, breathing loveliness of her. You could stare at her like a fool for fifteen seconds, soaking in her beauty, then turn away and not trust your own recent memory of her perfection, so you would have to look again to be sure.

And I don't know if she made her own dresses or bought them, but how she got them to cling to her—as I wanted to do—is something I haven't figured out to this day.

Pearl worked in old man Snyder's store and lived alone in a little room upstairs. She was a hard worker, kept the place real clean and organized, made perfect change, and balanced the books. About the time I turned fourteen, I started loitering around the store quite a bit. I didn't have any money to buy anything, and Pearl probably knew it. I think she took pity on my innocence, but maybe she just took advantage of it.

She got me to run all kinds of errands for her, taking groceries to old folks who couldn't get around and things like that. There wasn't any money in it for me, just a nice word from Pearl every now and then, maybe a smile. Once in a while she would stroke my sweaty mop of boy's hair with her sensuous fingers. I guess she was just scruffing up my hair a little bit, but it felt like the embrace of pure tingling passion to me.

I was only vaguely aware back then of Pearl's reputation. I had heard some old biddies refer to her as "white trash." I figured they were jealous. Then one day Cecil Peavy, my friend and fishing partner, called her a slut, and we had a knock-around fight over it. Us boys from proper families grew up sort of innocent back then. I wasn't even real sure I knew what a slut was, but the way Cecil said it made me mad.

Slowly it began to dawn on me as I caught morsels of men's talk about her, and listened to some new instinct of my own, what the secret was about Pearl. It took some thinking to sort it all out, and some time to verify it—and even then, I was still a little fuzzy on the details—but the truth was that Pearl could be bought, if a fellow was lucky enough to come by her fee.

Learning the secret about Pearl didn't lower my opinion of her. In fact, it made her all the more fascinating. You have to remember, a fourteen-year-old boy doesn't decide his own morals. His glands do it for him. What preachers and church choir sopranos regard as scandalous, a fourteen-year-old boy might consider cause for sainthood. So, when I finally found out why everybody called Pearl "Pearl"—her real name was Carol Anne—her beauty in my eyes doubled, if it's possible to double an absolute.

If I could see, today, the same Pearl I knew back then, I wonder if I would find her as beautiful. Probably not. I'm more suspicious and critical of women now, as I am of people in general. I haven't seen pure beauty since Pearl, and that may only be because I remember her as she was that summer. Or more correctly, because I remember her with the memories of who I was then. When the summer was over, that Pearl was gone forever.

Anyway, my new hero, Billy Treat, had a lot more self-control than I did, and he only ogled Pearl for a second or two before heading back down to the wharf with me in tow. We brought all the people injured in the explosion to Snyder's store and took care of them as best we could until the doctor could arrive from Marshall.

That's when things started confusing me. I guess that's when my simple boy's life became complicated, and it's been getting more complicated since that day. I was given the job of carrying cold well water in by the bucketful so it could be used to ease the suffering of burns. Every time I entered the store, I couldn't keep my eyes off of Pearl for very long, of course, but the thing was that she couldn't keep her eyes off of Billy Treat. And Billy Treat was not exactly avoiding the occasional glance at her, either.

It was odd, because I had never been jealous before, and men gawked at Pearl all the time. But now it was Pearl doing most of the gawking—at my newfound hero. I caught them actually looking at each other once, for a mere second. Their eyes shared some common brand of remorse that I wouldn't understand for years. Suddenly, it wasn't such fun having a hero.

The first man Billy saved died before the doctor could arrive. Four of the firemen who had been stoking the furnace when the boilers blew also died. Two of them were never found. Caddo Lake took what was left of them and buried them somewhere. The other two casualties were Captain Gentry and a young man from Dallas who happened to have been walking down the saloon, directly above the boilers, when they blew. We all figured he had been heading for the toilets that hung over the stern.

It would take me years to prove that Judd Kelso murdered all seven of the victims for his own personal gain. When the scalded black man died quietly in the store, Kelso was still down on the wharf, his hands covering his face. I guess even Judd Kelso possessed something resembling a conscience.

4

THE *GLORY OF CADDO LAKE* DISASTER LEFT SEVERAL MEN UNEMPLOYED. Most of them boarded the next steamer and went to find work. But Billy Treat stayed. Widow Humphry said she was too old to be cooking for her guests and boarders, and since Billy was a cook, she would provide him with room and board plus a small salary to fix meals at her inn. Billy said it would do until he found something else.

This all made me a little nervous at first, because Widow Humphry's inn was just across the way from Snyder's store. But after about a week went by, I began to relax. I didn't notice anything out of the ordinary going on between Billy and Pearl. I saw him go to the store once for supplies, and I followed him in there to spy on him, but he hardly spoke three words to Pearl.

"Thank you," she said to him when she gave him his change. That was something, because I had never heard Pearl thank anybody other than me. But Billy only nodded at her before he left. He was my hero, but I thought he must have been a little crazy. When Pearl Cobb came right out and spoke to you, you were supposed to try to speak back. This Billy Treat was a funny character.

One day right after lunch when Cecil Peavy, Adam Owens, and I were chucking rocks at a squirrel in a tree out behind Widow Humphry's inn, Billy came out the back door and called my name.

"Ben, bring your friends over here," he said in that detached voice of his.

They looked at me with their eyes popping out. I had been bragging on how chummy I was with the new local hero, but they didn't believe me till then. To tell the truth, I didn't believe myself till then. I wasn't sure if Billy even remembered who I was. I trotted happily to the back porch with Cecil and Adam behind me, to see what Billy wanted.

"Hi, Mr. Treat," I said.

He waved off the formalities. "Call me Billy. Listen, how would you men like to make a little money?" He was sitting on the porch steps, his sleeves rolled up over his rippling forearms as he adjusted a smart little straw hat on his head.

Us boys just looked at each other with our mouths open for a moment or two. None of us had ever owned more than a nickel at a time. "I guess so," I said. "How?"

"I need some fresh catfish. The fellows down at the fish camp have been selling me day-old fish, and it just doesn't taste as good as it should." He spoke to us in a very professional tone, as if we were negotiating the biggest deal in history. "If you boys could catch some catfish and keep them alive in a holding tank somewhere until I need them, I'd pay you a penny a pound."

I looked at Adam Owens in astonishment. "Sure!" I said, speaking for all of us.

But Cecil Peavy was a cynic, even at fourteen. "Is that live weight, or cleaned?" he asked. Cecil made good in life. Last time I saw him alive, down in Nacogdoches, he owned a whole city block.

"Live weight," Billy answered.

"Sure!" I repeated.

"Wait a minute," Cecil said. "Where are we gonna keep them? How are we gonna catch them?"

"My daddy has a trotline in the barn," Adam said. "Never been used. Got new hooks and everything."

"Do you think he'd miss it?" Billy asked.

Adam grinned and shook his head.

"Where are we gonna keep them alive?" Cecil repeated.

We thought in silence for a moment, then it struck me. "The old horse trough at the Packer place!" It was perfect—a big, round cypress trough, full of spring water, on an abandoned farmstead only a mile from the lake.

"That's a lot of work for a penny a pound," Cecil said.

"Take it or leave it," Billy replied sternly, smirking at him.

Adam and I looked anxiously at Cecil.

"Well, all right," he finally said. "We'll give it a trial to see how it works."

"Good," Billy said. When he shook our hands, we were bound.

"Go get that trotline," I said to Adam, all excited. "We can used old Esau's skiff to run the line."

"What are we gonna use for bait?" Cecil asked.

"We'll wade for some mussels."

Suddenly Billy perked up, and I saw a new light flash in his eyes for a second. "Mussels?" he said. "Do these waters bear a lot of mussels?"

"They're all over the dang place," Cecil said.

Billy glanced at a watch he pulled out of his pocket. "I think I'll come with you," he said. "I'd like to see these mussels."

Adam snuck his pop's trotline out of the barn along with a couple of cork floats and a good supply of hooks. Billy walked with us the two miles between Port Caddo and old Esau's saloon located on an inlet of Caddo Lake known as Goose Prairie Cove.

Esau was a friendly old man who drank whiskey all day, but never seemed to get drunk. He was dark-skinned and claimed five-sevenths Choctaw blood. I asked him one time how he figured that, and he said, "I've got seven ancestors, and five of them was Choctaw." I think he was really pure Indian and just liked to pull my leg. He kept his hair cut and dressed like a regular civilized man. With his saloon and fishing camp down at Goose Prairie Cove, he managed to make a living that he supplemented by hunting wild game and running a few hogs in the woods. He had several old leaky boats at his camp and never refused them to us boys.

Esau always ran us off after dark, though, because sometimes fights broke out between drunks at his place. But there were a few knotholes in the walls, and we often snuck back and looked through the knotholes to see what barroom life was like. One night when we were peering through the knotholes, Esau walked casually over to a chair by the wall, sat down in it, and sprayed a mouthful of whiskey in Adam Owens' eye through a knothole. I never did figure out how he knew we were out there.

Anyway, when we got to the fishing camp, we found Esau and Judd Kelso sitting in the shade of a big mulberry, sipping whiskey. Judd Kelso had been hanging around Port Caddo ever since the disaster. I didn't think anything of it at the time, but he should have been looking for work somewhere. Kelso was not independently wealthy. However, his family lived over at Long Point, not too far away, so it didn't seem unnatural to me for him to stay in the area after the boiler explosion.

Esau stood up to greet us when we got there. We introduced Billy and they shook hands. Esau offered Billy a whiskey flask.

"I never drink," Billy said.

Esau didn't bat an eye, just put the flask in his pocket. We asked him if we could use a skiff to throw mussels in and run a trotline, and he told us we were welcome to, as long as we brought the skiff back.

"Howdy, Treat," Kelso said, waving glassy-eyed, sprawled across a wooden chair in the shade.

Billy just flat ignored him and went with us boys to the lakeshore. My friends and I waded barefoot into the shallows, towing a skiff behind us. I had worked up a sweat on the walk from Port Caddo, and the water felt good. Billy kicked off his shoes, put his pocket watch in one of them, and followed us in.

It didn't take long for me to find the first mussel. I was probing through the mud with my toes when I felt it, a hard ridge in the muck. I dug it out with my toenail, then used my foot like a shovel to lift it up to where I could grab it in my hand.

It was a pretty good-sized one, but nothing extraordinary—about as wide as the palm of my hand—a dark brown, clamlike shell plastered with mud. I threw it into the skiff Adam was holding by the rope and went on hunting with my toes. Billy sloshed over to the skiff, grabbed the mussel, washed it off, and studied it. I saw that light in his eyes again. He seemed fascinated.

"How many catfish do you expect us to catch?" Cecil asked, throwing a small mussel shell into the skiff.

Billy dropped the mussel he had been looking at and started feeling around with his feet as us boys were doing. "Enough where I can fry a catfish dinner twice a week or so."

We hunted for almost an hour, joking and taunting each other, as boys will. Billy hardly said a word to us. He just searched silently for mussel shells, finding a few, studying them, comparing them. I still idolized him, but I was beginning to think he was a little peculiar. "How many varieties of mussels live in this lake?" he asked us at one point. We didn't know.

When we had waded out to our chins, and Billy to his chest, we finally had enough mussels to bait our trotline. We towed the skiff back to shallower water and sat on an old pier that stuck up just above the water level. We decided to go ahead and open the mussels there, so we could bait our line quicker when we set it out.

There's a trick to opening mussels. Between those two shells they're almost nothing but solid muscle, and they don't open easy. It's a little dangerous. You're likely to slip and cut your hand if you don't watch yourself.

The way Billy had been studying the mussels we found, I was of the opinion that he had never seen one before that day. So, when we got our pocket knives out, I thought I'd show him how to open mussels. I didn't want my hero sticking himself. And, to tell the truth, I wanted to show off a little.

"Hold it like this, Billy," I said, "and stick your knife in right here, then twist it open." I wrestled with the mud-slick mussel shell for some time, poking clumsily at it with the knife, until I finally pried it open. I pulled out the shapeless little animal, threw it in a bait bucket holding a little water, and handed Billy one to try on his own.

His knife moved so quickly that I couldn't follow it. In less than a second, the shell was open in his hand. He pulled out the mussel and felt it between his fingers, as if looking for something hidden in it. He dropped it in the bait bucket, then ran his finger along the pretty purple inside of the shell. He angled it in the sun to catch the iridescent rainbow sheen of the shell lining. He had that look on his face again. His eyes darted and sparkled, and he almost smiled. Then he grunted, tossed the shell in the water, and grabbed another mussel.

He looked at me and found me staring. "What are you looking at?" he said.

"Nothin'," I answered.

Cecil and Adam hadn't noticed anything unusual. They were arguing about where to put the trotline.

"The best place is over on the edge of Mossy Brake, right across from Taylor Island," Cecil said. "That's where all them big opelousas cats live."

"You've got to have live bait to catch an opelousas cat," Adam argued. He didn't know too much, but there wasn't a thing about hunting and fishing he didn't know. "We won't catch anything but willow cats on these mussels."

"Maybe some humpback blues," Cecil suggested.

"Not in Mossy Brake. You have to go out in the Big Water to catch them."

They went on arguing and shelling mussels until only a few were left. I was listening to them yammer and trying to figure out how Billy could get those mussels open so quickly, when I realized he was just sitting there on the pier with his feet in the water, staring at an open mussel shell in his hand.

It was a big washboard mussel—the kind old Esau scraped his dead pigs down with when he was slipping the hair from them at butchering time. The inside of the shell glistened a kind of pink rainbow color. I didn't see what had Billy so captivated until he nudged the mussel with his finger. Then I saw him uncovering a perfectly spherical bead of translucence perched on the rim of the shell. Billy Treat had found a pearl.

"Wow," I said, before I could consider all the ramifications of the find. "Hey, y'all, Billy found a pearl!"

Cecil and Adam stopped arguing and looked. They jumped to their feet and hung over Billy's shoulders to see. Billy had that faraway look in his eyes again, as if he was thinking of someplace else. It almost seemed like he was afraid of that pearl.

"Hey, Esau!" Cecil shouted.

"Esau!" Adam repeated.

"Billy Treat found a pearl!" they yelled together, as if they had rehearsed it.

Esau rose slowly, but Judd Kelso floundered as if wasp-stung getting out of his chair.

I envied Billy something terrible at that moment, and resented him a little, too. What was he going to do with that pearl? I knew what I would have done with it, if I could have found the nerve. But I didn't have the pearl. Billy did. And in my eyes, he had nerve enough for ten men.

I had heard about Caddo Lake pearls all my life, and had seen several girls wearing lopsided ones given to them by their beaux who had been lucky enough to find one. But this was the most beautiful one I could imagine. It was fairly large—bigger than a raindrop. It had an overall white color, but little windows of blue and green and red and purple kept appearing within it, blurred and indefinable. A prismatic haze seemed to cling to its surface like a fog.

I smelled whiskey over the stench of the mussels when Esau and Kelso arrived.

"Well, I'll be damned," Kelso said.

"That's one of the best I ever seen, and I've lived on this lake forty years," Esau said.

Billy looked up at the old Indian. "Pearls are common to this lake?"

Kelso was squinting his gator eyes, scheming.

"Maybe not common," Esau said, measuring his words. "But they turn up. I've found a couple myself over the years. Nothing as pretty as that one, though."

"What do people do with them?"

"Well," Esau said, glancing at Kelso. "A young man might give it to his sweetheart, if he's got one. A daddy might give it to his daughter to play with."

"Nobody ever sold them?" Billy asked.

Esau wrinkled his old dark face. "They ain't worth nothin'."

"They's worth somethin' to me," Kelso blurted. He pulled a large roll of bills out of his pocket and peeled one off. "Here, I'll give you five dollars for it."

"Where did you get all that money?" Billy asked, his voice flat and emotionless as ever.

"None of your business. Here's five. Now, give me that shell slug."

"For five dollars?" Billy said.

"All right, ten!" Kelso peeled off another bill and shook it in Billy's face.

"Don't sell it, Billy," Cecil said. "Use it yourself."

I pushed Cecil and he looked at me as if I was crazy, but the whole incident was making me mad. I didn't want Billy using the pearl the way Cecil was suggesting.

"Use it?" Billy said. "Use it for what?"

Kelso laughed. "I'll use it. I'll take it over to Pearl Cobb and get my piston stroked." He peeled another bill from his roll. "Fifteen. That's as high as I'll go, Treat."

Billy looked up at Kelso. "What do you mean by 'getting your piston stroked'?" he asked.

Now, even I knew what he meant, and I was only fourteen years old, but I guess Billy wanted to be certain.

"Pearl's a whore!" Cecil said. He was so red in the face, you would have thought *he* had found the pearl.

I shoved him hard in the chest. "She is not!" I shouted. I was getting really mad now, and so frustrated I thought I would cry.

"She'll be a whore tonight!" Kelso said, grinning idiotically.

Billy looked up at Esau.

The old Indian took a sip from his whiskey flask. "She ain't a regular whore for a man who just wants to spend some money," he said in his slow, careful voice. "But if you have a pearl—"

"And I just bought me one!" Kelso shoved the three fivers into Billy's shirt pocket and reached for the pearl.

Quick as he had opened the mussel, Billy slammed it shut in his left hand, the pearl clamped safely inside. With his right hand, he grabbed Kelso by the back of the collar. The speed and strength he moved with shocked me out of my anger and frustration. I saw Kelso fly headfirst from the pier into the water, but Billy did not let go of him. He held Kelso under, facedown. Kelso thrashed like a snared gator. That Kelso was a bundle of muscles and it took some power to hold him down. Billy did it with one hand. His left hand still clutched the pearl mussel.

"What's this about Pearl Cobb?" Billy asked, speaking as smoothly as if he were sitting in someone's parlor. Kelso continued to claw at him ineffectually.

"Her real name's Carol Anne," Esau answered. "She likes pearls, I guess. Does a man favors for 'em. That's how she got her nickname."

Billy shoved Kelso deeper. The man's face must have been in the mud. His feet came up and splashed muddy water everywhere with their flailing.

"What does she do with them?"

Esau reached for the flask again. "I don't know. Keeps them in her room, I think. A fellow told me one time he took her a pearl and she had him put it in a tobacco tin with a bunch of other ones, then—" He looked toward us boys and decided against giving further details. "You gonna let him up for air?"

"A man can hold his breath a long time when he has to. Isn't that right, Ben?"

I was speechless. I didn't know who or what Billy was anymore. Was he a murderer who drowned his enemies? A hero who saved drowning men? Was he my friend, or my rival for Pearl's attention? I didn't stand a chance of impressing her with Billy waving pearls under her nose. Of course, I wouldn't have stood a chance anyway, but I was fourteen and too infatuated to figure my chances realistically. All I knew was that *I* should have found that pearl. It was meant for me, and Billy had stolen it from me.

It was funny, because I had known for some time who Pearl Cobb was and what she did. It didn't bother me that she had had all those men who brought her pearls. I figured she was just generous. And if she could be generous with them, why not with me? But this Billy Treat was dangerous. I don't know how I knew, but I sensed he might take all of Pearl's generosity for himself.

"He stopped kickin', Billy," Adam said, staring fearfully at Kelso's legs.

Billy pulled the man up. Kelso sucked in some mud and water with his first breath. He coughed and gasped with horrible sounds as Billy shoved him toward the shore. While Kelso caught his breath, Billy opened the mussel shell and removed the pearl. He pulled the mussel out, too, and threw it into our bait bucket.

"Goddam you, son of a bitch!" Kelso wheezed, scooping mud away from his eyes.

Billy took the three bills from his shirt pocket, wadded them up, and threw them at him. "Don't cuss me, Kelso."

Kelso got up and staggered toward Esau's saloon. "You better watch over your shoulder, Treat," he said.

When Kelso was out of the way, Adam asked, "Can I see the pearl, Billy?"

Billy let him look at it as he stepped back up onto the pier. Adam handed it to Cecil to look at, then Cecil gave it to me. I wanted to rear up and throw that pearl back out into the lake, but I didn't know if maybe Billy might hold me under, too. I just stood there, looking at it in my open palm, nudging it around a little with my finger. It was almost as beautiful as Carol Anne Cobb.

"What are you going to do with it?" I asked Billy.

He looked at me, those pale blue eyes drilling me like skewers. "What would you do with it if you were me?" he said.

I swallowed and felt a red flood of anger and embarrassment engulf my face.

Billy smirked at me. "That's what I thought," he said.

"Is that what you're going to do with it?"

With a sudden upward flick of his palm, Billy tapped the back of my hand, propelling the pearl into the air. He snatched it right in front of my eyes, quick as a frog's tongue. "Learn to mind your own business, Ben," he said.

He stared at me, knowing everything I was thinking. His eyes were inscrutable and mysterious, like sky-blue pearls, flecked with shafts of danger, bored with big dark holes. Oh, that Billy Treat could see your naked soul with those eyes.

5

PEARL LOCKED THE FRONT DOOR OF SNYDER'S STORE AND FOUND HER WAY by starlight to the stairs around back that led to her room. Her entire life consisted of the store by day and her room by night. She rarely went anywhere else. Not to church, for no congregation had embraced her. Nor to visit friends, for she had none—with the possible exception of old man Snyder and young Ben Crowell. Hattie Hayes, the constable's wife, was civil to her, but she couldn't really count her as a friend.

She entertained an occasional guest.

Where would she go when the town died and the store closed? She had nothing else. The job she did was the only thing she took pride in, though it paid little. She was not proud of her beauty. Her looks were a curse.

She had a can of beef stew in her hand as she climbed the stairs. She would have the stew for supper, if she found an appetite. She opened the door and entered her dark room. She felt for the matches and lit the tallow candle. No need to light the lantern. It was better to save the coal oil.

When the candlelight filled the room, her eyes went immediately to the tobacco tin on the shelf above her bed. The pearls lay within like pebbles of shame . . . her only links to the social fabric of the town.

Carol Anne had come to Port Caddo years before with her mother, a notorious Creole quadroon from New Orleans, renowned for her beauty and wiles. Her father was a gambler named Cobb, whom she never met. When she was six, her mother became the mistress of a rich planter on the Louisiana side of Caddo Lake. For four years, she and her mother lived well in a white frame house at Mooringsport. Carol Anne dressed primly and went to school.

Then the Civil War came on. Her mother's keeper became a lieutenant and died in one of the first battles. When the money ran out, they drifted across to the Texas side of the lake and landed in Port Caddo. Carol Anne's mother rented a small house on the edge of town where she established a practice among the riverboat men, sawmill hands, farm boys, and fishermen.

Carol Anne didn't go to school anymore. There was no public education system, and none of the girls' academies would enroll the daughter of a known prostitute. No white girl of proper family was allowed to befriend her. She played some with the black girls whose mothers washed laundry on Gum Slough, but Negro society was as suspicious of her as whites were righteous above her.

Malaria ruined her mother's health and trade, and eventually left Carol Anne alone in the world. She was fifteen. Kindly old Jim Snyder gave her a job at his store in exchange for room and board. In a couple of years, she was running the store on her own, earning a salary, and giving Jim Snyder more time to look after other business concerns.

She was getting prettier, and growing out of awkward girlishness into womanhood. She had contact with many townspeople through the store, and some of them began to let the memory of her mother fade. She might have had a respectable future in Port Caddo if not for the pearls.

A few of the proper girls who came into the store wore freshwater pearls their beaux had found and given to them. They wore them around their necks on simple silken threads or on slender chains of gold. They flaunted them, rolling them between their fingers as they shopped for white silk. Some wore their pearls mounted in golden ring settings, or on the ends of silver hairpins. A pearl from Caddo Lake was a proposal for marriage when given to a girl. Carol Anne wished she could have one.

A promising young man from a South Shore plantation came to Carol Anne's door one night and asked if he might come in. He held her wrist and pressed a pearl into her palm. It was a fine teardrop of blue smoke and luster. He was in love with her, he said, but he couldn't let anybody know. Their love had to remain a secret until he turned twenty-one. His family already had his bride chosen for him, and might deny him his trust fund if he married the wrong girl. He told her this, then kissed her and went away.

She lay awake that night with the blue pearl in her hand and dreamed of wearing it someday—a pendant set in gold. She dreamed of the boy, too, and their plantation home, their children, her flower garden.

He returned two nights later and kissed her as he came in the door. He said he had been thinking of nothing but her. He snuffed out the candle and led her to the bed. She found little reason to resist. She was ready.

For weeks, they guarded their secret with care. Carol Anne would fondle the teardrop pearl after he left and dream of their wedding and their life together. Then he stopped coming. She read in the *Port Caddo Steam Whistle* that the boy had been accepted at West Point and had a promising military career ahead of him.

It didn't take long for Carol Anne to realize that before he left, he had boasted to his friends about how he had seduced her, the daughter of the dead town whore, with a worthless shell slug.

Not long after that, someone else knocked on her door. She found a farm boy standing at the top of the stairs. He said he had found a pearl that he would give her if she would let him come in. She almost pushed him down the stairs, but then the farm boy opened his hand to show her, and in the candlelight, she saw the mystical glow of the yellow oval. In its pearlescence she saw the same kind of visions she had seen in the smoky-blue teardrop. She saw family, home, and happiness. The ghostly colors swam in darting schools around the gem.

She let him in, took his pearl. He never came back.

After that, she forgot their faces, but remembered their pearls. Each held for her its own fantasy images of hearth and kin. She pretended they were men they could never be. In her room at night, she lived multiple lives—perfect lives encrusted safely in nacre. She became a collector of pearls. She became Pearl.

Pearl put her can of beef stew on the table and lay down on her bed. She arched the stiffness from her back and stretched her arms toward the ceiling. She reached the tobacco tin, lowered it to her stomach, and opened it. She probed the folds of the velvet cloth that cradled the pearls. With her fingers, she felt the keepers of her fantasy lives. She knew most of them by touch alone. She closed her eyes and let the visions swarm.

She had almost fallen asleep when she heard footsteps on her stairs. It was probably Jim Snyder, the grandfatherly old man she loved. He came to talk to her occasionally on her stairs, but would never enter her room.

When the knock came, she opened the door and found Billy Treat standing at the top of the stairs. He held his straw hat in his hand; he smelled faintly of kitchen smoke. She wished she had taken the time to look in the mirror and straighten her hair.

"Are you Carol Anne Cobb?" he asked.

She nodded.

"I've heard you collect pearls."

She felt confused, and maybe a little ashamed, though she had learned to hide her shame. Since the day she first saw him; she had dreamed of him climbing the stairs to her room. But in her dreams, he never spoke of pearls. "So what?" she said, rather defensively.

"Well, if you don't mind, I'd like to see them."

"What for?" she asked, suspiciously.

He crumpled the hat brim in his hand. "You might say I used to collect pearls, too. Saltwater pearls, mostly. I'd like to see yours, if you don't mind."

She looked in his eyes. It was like looking into a mirror. His stare couldn't meet hers. He diverted his line of sight. He was trying to get by some shame of his own.

"All right," she said, stepping aside to let him in. "I wasn't expecting anybody." She put the can of beef stew behind the curtain on the windowsill, fluffed her hair a little, and pulled the bedspread tight where she had been lying on it.

Billy stood uncomfortably in the candlelight. "Mind if I light the lantern? I can grade the pearls better in lantern light."

"Grade them?" she said, handing him the lantern from her bedside. "What do you mean by 'grade' them?"

Billy held the burning candlewick under the globe and lit the lantern. "See how much they're worth. I'm not up on today's prices, but I can give you an idea of what they'd sell for."

Pearl wrinkled her pretty nose. "Pearls from that old muddy lake aren't worth anything."

"A pearl is a pearl, Miss Cobb. It doesn't matter if it comes from a Caddo Lake mussel or a South Seas oyster. They're all graded the same way."

She stared across the room at him. He was an unusual man to know so much about pearls. Who was he? What had he come here for?

Billy shuffled nervously. "Well, where are they? If you don't mind . . ."

"They're in here." She picked up the tobacco tin from her bed.

They sat across from each other at her table and he opened the container. He angled the box to catch the light, then reached in with his fingertips and nudged apart the square of velvet bundled around the pearls, to get a glimpse of them. "You've got a lot of them," he said.

Pearl shrank into her chair with shame, and Billy looked as if he regretted commenting on the extent of her acquisitions. Perhaps he hadn't meant anything by it. He removed the piece of velvet from the tobacco tin and spread it across the tabletop, letting the light strike and dance upon the pearls.

There were more than twenty pearls of many shapes and colors. About half of them were white. The others varied from blue to purple to pink to yellow to gold. Only a few were perfect spheres. Some were flat, others long and thin like spikes; still others were shaped like flower petals or angels' wings. Then there were the smoky-blue teardrop and the yellow oval.

"You like pearls?" he asked as he pushed them into groups, studying them.

"All girls like pearls." She looked at him blankly, coolly. "I like the white ones best." She felt compelled to speak something she had never said to anyone else. "The colored ones are pretty, but the white ones look like the moon through a rainbow."

He glanced appreciatively into her eyes. "In the South Sea islands," he said, turning back to the pearls, "there's a legend of a god called Oro who rides to Earth on a rainbow." He held a round white pearl up to the light. "And he leaves a little of that rainbow color on the pearls wherever he goes."

She felt her heartbeat quicken. "How do you know things like that?" she asked, fascinated by his manners and his talk.

"Like I said, I used to collect pearls. And I've read everything ever written on them, I guess." He spoke as if pacing his words while he herded the gems into piles, comparing them, moving them from group to group. "The Greeks thought they were caused by lightning striking the water. And the Romans . . . well, the Romans thought they were the tears of angels. Christopher Columbus theorized that they were caused by dewdrops falling into the water from mangrove plants. . . ."

She felt as if she were in a dream. No one had ever spoken to her of such fanciful ideas. That was not bayou talk. "Whatever got you so interested in pearls?"

He shrugged. "My father was a jeweler."

"So? My father was a gambler. You don't hear me going on about cards and dice."

Billy glanced up at her and smiled. "Well, we had a summer home in the country in New Jersey. A stream nearby had mussels in it that my mother liked to fry. She'd send me out to collect them."

"And you found a pearl in one of them?"

"Only after it was cooked and on my plate. The cooking had ruined it. My father said it would have been worth five hundred dollars. It was a big round one. Anyway, that's what got me interested in pearls. I'm out of the business now, though. I had some bad luck with it."

She watched in silence for some time as Billy studied the pearls with a serious look on his face.

"See," she said, mistaking his expression for one of disappointment. "I told you they weren't worth anything."

He looked up at her and squinted his eyes. He smiled slightly. "This blue teardrop is your best one, by my judgment. It'll fetch seven hundred. All together, Miss Cobb, I'd say you have between three and four thousand dollars' worth of pearls here."

Pearl looked back and forth between Billy's face and the collection of Caddo Lake pearls. This Billy Treat was out of his mind! "That doesn't make sense. How come nobody ever sold them before?"

"Probably because nobody knew they were worth anything. The South Sea islanders used to play marbles with theirs, until they found out they could sell them."

That was the third time he had mentioned the South Sea to her. "Have you been there? To the South Sea?"

He looked away from her and nodded. "Yes. Years ago. Listen, Miss Cobb, I know a pearl-buyer who works out of New York City who would probably be interested in buying these from you. If you want me to, I'll contact him for you and have him come take a look."

Pearl got up from her chair to stand beside the table. "I never wanted to sell them," she said, wringing her hands.

"Why not?"

"They're mine. I like them."

Billy sighed. "Look, Miss Cobb," he said, "I know how you came by these pearls. I don't understand why you'd want to keep them. But if you sell them, you can use the money to get out of this town. You can make a new start. You know how to run a business. You could buy one of your own."

Pearl's anger flared. She put her hands on her hips and scowled at him. "Well, you've got gall to talk to me like that. Anyway, since you know how I came by these pearls, I guess you also know that if I sell them for money, it makes me a whore . . . an expensive one, to hear you talk." She didn't raise her voice, but charged it with deep indignation.

"Whether you do it for pearls or for money," he said, "it seems about the same to me. What I'm telling you is that you've got a chance to turn your adversity into something valuable. That's how pearls are made."

"What's that supposed to mean?"

"A pearl starts out as something that galls the shellfish—whether it's an oyster or a mussel. It could be a grain of sand the creature can't get rid of. Could be that some pearls start as parasites living off of the shellfish. Anyway, the animal takes this thing that frets it, and covers it with the same stuff it coats the inside of its shell with. Covers it and covers it until it's not a problem anymore, but a thing of beauty."

She turned her mouth into a voluptuous smirk. "What about the tears of angels?"

"There may be some truth to that, too. Don't you believe in angels?"

"Yes."

"Don't you believe they cry?"

She paused, thinking. "Yes." She spoke now with less bitterness. "I even know why."

Billy nodded. "Sell the pearls and use the money to your advantage. That's my advice."

She folded her arms in front of her. "I don't need your advice. They're *my* pearls. I won't agree to sell them just because you come in here with a bunch of stories and put a high price on them." She scoffed. "What makes you think I believe you? What do you care about me?"

He shrugged. "Well, if you change your mind, I'll contact the pearl-buyer." He stood, pulling a handkerchief from his pocket. "I found something today. I want you to have it." He came around the table as he untied a knot in the handkerchief. He turned the corners back and revealed the white pearl from Goose Prairie Cove. He picked it up and placed it in her hand. "This one's worth another hundred and fifty or so."

Carol Anne was seething. Now she had him figured out. He knew what she was, and she knew what he wanted. In spite of his fancy talk and his good looks and his heroism, he was just another riverboat man. She suddenly doubted that he had ever read about pearls at all, or had ever been to the South Sea. He was just making it all up to exaggerate the value of the gift, hoping she would respond in kind.

Still, she was ready to earn that pearl. He didn't know about her power. She could snuff the lantern and turn him into someone else. He would never even realize it. She would keep the pearl, and under its rainbow luster, imprison a million visions of bliss. She didn't need him. She only needed his pearl. She closed her palm around it and began deciding who he would be when he crawled into her bed.

"Like I said, I've had some bad luck with pearls. I'd just as soon somebody else had it who appreciates it." He went to the door and put on his hat. "Like the moon through a rainbow." He smiled. "I'll remember that." Then he was gone.

Carol Anne opened her hand and looked at Billy's gift. She angled her palm and let the perfect sphere roll down her fingertips, onto the velvet. It bumped against another pearl and quenched, in an instant, all the silly images associated with it. Like a ripple from a stone thrown in the water, the power of the new white pearl spread outward and rinsed the fragile fantasies from each of the others, leaving them quiet and dead. Now only Billy's pearl remained animated with hopes and desires.

She burst through the door and ran down the steps. She sprinted around the corner of the store and saw him crossing the street toward Widow Humphry's inn.

"Mr. Treat!" she cried.

He turned.

"Contact the pearl-buyer."

He nodded and waved. "Call me Billy."

6

THERE IS NO SUCH THING AS A FOURTEEN-YEAR-OLD GENTLEMAN. IF YOU think you've found one, he's got you fooled. I don't care how often he says please, thank you, and yes ma'am—in his private mind, he's another person.

Take me, for example. I was well-liked by adults in Port Caddo. They thought of me as a fine boy. Of course, a few of the men who could remember being fourteen were on to me, but the ladies had no clue. My mother, I am sure, thought never a lecherous idea crossed my mind. She would have been horrified had she known the truth.

Cecil Peavy's old man, Joe Peavy, was a horse trader in Port Caddo. He was an expert judge of horseflesh. He could look at horses' legs and tell you how it would feel to ride them. He would comment on the muscling of the thighs, the curvature of the hips. He liked horses spare in the flank and round in the loin. He knew them from throatlatch to tail, from hock to knee. He could even look at a mare and tell you whether or not she would ever "fall apart," meaning to break down and lose her fine conformation at a certain age.

Well, that summer I started applying Joe Peavy's principles to females of the human species. There was nothing gentlemanly about the way I ogled girls and young women, sizing them up like horseflesh. I too liked them spare in the flank and curved in the hips. And I could give you my opinion as to whether or not they would fall apart before the age of twenty-seven.

I knew every vantage in town that facilitated a regular look at girls, and many of them were situated around Snyder's store, for Pearl Cobb was the ideal against which all other specimens were judged.

Behind the store there was a large oak tree with a comfortable fork about twenty feet up that afforded a perfect view of the stairs leading to Pearl's room. I often perched there after dark, hoping to see her ascend. Then I would watch the window and wonder what she was doing. Occasionally I would see her through the curtains. I wasn't exactly a Peeping Tom, for I had no real malicious intent. I was just a fourteen-year-old boy with raging curiosities.

I was there in the oak tree when Billy Treat went up to Pearl's room, and I hated him. I thought I knew what he was going to do with the pearl that should have belonged to me. That's why I was so surprised to see the lantern come on. I saw them sit together at the table. They talked. Then they stood. Then he left.

I didn't know what to make of Billy. I was at first relieved. He hadn't used his pearl as others had used theirs before him. He wasn't trying to trade it in for the vague pleasures of Pearl in the dark. Then, somehow, I knew that that was what made him dangerous. He was a gentleman and I was not.

I saw Pearl run from her room, down the stairs, around the store. I heard her call out to him. She came home alone.

It confused me. Was he going to ruin everything Pearl Cobb was, or was he going to rescue her as he had rescued me from the sinking riverboat? I feared and respected him, admired and hated him. He wasn't a particularly nice fellow to be around, but I liked him. I feared he would find work elsewhere and leave town, and at the same time, I couldn't wait for him to go.

Thankfully, something happened in Port Caddo that took my mind off of Pearl Cobb and Billy Treat for a while. Some workmen came up from Shreveport in a government snag boat to remove the remnants of the *Glory of Caddo Lake* from the bayou channel. The snag boat had been built to winch stumps and dead trees up from the waters and cut them into harmless pieces. Those snags, as they were called, had ripped open the thin wooden hulls of many a riverboat.

Every snag boat I ever saw floated on two hulls that would straddle a snag. A steam winch between the two hulls would lift that snag out of the water where the steam-powered saws could cut it up. The snag boat was invented by Henry Shreve, the old riverboat genius and founder of Shreveport. For years, the government employed him and his snag boats to clear the Great Raft from the Red River, so steamers could navigate above it. Shreve had been dead more than twenty years that summer, but his inventions were still whittling away at that immense logjam on the Red.

This snag boat that was pulling the old *Glory* apart usually worked at removing the Great Raft, but had come up through Caddo Lake to clear the wreck from our channel for us.

Between baiting our trotline and checking it for fish, Cecil Peavy and Adam Owens and I spent a lot of time on the Port Caddo wharf watching the snag boat work. Billy Treat also came out to watch when he wasn't cooking or cleaning up the kitchen in Widow Humphry's inn. He seemed very interested. Every evening when the snag-boat men quit work, he asked them what they had found.

One day a steamer came up Big Cypress Bayou and instead of tying up at the Port Caddo wharf, it anchored first beside the snag boat in the channel. The rousters put a gangplank between the two boats and we saw a fellow in alligator shoes and a silk tie cross the gangplank to the snag boat. He poked around for a long time, asking questions and writing things down. Then he had one of the snag-boat men bring him to the wharf in a rowboat.

"That's him," the snag-boat worker said, pointing at Billy, who was standing on the wharf at the time.

"Are you Billy Treat?" the man asked, stepping up on the wharf.

He was a chubby fellow of about forty, dressed in slick New Orleans styles, stained with sweat. He grew little-bitty mustaches that looked like they had been drawn on with a pencil.

"Yes," Billy said.

"You were the cook on the *Glory of Caddo Lake?*"

"Who are *you?*" Billy asked.

The man stuck out his hand. "Joshua Lagarde, Delta State Insurance Company, New Orleans. We hold the policy on the *Glory of Caddo Lake*. The owners have put in a claim."

"The owners?" Billy said. "Captain Gentry was the only owner I knew of."

Lagarde mopped his neck with a handkerchief and shook with a chuckle. "Gentry didn't own the boat, Mr. Treat. He sold it six months ago to pay off some gambling debts. The new owners simply insisted that he continue to pose as captain and owner so as not to damage trade. At least that's the story they give."

"Who are these new owners?" Billy asked.

"I'm not at liberty to say. I would appreciate your cooperation, Mr. Treat, but you'll have to let me ask the questions."

I nudged Adam Owens. "Run to my pop's office and tell him there's a story on the wharf," I said. Adam wasn't listening to what was going on anyway. As long as I knew him, he never cared much for gossip and intrigue. He died a simple working man. He took off at a run toward my pop's newspaper office, delighted to have something to do.

"Now, Mr. Treat," Lagarde said, "the fellows on the snag boat have brought up the steam engines and all their fittings—the throttle, the valves, etcetera. I've found something quite curious about them. All the valves were closed at the time of the explosion. Do you have any idea why?"

"Yes, I do," Billy said. "There was nobody in the engine room when the boat blew up. . . ." He went on to tell how the explosion had occurred, and he told it in such detail that it gave my pop time to arrive. Pop walked up real casual and pretended to be watching the snag-boat work. But he was in easy listening distance of the insurance man. Billy was just finishing up by explaining how the *Glory*'s engineer had climbed into the yawl only minutes before the boilers blew.

"Why would he do that?" Lagarde asked.

"His story was that he wanted to check something on the paddle wheel as the boat got underway."

Lagarde scribbled something down in a notebook. "How much do you know about steamboats, Mr. Treat?"

"I worked on the *Glory* for a year and a half. I knew her pretty well."

"Do you know what this is?" He motioned to the man in the rowboat, who handed up a large iron cylinder, pretty badly mangled.

Billy took it in one hand. "Used to be a safety valve."

"Notice anything unusual about it?"

"Yes. The valve lever has been loaded down with extra weight."

"What does that mean?"

"I think you know what it means, Lagarde. It defeats the purpose of having a safety valve in the first place, doesn't it?"

Lagarde chuckled again and took the valve back. "The men couldn't find the other two safety valves. This one came from the only boiler that didn't explode. Who do you suppose might have loaded the lever down?"

"You'd have to ask the engineer."

"I have a Mr. Judd Kelso listed as the engineer."

"That's right."

"Any idea where I might find him?"

"Right now," Billy said, "he's probably over at old Esau's saloon."

Lagarde's eyes widened. "He's still here? He hasn't left town?"

"No. I hear he's got family around here."

"Have you noticed him spending money freely, making any large purchases?"

Billy Treat glanced at me. "He's been flashing a big roll of bills."

"That's right," I said. "I've seen it."

Cecil stepped up. "Me, too. That big around." He made a circle with his fingers.

Joshua Lagarde mopped his face and smiled. "Where is this saloon?"

"A couple of miles from town," Billy said. "I'll walk over there with you, if you'd like."

"Why not drive?" Pop said, turning suddenly and stepping up to the men. "I was thinking about taking a buggy over there and having a little drink this afternoon anyway." He nudged Lagarde.

The insurance man smiled and licked his lips.

I don't know how my pop did it, but he could tell you half a man's life just by looking at him. That's what made him such a good newspaper man. He had Joshua Lagarde pegged as a drinker the instant he saw him. Pop wasn't normally a drinker himself, but he'd swallow a few to get in on a good story.

"Ben, you and your friends go hitch the buggy," he said, even before Lagarde accepted his offer.

Well, we didn't own a buggy, but I just sang out "Yessir" and ran to Cecil's daddy's livery stable with Cecil and Adam, and we led a horse and buggy back down to the wharf. My pop often used us boys as his special agents to run errands and ferret out good newspaper stories, and we loved it.

"What kind of business are you in, Mr. Crowell?" asked Lagarde as he and Pop and Billy Treat got into the buggy.

"I own a print shop," Pop said, never mentioning the newspaper. It was true. He did a lot of printing on the side.

Us boys didn't get to ride to the saloon with the men, but I found out later what happened. I asked Pop about it, and read his report when it came out in the paper. Years later, I came across the notes he had made after the meeting at the saloon. He had amazing recall for details and could repeat a conversation almost to the word after the fact. In his *Port Caddo Steam Whistle* article, he didn't use much of the conversation that took place at Esau's saloon, because it didn't prove anything conclusively, and Pop didn't print rumor or speculation. But his notes say the meeting went like this:

> *Lagarde*: Mr. Kelso, were you the engineer on the *Glory of
> Caddo Lake* the morning she blew up?
> *Kelso*: I damn sure was.

Lagarde: Were you on the boat when she blew?

Kelso: Of course.

Lagarde: Mr. Treat says you were in the yawl.

Kelso: Well, I was, but I was right beside the boat. I was going to have my apprentice tow me behind the boat so I could listen to a thumping sound I heard in the paddle wheel and try to figure out what was making it. (Kelso very indignant toward Treat.)

Lagarde: Why wasn't anyone in the engine room when the captain gave the signal to steam ahead?

Kelso: I told my apprentice to let the yawl down and get back into the engine room. He was slow, I guess.

Lagarde: Where is your apprentice now?

Kelso: I don't know. He went off looking for work.

Treat: He rode the *Sarah Stevens* down to New Orleans to find a job. His name is Reggie Swearengen. (Kelso glowering at Treat. Lagarde writing notes.)

Lagarde: Mr. Kelso, in your opinion, what caused the boilers to explode on the *Glory of Caddo Lake*?

Kelso: They were old, and the niggers threw too much wood under them.

Lagarde: As far as you know, were the safety valves on the boilers in good working order?

Kelso: Yes.

Lagarde: How do you know?

Kelso: I set them myself.

Lagarde: Did you hear them releasing steam at any time before the explosion?

Kelso: I didn't notice. I guess they did.

Lagarde: Mr. Kelso, we have recovered a safety valve from the wreck. It was loaded down with extra weight. Can you explain that? (Kelso nervous. Goes outside to relieve himself. Gone two minutes.)

Lagarde: About the safety valves, Mr. Kelso.

Kelso: Yes, I just remembered. Captain Gentry checked

the valves the night before the blowup. I saw him.

Lagarde: What are you saying?

Kelso: I'm saying he checked them.

Lagarde: Why didn't you mention that before?

Kelso: It didn't seem worth it. He was always going behind me and checking things.

Treat: He never checked my work.

Kelso: (Angry.) You're just a goddamn cook, Treat!

Lagarde: Mr. Kelso, are you suggesting that Captain Gentry may have intentionally blown the boat up?

Kelso: If the safety valves were loaded down, he must have done it. I know I didn't.

Lagarde: Why would Captain Gentry want to blow up the *Glory of Caddo Lake*?

Kelso: You're the investigator. You tell me.

Lagarde: Captain Gentry had nothing to gain. He didn't have the policy on the boat. He didn't own it.

Kelso: (Doesn't seem surprised.) Maybe he did it for whoever it was that did own it. The son of a bitch! He could have blown us all to hell, but just ended up killing himself! (Laughs.)

My pop's notes also mention that Billy didn't drink, that Kelso insisted on paying for Lagarde's drinks from a large roll of cash he carried in his pocket, and that after a few rounds, Lagarde let it slip that the owners of the *Glory of Caddo Lake* were suspected in a number of other insurance-fraud cases.

In his article, Pop only mentioned that insurance fraud was suspected and that the explosion might have been intentional. He didn't even print Kelso's name, but word got around town that Kelso was a prime suspect. Before long, it was plain that everybody in Port Caddo considered him a murderer. But Kelso was hardheaded and stayed around. He avoided nobody. It seemed he wanted to taunt us. He was an idiot. The days of vigilante lynch mobs were not that far behind us.

I guess he figured he was protected because he came from a big family of ruffians, all of them living over at Long Point.

Joshua Lagarde didn't stay in town long. He took the mangled safety valve from the *Glory of Caddo Lake* back to New Orleans as physical evidence. His investigation would eventually prove that Kelso had blown up the *Glory* for a price.

I didn't find out about that until years later, and by that time, the proof was worthless, seeing as how Kelso was already dead. He was knifed to death in Carol Anne Cobb's room and nobody to this day can prove who did it. But I'm getting ahead of myself, because Kelso wasn't killed until September—after the rise and fall of that wondrous event called the Great Caddo Lake Pearl Rush.

7

THE GANGPLANK BENT AND SPRANG UNDER THE WEIGHT OF TREVOR BRIG-ginshaw as he bounded down it to the Port Caddo wharf. He carried a large leather satchel, buffed with age around the corners, etched everywhere with hairline cracks, and stuffed to bulging with unknown contents. In spite of the July heat and humidity, he wore a white cotton jacket that strained at the seams around his bulk, like an overfilled grain sack.

He looked like a huge animated hero from a romantic painting, his neck rigid, beard full and jutting, chest barreled, legs consuming ground in great, powerful strides. He hummed an Australian marching song as he strode up the bayou bank to the cobblestones, where the business district of Port Caddo began.

People stopped to watch him pass. His size alone made him conspicuous. He stood six-foot-five and carried two hundred fifty pounds as if chiseled from a great trunk of oak. Despite his size, he did not appear fearsome. In fact, there was something engaging about his energy and lively swagger.

"You there!" he shouted to Robert Timmons, the tinsmith, as he reached high ground. "You, mate! A word, please." His deep Australian brogue pinned Timmons in his tracks. Brigginshaw swept his panama hat from his head as he descended on the local informant. "I'm looking for a Miss Carol Anne Cobb. Where can I find her?"

Timmons pointed up the street as he tried to take in all of Trevor Brigginshaw and make some kind of sense out of what such a character would be doing in Port Caddo, Texas. "Snyder's store," he said. "The building with the red brick front, up the street. She works there."

"Good man!" Brigginshaw said through a toothy smile. He slapped the panama back onto his curly head and hiked up the street on swinging cassowary legs.

The brass bell on the door of Snyder's store jingled in alarm as the huge Australian burst in. His size in the doorway brought the darkness of storm clouds into the building. Pearl stepped back from the counter in surprise and three wives looked up from their shopping lists.

Brigginshaw's eyes fell on the exquisite form of Pearl. "Miss Cobb?" he said.

She nodded.

The worn leather satchel blew dust from the cracks as it hit the hardwood floor. Brigginshaw dragged his panama from his head and onto his gigantic heart. He strode as if entranced to the counter between himself and Pearl. "Billy Treat is a bloody fool to have understated your beauty." He reached for her fingers, bowed over the counter, and kissed the back of her hand.

Pearl pulled her hand away. The three customers were agog, watching from the aisles between the store shelves.

"Who are you?" Pearl said.

"Captain Trevor Price Brigginshaw—Sydney, London, and New York."

"Well. . . . What do you want?"

"I've come to purchase your pearls."

"You're the pearl-buyer?"

"The pearl-buyer?" Brigginshaw bellowed. "Is that how the wretch refers to me? The pearl-buyer? Doesn't he have the common decency to name me? He that saved Billy Treat from pirates among the Pearl Islands of the Southern Seas? I'll thrash the lout when I see him again!" He laughed to keep from shocking her.

"I don't think he meant anything by it," Pearl said.

"You think not? Billy's a calculating bloke, Miss Cobb. He doesn't do anything without purpose. Now, where do you keep this collection of exquisite pearls? If they are as beautiful as you, I promise I cannot afford to buy them."

"Now? I'm working right now," she said. But when she thought of ridding herself of all those angel tears, as Billy had said the Romans called them, she couldn't wait. "Oh, all right, I'll get them." She turned to the customers. "You ladies make your own change," she said, and swept past Trevor Brigginshaw to the door.

When she came back from her room with the tobacco tin, she found the pearl buyer opening his satchel on the store counter. "Not in here," she said. "Over at Widow Humphry's inn. Billy works there."

"I insist on business before pleasure, Miss Cobb. Let's have a look at the pearls and strike a deal, then we'll see Billy."

"Let's see Billy first," Pearl said, sternly. "I don't know anything about grading pearls. You might swindle me."

"I? A cheat?" Brigginshaw roared.

Pearl looked away, as if bored.

The big Australian began to laugh. He laughed so loud that one of the customers covered her ears. "Has Billy mentioned only my vilest characteristics, Miss Cobb? I'd brain another man for less, but with a skull as thick as Billy's, it would benefit him no more than it would a hammerhead shark." He buckled the leather satchel. "Is the Widow Humphry as beautiful as you?"

Pearl Cobb and Trevor Brigginshaw caused a sensation crossing the main street of Port Caddo together. Robert Timmons had already alerted the town to the arrival of the big Australian. When Pearl and Trevor reached the inn, the women in Snyder's store dispersed without buying anything or making any change, and went to spread the news.

The buyer and the seller found Billy in the kitchen, cleaning up the dinner mess.

"My God, can it be?" Brigginshaw said. "The king of Mangareva's become a lowly galley rat!"

Billy wheeled. His eyes fell on Pearl first, momentarily. Then he shifted his pale gaze to the Australian. "Trev," he said.

Pearl saw a new Billy. Life leaped into his eyes and molded his face with a smile. He wrung his greasy hands on an apron as he marched forward and fell into the crushing embrace of Trevor Brigginshaw. They shook the whole inn, hopping in each other's arms like boys, each slapping the other's back as if trying to put out a fire.

A couple of the most avid gossips in town happened to come visiting at Widow Humphry's just as Pearl and the two men retired to Billy's room. It was scandalous. The two men went down the hall laughing and talking, and Pearl followed them into the room with her tobacco tin.

When Captain Trevor Brigginshaw took off his white jacket, Pearl almost gasped at the revolver stuck under his belt, its handle inlaid with mother-of-pearl.

"Nothing to fear," he said, sensing her apprehension. "The weapon is intended strictly for security of the company's property. I rarely have to use it."

"The company?" Billy said. "What company?"

"International bloody Gemstones," Trevor said with a snarl.

"I thought you were independent."

"The company's only a temporary inconvenience, mate. Until I can afford another boat and get back among the Pearl Islands."

"What happened to the *Wicked Whistler?*"

"Hurricane, last year on Jamaica. Now, let's not take up any more of Miss Cobb's valuable time with our personal business. I'll tell you all about it later." Captain Brigginshaw opened his satchel, took out a rolled piece of black velvet, and spread it across Billy's table. "The pearls, if you please, Miss Cobb."

She gave him the tobacco tin. He opened it, poker-faced, and shrugged as he poured the pearls onto the black velvet. He began sorting them, as Billy Treat had done in her room. He hummed as he made piles, his rich baritone voicing an occasional phrase. Pearl looked at Billy. He smiled at her.

"They pale in comparison to your loveliness, Miss Cobb," Trevor said after several minutes of sorting. "I'm afraid they disappoint me."

Billy scoffed and chuckled.

"Let's start with these small ones. They're little better than seed pearls. I can pay no more than thirty-five dollars for each."

Billy laughed. "Seed pearls! There's not a pearl there smaller than ten grains! Even the baroques are worth eighty dollars each."

"You've been out of the business too long, Billy. These dogtooth and wing pearls are virtually worthless on today's market. . . ."

They haggled for fifteen minutes and finally arrived at a figure of seventy-five dollars apiece for the first batch of ten pearls. Trevor removed a ledger book from his satchel and mumbled as he penciled in the first purchase:

"A clutch of ten *seed* pearls . . . seventy-five dollars each . . . Miss Carol Anne Cobb."

His thick fingers picked up the ten pearls one by one and put them in a case with velvet folds in it to keep the gems from rolling around. "Now, for this group of seven, I'll pay eighty dollars each. They're hardly superior to the first clutch."

Billy laughed again. "You see what he's done, Carol Anne? He's separated your best pairs. See these two pear-shaped specimens? They're perfectly matched, and worth more when sold together, for making earrings. But Trev here has put them in different batches! Same with these two egg-shaped pearls."

The haggling commenced again, and went on for half an hour. The men regrouped the pearls several times and finally agreed on a clutch of five that would sell for one hundred twenty dollars each. Billy looked at Pearl. She nodded. Trevor made the notations in the ledger book.

The eight finest pearls remained on the black velvet. In an hour,

Billy and Trevor had agreed to put six of them in a batch to sell for two hundred each. Billy looked at Pearl for approval.

"Not that one," she said, indicating the pearl of living visions that Billy had given her. "It's not for sale." She removed it from the group and held it in her hand.

Billy's face revealed nothing to Trevor Brigginshaw.

Only two pearls remained unsold. Brigginshaw tried to group them together, but Billy insisted on bargaining for each separately. He graded the yellow oval at nineteen grains. Trevor said it was only fifteen. He took the pieces of a small scale from his satchel, put it together, and weighed the pearl at almost exactly nineteen grains. Billy mentioned its superior shape, luster, and overtone. He would settle for no less than three hundred dollars. Pearl agreed. Trevor relented after forty-five minutes.

They spent a full hour dickering over the smoky-blue teardrop that had begun Pearl's collection six years before. Thirty grains, Billy said. Trevor shook the inn with laughter. But the scale and the pearl's shape, color, and orient ultimately demanded seven hundred and fifty dollars, despite the Australian's fiercest negotiations.

Brigginshaw sighed as he made the final entry in his ledger. "Miss Cobb, my trip to Port Caddo has hardly been worth my time at these high prices. What little gratitude Billy has shown me for saving his life from pirates in the South Pacific."

"Don't let your conscience bother you, Carol Anne," Billy said. "This man's a pirate himself when it comes to pearls. Those big hands have held more pearls than all the royalty in the world put together ever did."

Brigginshaw chuckled. "Now, about that last pearl," he said. "May I have another look at it?"

Carol Anne opened her hand and put the pearl on the black velvet. The buyer picked up a pearl case and probed through a few of the folds. "No, not that one," he mumbled. "No, too small. Wrong color. Ah! Here it is. A perfect match." He removed a white sphere, identical to the one on the velvet cloth. "This one came from Pennsylvania. Since it matches yours, I can offer an extra fifty. Two hundred fifty dollars, Miss Cobb. What?"

Carol Anne took her pearl back into her hand. "This one's not for sale," she said.

"Three hundred?"

"No. It was a gift." She folded her fingers around it protectively.

Billy remained silent.

Carol Anne was about to ask how International Gemstones would pay for the pearls when the Australian lifted a stack of bills from his satchel. He slowly and methodically counted out thirty-four one-hundred-dollar bills.

Before handing them to her, he said, "I insist on one stipulation before making this deal complete."

"What now?" Billy asked.

"Both of you must keep your mouth shut about these ridiculous prices. I won't be taken this badly again if there are any other pearls to be purchased about here. Agreed?"

"I'll agree," Billy replied.

"Yes, that's fine," Carol Anne said.

After the money changed hands, Trevor wanted to celebrate. But Carol Anne said she had to get back to the store. Mr. Snyder was probably furious at her for taking the entire afternoon off. And Billy had to prepare supper for the boarders.

"Just as well," Trevor said, covering his weapon as he put on his jacket. "That will give me just enough time before supper to do a little business in town. Set an extra plate, Billy. I hope you're a better cook than friend."

The inn's parlor had seldom seen as much socializing. When Carol Anne and the two men left Billy's room, a hush enveloped a dozen or more town gossips, men and women. Carol Anne went out first, ignoring the eyes that followed her.

"Who's your friend, Mr. Treat?" someone asked, before Billy could turn into the kitchen.

"Captain Trevor Price Brigginshaw," the big Australian said, letting Billy go with a wave.

"Staying with us tonight, Mr. Brigginshaw?" Widow Humphry asked.

"I would be pleased to, Madam. I was hoping you would have accommodations available."

"Oh, yes. We haven't filled up since before the war. Shall I have the boy take your suitcase up?"

"No, thank you, my good woman. It never leaves my side. It's because of this bloody case that I have never married. It's a terrible burden in bed."

Some of the men laughed, a couple of ladies giggled, and the others gasped. Widow Humphry urged the owner of the case in question to sign the register.

"Whatever you've got in there, it must be important for you to take it to bed with you," said Robert Timmons.

"It is filled with things of great value and beauty," Brigginshaw said. "Things that I am bound to protect with my life."

"Your accent is delightful," said an infatuated young woman. "Do you mind our asking . . . ?"

"Not at all. I've heard that you Texans are a great deal like us Australians—never pass up an opportunity to boast whence you hail. Sydney, Australia, is my home, though I keep residences in New York and London as well."

"Put the name of your firm here, if you wish," Widow Humphry said. She made knowing faces at the locals over the big man's back as he bent to write in the space she had indicated. "Your room will be upstairs. First on the left. Supper at six."

"Thank you, my good woman. Now, if someone will direct me to the local newspaper office . . ."

Several volunteers rendered the directions and the pearl-buyer left, tipping his panama as he stepped out. There was a general rush to read the register when he was gone.

•   •   •

In two minutes, Trevor Brigginshaw had found the offices of the *Port Caddo Steam Whistle*. John Crowell knew about him already, and had been receiving reports from news-gathering spies all afternoon. He was busy setting type, however, and couldn't get out of the office to do any snooping on his own. He was happy to see the news come to him for a change.

"It's my pleasure to meet you," Crowell said, shaking the stranger's powerful hand. "I've been saving a place for you at the bottom of page one. My instincts tell me some import accompanies your visit."

"God bless a bloke who follows his instincts. Mine have kept me alive for many years. Getting an issue together soon, are you?"

"Going to press tonight, as a matter of fact. Your timing is very good."

"Between my timing and your instincts, we may just benefit each other, Mr. Crowell. We very well may." He sat down in front of the editor's desk, holding his satchel in his lap. "I'm here to buy pearls. I've already made one confidential purchase this afternoon, and I'd like to advertise for more in your paper. What are you laughing at, mate?"

"I'm sorry," Crowell said, wiping his inky hands on his apron. "It's just that everybody in town already knows about your 'confidential' purchase."

"That I gathered. But the details will have to remain confidential. I can say only that the local collector had many pearls valued at about ten thousand dollars."

The smile slid from John Crowell's face. "Did you say *ten* thousand?"

"Roughly. Don't press for details, Mr. Crowell. I can't tell you any more than that. The collector insisted."

"Ten thousand dollars! How many pearls did she have? She couldn't have had more than twenty or twenty-five."

"I'm not at liberty to say."

"Ten thousand dollars!" The editor got up to look at the hole in his front-page plate. "I had no idea those pearls would bring such high prices."

"I wish I could give you more details of the sale for your front-page story, Mr. Crowell, but the collector wants to avoid publicity. I, on the other hand, want to feed it. I wonder if a quarter-page advertisement might make a good start."

"It might," Crowell said. "But a half-page—and a story at the top of page one instead of the bottom—might attract a good deal more publicity. Yes, a good deal more."

Trevor Brigginshaw smiled as he opened his money case. "A sensible newspaper man is more difficult to come by than the finest paragon of pearls. You, mate, are a gem!"

8

YOU KNOW WHEN I GOT RELIGION? WHEN I FOUND OUT JESUS WAS A FISHerman.

I have lived within casting distance of water all my life, and I guess I've caught fish every which way known to man. I've sailed the Gulf of Mexico and hooked tarpon bigger than calves. I've climbed the Rocky Mountains to fly-cast for rainbow trout in waters barely ankle-deep. I've waded the mouths of big rivers and speared flounder by lantern light with a pointed stick.

But the best fishing waters I know of in the world are right here at Caddo Lake. If you could take all the fish I've caught here in my life and put them together at one time, they would fill up the lake they came from. I'm mainly a sport fisherman now, and just plug some for bass around the lily pads. Bass are good fighting fish and not bad eating. I also enjoy fishing with live minnows on cane poles for white perch. And I once made pretty good money catching those spoonbill catfish around spawning time to pass their eggs off as caviar.

But back in my younger days is when I really caught fish. I would load them in barrels to ship to Marshall, Jefferson, or Dallas. That and duck-hunting and hogs and boat-building have gotten me through some lean years when the sawmills and railroads weren't hiring.

I used to set gill nets and trammel nets in the Big Water and up Jeem's Bayou to catch carp and buffalo by the hundreds every night. Old Esau showed me how to shoot them with a bow and arrow, tying a stout cord to the arrow. I once shot a hundred-and-twenty-pound alligator gar that fought for over an hour before I clubbed it senseless with an oar.

After Billy Treat taught us how to hold our breath for a good long time, Adam Owens and I became famous around here for hand-grabbling those big opelousas cats out of hollow logs and out from under washed-out banks.

But of all the fishing I have ever done, trotlining gives me the biggest thrill. I like it even better than those hooking those huge tarpon in salt water or catching those rising trout from the mountain streams. People who consider themselves sport fishermen scoff at the trotline, but I know of no finer tool for recreation or livelihood, and it all started for me that summer back in 1874, when me and Cecil Peavy and Adam Owens were catching cats for Billy Treat's kitchen.

We were on the lake at sunrise the day the Great Caddo Lake Pearl Rush began. It looked like any other summer day to us as we launched old Esau's skiff and started paddling toward our trotline over near Mossy Brake. We were talking about Captain Trevor Price Brigginshaw, who had come to town the day before.

"He's big as ol' Colored Bob over at the sawmill," Adam claimed.

"He's not that big," Cecil argued. "Colored Bob has to duck to go under doors."

"Well, he talks funnier than Colored Bob." Adam had his own strange way of winning arguments.

As they paddled and contradicted each other, I opened mussels to bait the trotline with, and of course I checked them all for pearls.

"Ben," Cecil said, "what are you gonna do if you really find a shell berry in there? Are you gonna trade it in for ten thousand dollars, or a hump with Pearl Cobb?"

"One pearl ain't worth ten thousand dollars," I said, avoiding the more interesting half of the question.

"I thought you said today's paper was gonna talk about Pearl Cobb selling a pearl for ten thousand dollars."

"It doesn't say it was Carol Anne, and it doesn't say it was just one pearl. Don't you ever listen?"

"I guess she probably sold that Captain Brigginshaw a couple of hundred pearls to get that much money. Lord knows, she's got a thousand of 'em."

"Shut up, Cecil," I said.

"You like her, don't you?" Adam asked.

Before I could think of an answer, Cecil said, "Like her? He's in love with her, boy, can't you tell? If Ben found a ten-thousand-dollar shell berry right now, he'd give it to Pearl Cobb for one hump, when he could get a couple of thousand humps for it over at the nigger whorehouse."

"How would you know, Cecil?"

We aggravated one another like that until we saw our trotline floats bobbing. The second-biggest thrill in trotlining is seeing those floats bob. When you see that, you know you've caught something. We had good-sized cork floats on our trotline, and we hadn't yet caught anything big enough to pull one all the way under. But that morning, as we approached, we saw the cork stay under for five seconds, and we knew we had hooked a monster.

Cecil was businesslike, as usual. While Adam and I were almost falling overboard with excitement, he said, "Take it easy! We'll run it from the north end, like we always do. Whatever it is that's on there, it won't go anywhere. Probably just a big snappin' turtle or an alligator gar, anyway."

We had been using mussels to bait the line and had been catching mostly willow cats, because they don't mind eating dead bait. Billy had been very pleased with our catches. They were mainly in the three-and four-pound class. A fresh willow cat of that size—skinned, filleted, and fried—is the best-eating fish in the world. The biggest we had caught was maybe ten pounds. We all knew that if we wanted to catch a huge opelousas catfish, we needed to put something live on the hook.

We had also caught a few carp, which we gave to some colored folks we knew, but I didn't think a carp would get big enough to hold the cork float down that long.

Figuring Cecil was probably right, I got a little nervous. An alligator gar big enough to pull that cork under like that would have a snout a foot long, lined with razor teeth. A snapping turtle of the same size could take your fingers off with one snap, quicker than you could blink.

But whatever it was, it wouldn't get *my* fingers. It was Adam's job to take the critters off the hooks. He had a knack for handling thrashing catfish without getting barbed, and I figured he could handle a gar or a snapper, too. Maybe he would just cut the line and let the monster go, the hook still in its mouth.

I figured it was a gar. We hadn't yet taken any turtles off the line on the morning runs. Turtles usually won't bother a trotline at night. Yes, I was pretty sure it was a gar, but that was part of the lure of trotlining. When you see those floats bobbing, you never really know what you've got until you hoist it up from the deep.

We paddled to a big cypress standing in the water at the edge of Mossy Brake. We had one end of our line tied to a cypress knee next to the tree. From there it ran down into a channel where those willow cats liked to prowl. Some people, as a matter of fact, call them channel cats for just that reason.

Adam sat in the front of the skiff. He would grab the line, pull the boat along, and take the fish off the hooks. I was in the back of the boat. I kept the boat straight, helped pull on the line, and put fresh bait on the hooks. Cecil was useless except as a counterweight. With Adam and me hanging over the right side of the skiff, it was helpful to have Cecil sit on the left side, to keep the boat as level as possible. As long as I knew Cecil, he always preferred to let other people do the work for him while he sat back and counted money.

The sun and the rich, rotten smell of the lake were hitting us when Adam began working the line. We pulled the skiff along, passing the rock we had tied on to pull the line to the right depth and keep it tight. Along the main line were lighter cords, about a foot and a half long, tied at six-foot intervals, and on these lighter cords were our hooks. The first few were empty. I untangled the twisted cords and baited their hooks with fresh mussels. Then I felt the first tug, despite Adam's hold on the line.

The biggest thrill in trotlining is feeling the fish tug from down deep. Even a little catfish can pull the line pretty hard. As we approached the next hook, I saw the flash of gray down in the brown, muddy water. Adam was smiling. He lived for simple pleasures like that. He pulled a three-pound willow cat to the surface. It splashed us pretty good before he got it unhooked and into the boat.

Catfish have bony barbs on their pectoral fins, and one on their dorsal fin, too. If they stick you, it aches something fierce for a long time. The skin has some kind of poison in it, I've heard. But Adam Owens wasn't afraid of anything you could pull out of the water, and he knew how to grab a catfish around those bony barbs where it couldn't jab him. He knew how to grab alligators, water moccasins, wild hogs, and snapping turtles, too.

He carried a pair of pliers in his pocket and had the hook out of the fish's mouth in no time. He threw it between the bulkheads at Cecil's bare feet.

"Hey, watch it!" Cecil said as the cat flipped and flopped around. "That thing will stick me!"

"Oh, shut up, Cecil," I said, still put out over what he had said about Carol Anne. "Just keep the boat steady."

We worked down the line, me and Adam feeling anxiously for the tug of every fish we had hooked, and getting more excited as we came closer to the place where something big was pulling the cork float under.

"All right, here it comes!" Adam said. We were only a couple of hooks away. "Hold the line tight, Ben. Don't let it pull a hook through your finger."

"Can you see it yet?"

"No, not yet. But, by gosh, I can sure feel it!"

The plunges of the creature on our line were rocking the boat like crazy.

"Just cut it loose as soon as you can," Cecil said, calmly. "Don't let it tear up our whole line. Hey, maybe it's a little gator. Watch your hand, Adam!"

"I'm watchin'! Gosh, it pulls hard!"

We worked the skiff forward and Adam grit his teeth lifting the catch. Then I saw it. A huge, flat head rose in the muddy water, then turned for the deep as if the light hurt its beady eyes. A broad tail flipped and splashed a wall of water toward me, even though the fish was still completely submerged.

"What is it?" Cecil demanded.

"It's the biggest damn opelousas cat I ever seen!" Adam's muscles were popping from his thin arms like twisted steel cables as he fought to pull the fish up. The line was all but cutting through his hand.

"Hold on tight, Adam!" I said.

He gave a loud grunt and hoisted the monster from the deep. It looked like a dinosaur coming up from Caddo Lake. Its broad, flat head told us it was an opelousas cat. Its mouth looked like the opening to Captain Brigginshaw's money satchel, with a jutting lower lip.

When it broke the surface, I saw its three bayonet-sized barbs, then lost them behind a spray of brown froth. The boat almost pitched Cecil off of the high side. Adam hollered for joy as he reached into the gill under the monster's head and took a firm hold.

"It must weigh seventy-five pounds!"

"Get it in here, then!" Cecil said. "It's worth two bits to each of us!"

The catfish lunged, beat its head against the boat, and splashed bucketfuls all over the place, but Adam hung on. He didn't fool with the hook. He just cut the line that the hook was tied to. He almost fell over backward pulling the fish into the boat, and still wouldn't turn loose of the gills for fear the biggest fish he had ever seen would jump out of the skiff. The thing was fat and grotesque out of the water, beating itself stupidly against the bottom of the skiff and slapping the smaller fish with its tail.

"I guess you were wrong!" Cecil said triumphantly to Adam. "I guess you *can* catch an opelousas cat using dead mussels for bait!"

"No, I was right all along!" Adam said, panting. "Look!"

He pulled the lower jaw of that monster catfish open and we saw a smaller fish in the big one's mouth. About a seven-pound willow cat had taken our mussel bait and hooked itself. Then that giant opelousas cat had risen from its dark hole somewhere to eat the willow cat that had eaten the mussel. The hook alone probably wouldn't have held a fish that big. It probably could have bent it straight getting away. But when it swallowed that willow cat, the smaller fish set its barbs in the big cat's throat, and died holding it on our trotline for us.

Cecil had to take Adam's place running the rest of the line because Adam didn't trust him to hold onto the big fish. We baited as quick as we could, collected a few more normal-sized fish, and paddled back toward old Esau's saloon.

On the way, the *Lizzie Hopkins II* steamed within forty yards of us, en route to Port Caddo. The pilot rang his bell and blew his steam whistle when we showed him the fish. The passengers all crowded the rail to see. We felt like decorated heroes. Lucky ones, at that. We hadn't expected any steamers. The lake was getting almost too low to handle them. The *Lizzie* would be the last one of the summer, until the rains came back.

When we came around Pine Island and caught sight of Esau's place, we saw a big crowd of people standing on the shore, others wading, and some floating in boats. It was as if the news of our tremendous catch had preceded us and people had come out to see it. We didn't know what was going on, but we were thrilled.

"Too bad Pop already printed the paper," I said. "Now we won't be in it till next week."

"He ought to print an extra for a fish like this," Cecil said. "I wonder what all those people are doing at Esau's. Wait a minute. I know what they're doing. Look! They're hunting for pearls!" He laughed so hard that he had to quit paddling. "That's Captain Brigginshaw on the shore with his suitcase."

Cecil was right. Everybody in town had seen Brigginshaw's half-page ad and read about the big pearl sale of the previous day. Half the population of Port Caddo had come to hunt up a fortune in Goose

Prairie Cove, where Billy had recently found his pearl. Nobody had found anything yet, but a few disenchanted wives had brought old specimens their husbands had given them years before. Brigginshaw was dealing for them in the shade of a big mulberry.

"There's Billy standing beside that Brigginshaw fellow," I said.

"Good," Cecil replied. "He can pay us on the spot for this fish."

When we got closer, we started hollering to attract attention. We paddled in among the pearl-waders and let them look over the edge of the boat at our fish. Esau met us at the bank with Billy and Captain Brigginshaw. They made us feel good, bragging on us for bringing in such a monster whisker fish. Pop was there too, taking notes on the pearl-hunt, and he promised he would write us up on the front page next week. When Billy said he would pay a penny a pound, as promised, Esau doubled the stakes.

"Might as well fry up some fish to feed these hungry pearl hunters," he said.

Most of the pearlers had come out of the water to view our fish and hear our story. They took turns looking into the big cat's mouth, to see the smaller one lodged in its throat. I was bulging with pride. For the first time in my life, I was earning money and getting recognition for something besides being my parents' son. Even Billy was amazed at what I had done. I wondered what Carol Anne would think when she heard.

What had started out as a pearl-hunt was quickly turning into nothing more than a big fish fry. The novelty of opening mussels in search of riches wore off fast. Most of the men were content to stand around our huge opelousas cat and tell fish stories. As whiskey sales increased, Esau decided to buy every fish we had in the boat. And he hired us to skin and gut them.

A couple of men volunteered to carry our big fish up under a tree where we could hang it, whack it on the head to make sure it was dead, and go to work on it. We felt like local heroes as two dozen whiskey-sipping ex-pearl-hunters followed us up under the boughs of the shade tree. It was shaping up to be the most glorious day of my life.

Then it happened. A shout came from Goose Prairie Cove. At first, nobody paid any attention. Slowly, though, I realized that somebody was yelling his lungs out. I heard a body splashing madly through the water, and turned to see Everett Diehl floundering to dry ground, all wet and muddy.

"Pearl!" he hollered. "I found a pearl!"

9

I WAS ACCUSTOMED TO EVERETT DIEHL SPOILING MY FUN, BECAUSE HE taught school at the Caddo Academy where I took my lessons. But school had been out for weeks now and he still wasn't satisfied. He was trying to upstage my catfish with a measly shell slug. As soon as he hollered "Pearl!" every man standing around the big ugly fish hanging in the tree turned and stampeded to the lakeshore to see what he had found.

"I was just about to give up!" Diehl claimed as the crowd gathered around him. "I thought I'd open one more. I almost threw it back in before I saw the pearl stuck to the rim of the shell. Look!"

Captain Brigginshaw pushed through the crowd of men, his money case like a battering ram. He took one glance and said, "Button pearl. I'll give you seventy-five dollars for it."

Diehl's enthusiasm wilted a little. "Seventy-five? But the paper said they were worth thousands."

"Those were excellent specimens, and many of them."

"Still . . ." Diehl lamented. "Just seventy-five dollars . . ."

"No small wage for two hours of work," the captain said, opening his money case. "Seventy-five dollars, take it or leave it."

As Diehl groused, Billy took the mussel shell from him to examine the pearl. "I'd take it," he advised. "This pearl isn't worth fifty. Captain Brigginshaw sometimes inflates the prices in the early going to promote interest."

The big pearl-buyer sighed and frowned at Billy for revealing his tactics. Diehl decided to sell immediately. When his soft, pale fingers closed around the seventy-five dollars, all the men in sight—except for Brigginshaw, Billy, and Esau—turned and ran into Goose Prairie Cove like boys. It was then that the Great Caddo Lake Pearl Rush truly began. My friends and I didn't get to take part in that first stampede. We had to gut and skin catfish.

The hunting went on fruitlessly until about sundown, when Allen Byers, the sawmill owner, came up with a hundred-dollar pearl. Brigginshaw's luck had held out. The pearl fever would carry over to the next day.

By the second day of the pearl rush, I had established a daily routine. At dawn, I rode in the skiff and opened the mussels we had gathered the day before, while Cecil and Adam paddled to our trotline.

After running the line, we took the fish we had caught to our holding tank on the old Packer place. Like Billy Treat, those catfish could hold their breath a long time. The Packer place was a mile from the lake, but the fish could survive out of water until we got them to the big cypress trough.

By that time in the morning, it was hot, so Cecil and Adam and I were happy to go splash around in the water. Port Caddo must have been almost abandoned that second day of the pearl rush. It seemed every man in town was looking for mussels in Goose Prairie Cove. Some ladies had come, too. They didn't wade in like the men did because it wasn't considered ladylike for them to get their clothes all wet and sticking to them, but some of them opened the shells the men brought to the shore.

Cecil and Adam and I threw the mussels we found into one of Esau's skiffs. We would open them that afternoon, on our evening run to the trotline. First, though, we ate some lunch we had brought from home, and found some kind of useless way to occupy ourselves for a couple of hours along the lakeshore, or up in the woods.

By the time we shoved the skiff into Goose Prairie Cove that afternoon, Captain Brigginshaw had purchased three new pearls. As we were paddling away, someone came rowing into the cove, shouting. It was Junior Martin. He had found a two-hundred-dollar pearl somewhere on the North Shore. A new surge of excitement fluttered through the gathering of pearl-hunters.

"Where 'bouts did you find it, Junior?" somebody asked.

"The same old mussel beds I've been gittin' my trotline bait from for years. The best mussel beds on the North Shore."

"Where's that?"

"None of your damn business!" he said with a big grin.

Two men vowed to follow him all over the lake all night long to trail him to his lode. He was a good-natured fellow and challenged them to do just that. Junior was a lake rat and knew how to hide out in the brakes and swamps.

When we left to run our line, spirits were running high at Goose Prairie Cove, and folks were talking about scouting new mussel beds all over the lake.

On the third day of the rush, a couple of farm wagons showed up near Esau's place. The news had spread into the hills and fields. The crops were in the ground and wouldn't require much cultivation, except after a rain. A farmer could leave a couple of his older sons to take care of the fields and bring the rest of the family to the lake to hunt pearls.

On the fourth day, Goose Prairie began to look like a camp meeting. More wagons and tents appeared. Trevor Brigginshaw bought five pearls that day. People waded, napped in the shade, drank whiskey at Esau's, cooked, talked, laughed, and played.

Billy walked over to the cove between dinner and supper, and found me and Cecil and Adam watching a wrestling match between two farm boys.

"Ben, we have a problem," he said.

"*We* do?" Cecil asked.

"Esau can't keep fresh drinking water for all these pearl-hunters. I told him I'd talk to you men about it." He was always calling us "men" when he was trying to get us to do something productive.

"What are we supposed to do about it?" I said.

"Yeah, what are we supposed to do? Make it rain?" Cecil added.

Billy ignored him and talked to me. "Esau will provide the boats and water kegs if you men will row across the lake to Ames Springs every day and bring back water. He'll buy it from you."

Cecil ran to Esau's place and haggled over the price for a while before making the deal. Everybody in camp agreed to use lake water for washing, reserving the spring water for drinking and cooking. After we made our first water haul across the lake that day, we barely had time to run our trotline. My summer was getting busier than I had planned, but now I was making money off of spring water and catfish, and starting to think of things I would like to buy.

My pop's business was booming, too. He became Trevor Brigginshaw's most avid promoter. He was thinking more of Port Caddo than he was of the Australian, of course, but what was good for Brigginshaw was good for the town. International Gemstones continued to run a half-page ad in every issue, so pop went biweekly.

A regular pearl column appeared on the front page. Pop told where the best pearls had come from, what kind of mussels had yielded them, what they looked like, and what they sold for. By surveying pearl-hunters and analyzing the industry, he concluded that the average man would make a dollar a day in the pearl-hunt. But some lucky hunters would earn small fortunes.

Pop's editorials heralded the Caddo Lake pearl boom as the salvation for our town. Pearl money would replace the dying riverboat trade. He urged everyone in town to spread the news of the pearl rush. People would come from surrounding towns and farms. The stores would sell more goods, the inns would fill with weekend pearl-hunters. Everyone would benefit.

At his own expense, Pop printed fliers announcing a pearl rush of unprecedented magnitude on Caddo Lake, centered at our town. He sent them to surrounding towns. Local business people began to spruce up for a pearl boom.

Summer was supposed to be a slack time for trade. The lake had gotten too low for steamers to ply. But something new had come to Port Caddo. A glimmer of hope. People started talking about making the town a "pearl resort." Pop may have been a visionary, but he sure sold the town on his pearl vision.

The *Steam Whistle* carried regular stories of unusual pearl finds: A fellow came from Marshall and found a pearl in the first mussel he opened. A farmer found one lying loose on the shore—probably dropped accidentally by some careless mussel-opener. A camper gutted a fish and found a pearl in its stomach. A boy found a pearl caked in bird dung under a heron rookery.

Of course there were other news stories to report besides the pearl rush, and one article that caused a sensation around the middle of July dealt with the riverboat trade. After decades of work, the government snag boats were finally getting close to removing the Great Raft from the Red River.

I don't know if I've explained exactly why it took so long to get rid of the Great Raft. It was a huge tangle of driftwood, hundreds of years old, that fed itself constantly with trees washed down from upstream. At one time it blocked over a hundred miles of the Red River channel above Shreveport. It was a concern to Port Caddo, because to get into Caddo Lake, steamers had to skirt the edges of the Raft and find a bayou channel deep enough to navigate. The channels shifted constantly as they got choked with new drift logs.

The government contractors were now claiming, however, that the removal of the Raft and the clearing of a channel would make year-'round steamboat traffic possible on Caddo Lake for the first time ever. It seemed that the U.S. Government wanted to keep our steamboat industry afloat, even promising to mark channels to help pilots navigate. Port Caddoans began to talk about a new era of prosperity and a sustainable economy, based on pearls and riverboats.

George Blank, the blacksmith, was one of the first to take advantage of the new prosperity. He started building mussel rakes to sell to the pearl-hunters. He invented two models. One looked like an overgrown garden rake. The other resembled a huge pair of tongs, with two long handles. Both were designed to be used from a boat to get at mussels in water too deep for wading. They sold as fast as he could make them, for a while.

Charlie Ashenback, the best boat-builder on the lake, started taking back-orders. I regarded Charlie as a sort of artist. His skiffs and bateaux were the most graceful things in the water. He used only the best red cypress, and his hands were living tools. He could saw exactly three-eighths of an inch off of a board without even measuring. The boats he built would glide over the water like greased ice. If a fellow had to row all over the lake to find a pearl, he wanted an Ashenback under him.

Trevor Brigginshaw had Ashenback build a rowboat especially designed to carry his great weight, his money satchel, and an oarsman. He hired a young black man named Giff Newton to row the boat for him, while Brigginshaw himself sat in the bow with one hand on his satchel and the other on his pistol, watching for pirates. They made the rounds among all the best pearling spots, black and white.

Colored folks were in on the pearl boom, too. They generally kept to themselves, and hunted mussels where they were harder to get at. Us white folks got all the best mussel beds to ourselves.

Blacks and whites didn't mix much, of course. Around Caddo Lake, the colored population was double that of white folks in those days. Some whites were scared the coloreds would take over if they got education and the vote, both of which they were supposed to have, but didn't. There was a lot of severe harassing of any black person who tried to horn in on what the whites considered theirs.

But nature didn't discriminate against black folks, and they found their share of pearls. In fact, Captain Brigginshaw probably bought as many pearls from black folks as from white. Pop was careful not to print too many stories in the *Steam Whistle* about blacks finding a lot of pearls. He didn't want a bunch of high-handed nigger-haters attacking the black pearling camps and ruining the boom.

Anyway, about the only people in town who disapproved of the pearl rush at first were the preachers. The Reverend Bartlett Towne almost threw a hissy fit when half his congregation failed to show up the first Sunday of the boom. They were all out pearl-hunting. On Sunday! He preached against the evils of mammon for two weeks running, until he realized that not enough of that evil mammon was winding up in his collection plate. The third Sunday, he held services outside of Esau's saloon and asked God to bring luck to all good Methodist pearl-hunters.

And the luck came. Not just for the Methodists, but for all denominations. Most of the pearls found were just small things called seed pearls, or even smaller ones known as dust pearls. They sold for about twenty-five dollars an ounce, but it took a handful of them to make an ounce. Some people got in the habit of paying Esau with seed pearls for whiskey or drinking water. Cecil and Adam and I traded catfish for seed pearls sometimes. The seed and dust pearls enabled just about everybody to at least break even in the pearl-hunting business.

Several times a day, however, we would hear of something bigger than a seed pearl being found. Maybe it would be worth twenty-five dollars all by itself. Maybe it would fetch fifty, seventy-five, even a hundred. Those were tough times in the bayou country, and a hundred dollars could pay a pearl-hunter's expenses for the whole summer and still leave a profit.

Then there were the rare specimens everybody wanted to find: the pearls of fifteen grains or more, about the size of a garden pea, or bigger. Such a gem would sell for at least a hundred dollars. Edgar Burnett, who lived on the North Shore, found a metallic-green pearl that sold for five hundred. Wiley Jones, a woodchopper who came over from the Louisiana side of the lake, sold two matching egg-shaped pearls for three hundred apiece.

The pearl-hunters at Goose Prairie picked up a whole new vocabulary from Trevor Brigginshaw and Billy Treat. It was funny to hear the farmers, who usually sat around talking about bugs and the weather, saying things like "It had good overtone, but the luster was too low" when they talked about certain pearls.

After a couple of weeks, everybody in town knew the difference between a haystack and a turtleback. We could judge size, shape, and orient as well as any jeweler. Even Adam Owens could look at a pearl and tell you whether it was a wing pearl, a dogtooth pearl, a nugget, a ring-around, or a bird's-eye.

Camps of merry pearl-hunters sprang up all over the lake, and everybody made money. We owed it all to the stranger, Billy Treat. It was peculiar how the town idolized him, yet knew so little about him. He didn't hunt for pearls himself. He just continued to cook at Widow Humphry's place and wander over to Goose Prairie in the afternoons to see what was going on. He taught some hunters the finer points of judging pearls, so Brigginshaw wouldn't take them too badly, but other than that, he mostly stayed out of the pearl business.

He almost always seemed to be sulking over something, like there was a sadness in him he couldn't shake. At times, however, Billy would get to talking real poetic about pearls, and his mood would brighten. I heard him more than once quote a line from Shakespeare's *Othello*: "Speak of me as I am . . . of one whose hand, like the base Indian, threw a pearl away richer than all his tribe. . . ."

One day I came down from the catfish-holding tank and found Billy standing under Esau's mulberry tree with a crowd around him. "The Chinese," he was saying as I got close enough to hear, "believed in magical pearls that glowed and could be seen a thousand yards away. They believed the light of such a pearl would cook rice."

On another day, I was toting a water keg up to Esau's place and heard Billy telling how all the different ancient civilizations explained the formation of pearls. Angel tears, and things like that. "Some reasoned that a white pearl was formed during fair weather, and a dark pearl was formed during cloudy weather."

"What about our pink pearls?" someone asked. Caddo Lake produced quite a few pink ones.

"Maybe dawn or dusk, if you believe in that sort of thing," Billy answered.

He loved pearl legends and folklore, and I loved to hear him talk about them. It added an air of ancient romance to the muddy pursuits of us lake rats.

It was a wonderful summer. I will never forget it. I felt rich and free. It was a time like no other in my life. A time when I knew both the sterling excellence of innocence and the bewitching siren of temptation.

Pearls were my temptation. Mussel pearls and Pearl Cobb. I dreamed of finding the paragon of angels' tears. I dreamed of giving it to Carol Anne. It was the fabulous summer of pearls. I guess I thought it would last forever.

10

"No, thanks," Billy said, his back to the Australian as he finished drying the pots and pans.

Trevor Brigginshaw held his satchel in his hand. "Come on, Billy," he urged. "Just a drop. It won't hurt you."

"You know I don't drink," Billy said as he hung a heavy iron skillet over the stove. He turned to face his friend. "It's a waste of time and money."

"I'll give you the money."

"Who will give me the time?"

"For God's sake, mate, don't be such a stick-in-the-mud. You don't have to drink if you don't want to. Just come along for the fun!"

Billy took off his apron and hung it on a brass hook. "I like you when you're sober, Trev, but you're a mean drunk. There are happy drunks and sad, slobbering drunks and mean drunks, and you're the meanest of the mean if something rubs you wrong."

"So that's it? That time in Valparaiso?"

"And La Paz, and San Francisco, and Lahaina."

"Lahaina? Oh, now, that was different. The bloke kicked my dog, Billy. I was provoked."

"The *dog* bit the *bloke* first, and it wasn't even your dog."

"Well, I couldn't help that. I like dogs, I do. I've got a mind to get another one."

"What do you mean, 'another one'? You've never had a dog."

"I would have kept that one in Lahaina if you had bailed me out of the stinkin' brig before dawn!"

"And watch you tear another saloon apart? The brig's the best place for you when you're drunk, Trev. No, you go on to Esau's by yourself. I don't want to be there when the place falls in."

Trevor sighed and shook his head. "You've become a cautious soul, Billy. When are you going to stop blaming yourself for what happened on Mangareva and have some fun like you used to? You won't even hunt pearls with these Texans, and I know you want to."

Billy felt the guilt well up like an ocean tide. "I'm out of the pearl business. For good. You go on over to Esau's saloon. I have better things to do."

He stalked out of the kitchen, leaving Trevor there alone. He went to his room, washed his face, put on a clean shirt, and combed his hair. When he was sure the Australian had gone, he left his room, walked through the parlor, and went out the front door of Widow Humphry's place, into the dark. He crossed the street, nodding to a couple of locals who greeted him, and turned the corner of Snyder's store.

There was a light on in Carol Anne's room. He climbed the stairs and knocked on the door.

When Carol Anne saw him standing at the top of the stairs, her breath caught in her throat. She had been wondering if he would ever come to see her again. Billy had been spending so much time with Trevor that she was actually getting a little jealous of the big Australian. "Hi, Billy," she said.

"Are you busy?"

"No, not at all. Would you like to come in?"

"Yes, thank you."

They sat at the table and made conversation for a while, until Billy got around to telling her the reason for his visit. "I have a business proposition in mind that you may be interested in," he said.

"Business?" she asked.

"Yes. I've gotten to like some of the people around here, and I'm thinking about staying. I'm thinking about going into business, but I don't have the money to get started. I need some investors."

"Just a few weeks ago, people were talking about this town dying," Carol Anne said.

"That was before you started the pearl rush," he said with a grin. His smile was handsome and it made wrinkles line his eyes with character. "I believe that with a little organization, the pearl business could last here indefinitely. Trevor has already started talking to John Crowell about ways to protect the mussel beds. Crowell is going to try to drum up some interest through his paper."

"So, you're going back into the pearl business?"

"No, I'm through with pearls. I have another idea. The inn has been full now for two weeks straight. Widow Humphry says she hasn't had as much business in years. Those out-of-town pearl-hunters have taken every available room, and people are sleeping out on the open ground."

"You're going to build another inn?"

"Yes. And a store, too. And I'm going to buy a big wagon to take supplies out to the pearl-hunting camps so they won't have to come into town to shop. Maybe next year I'll buy a little steam-powered boat so I can reach the North Shore camps as well."

Carol Anne sat back in her chair and beamed at Billy. She loved his big ideas and his poetic talk of pearls. She was glad he was planning to stay in town. He had brought hope to Port Caddo, and he gave no one greater hope than he gave her. "How much do you need?" she asked.

"I have some money in the bank in New Orleans, but it's not enough. I'll need a couple of thousand more. I didn't know if you had any plans for your pearl money yet, so I thought I'd tell you first. I thought you might want to invest some of it."

She didn't want to appear overanxious. She wasn't going to throw herself or her money at Billy. She didn't think he'd respect that. He wanted a woman who could behave with a measure of self-restraint. He would admire her more if she thought it over for a while. "Thank you," she said. "Thank you for telling me before anybody else. I'll have to think about it, though. How soon do you need to know?"

"As soon as possible. I don't want somebody else getting the idea and beating me to it."

"I'll let you know tomorrow," she said. "I'm very interested."

Billy smiled. "Good." He got up. "Well, good night."

"Wait, Billy," she said before he could open the door. "I want to show you something."

She went to her old tobacco tin on the shelf above her bed. She put one knee on the bed to reach it. "I took the pearl you gave me to Marshall and found a jeweler there who could mount it," she said, opening the tin. She removed a gossamer chain of gold, adorned with a tiny pendant—a delicate crown of gold embracing the white orb. She draped it across her fingers so he could see.

Billy touched her hand as he examined the piece. "Nice job," he said. "Will you put it on?"

She shook her hair over her shoulders and reached behind her neck to fasten the chain. She had worn it only a few times, and only in her room. She started to get embarrassed when she couldn't hook the clasp.

"Let me help you," Billy said.

When she turned, he found the chain in her hands under her veil of shining black hair. She pulled her hair to one side so he could see the clasp.

"There," he said, turning her by the shoulders. He admired her for a moment. "It looks beautiful on you. I hope you'll wear it."

"I will," she said.

He studied her for a long moment. Then he smiled, turned away, and stepped toward the door. "I'll see you tomorrow. Think about my proposition."

"I will." She stood at the door to watch him walk down the stairs, along the back of the building, and into the dark. There was nothing to think about. Of course she would invest in his business ventures. Anything to root him to Port Caddo. The money meant nothing to her. There was nothing at all to think about.

But she did think, and by morning, Carol Anne was glad she had waited. She had come up with a wonderful idea. It was bold, but ingenious. She was going to tell Billy that she wanted to do more than just invest. She wanted an equal partnership.

When Carol Anne told Billy of her decision that afternoon, he accepted immediately. He would invest everything he had, and she would match it. They would split all profits down the middle. She would run the store and the inn, he would man the kitchen and drive the wagon to the pearl camps between meals.

Billy told Widow Humphry that afternoon that she would have to find another cook. Carol Anne broke the news to old man Snyder. She was afraid he would be angry, but he was delighted. She was like a granddaughter to him, and it elated him that Billy had taken an interest in her, even if it meant competition for his store.

The new partners spent the afternoon walking around town together, causing a stir. They looked at several likely sites for their business. A few buildings and lots were for sale, but they were located poorly, off the main street. There were a couple of lots available just above the wharf, but they were on low ground, only a few feet above the level of the bayou.

Billy asked around. Nobody in town could remember the water getting that high. He went to Goose Prairie Cove to ask Esau.

"I've lived on the lake for forty years," the old Choctaw said, "and I seen the water go that high just once, back in thirty-eight. That was a freak storm that year. I never hope to see the likes of it again. Big Cypress Bayou ran like a river for two days."

"But you don't think it will happen again?"

"It happened once. I guess it could happen again. There would be a risk building there. But if your place flooded there, so would my saloon. I'm no higher here than you would be there."

"It's a good location otherwise," Billy said. "Right next to the wharf."

"And just across the street from the jailhouse," Esau said. "You could visit your friend, Captain Brigginshaw. He almost landed there last night."

"Did Trev cause trouble?"

"Some, but me and the constable got him settled down. He's one of those mean drunks, Billy."

"I know."

Billy and Carol Anne agreed that afternoon to risk high water and construct a new building for their store and inn on the low ground just above the wharf. Theirs would be the first business the steamboat passengers saw when they disembarked.

They dined together that evening at Rose Turner's eatery. Billy had ham steaks and potatoes. Carol Anne ate broiled chicken and greens. She wore her pearl pendant. Rayford Hayes, the local constable, and his wife, Hattie, stopped by their table to congratulate them on their partnership. The news was all over town.

"I threatened to put your friend, Captain Brigginshaw, in the jailhouse last night," Rayford said. "He was picking fights out at Esau's place."

"I heard. Did he hurt anybody?" Billy asked.

"No, Esau got him settled down. He likes that old Indian for some reason. Did you know Brigginshaw carries a gun?"

"He's licensed to carry it. He provides his own security for the pearls he buys and the money he carries. He didn't pull a gun on anybody last night, did he?"

"No, but he pulled his jacket back where I could see it."

"He likes to fight a little when he gets drunk, but he won't draw a weapon unless somebody pulls one on him first, or goes for his satchel."

"He ought to leave that satchel locked up somewhere instead of carrying it around all the time," Rayford said. "Anyway, he apologized to me this morning and said he'd try to behave himself."

"I hope he does," Carol Anne said. She knew Constable Hayes as an old Confederate hero and the surest man in town with a handgun.

"That's a lovely necklace," Hattie suddenly said. "Is that a local pearl?"

Carol Anne was stunned to have one of the prominent local wives speaking to her in public. Hattie had always been civil to her in the store, but this was quite different. She figured she owed the honor to the fact that she was dining with the famous Billy Treat. "Yes, ma'am," she explained. "Billy found it at Goose Prairie Cove and gave it to me as a gift."

Hattie gasped joyfully and made all sorts of eyes at Billy. "So this is the famous Treat Pearl that started the pearl boom. It certainly is a beautiful one."

"Thank you," Carol Anne replied.

When Rayford and Hattie left, Billy asked, "What was all that about?"

Carol Anne rolled the pearl between her fingers. "Oh, she probably got the wrong idea. Used to be, around here, that when a fellow found a pearl, he would give it to the girl he wanted to marry. I guess I should have straightened her out."

Billy shrugged. "Let them think what they want to think. I gave you a gift. You shouldn't have to explain it to anybody."

The next day, the gossip hounds spread the word that Carol Anne was wearing the Treat Pearl. People stopped her on the street to look at it. She was amazed at the warmth they extended to her. It was as if she had never owned another pearl.

Billy bought lumber, paint, hardware, shingles. He hired carpenters and worked beside them. The happy cadence of hammers rang from sunup to sundown. The frame building was plain, but there would be time to add gingerbread later. The Treat Inn opened a month after the partnership was formed. The partners were seen together regularly around town.

Their inn offered three levels of accommodations. A large back porch enclosed in mosquito netting provided twenty cots where low-budget pearl-hunters could sleep for two bits a night and eat common fare for another two bits a day.

The first floor of the inn consisted of small rooms patterned after riverboat staterooms, six-by-six, with double berths. Common washrooms, one for men and one for women, stood at the end of the hall.

Upstairs, half a dozen suites had brass bedsteads, private washstands, mirrors, and armoires. Trevor Brigginshaw left Widow Humphry's place and took a suite in the Treat Inn. The good widow was actually a little relieved. The captain came home drunk once or twice a week, sang loudly in the middle of the night, and generally disturbed her other guests.

Billy's room adjoined the kitchen, behind the store. Carol Anne's room was above his. They were in debt by the time they opened, but immediately began catching up. The pearl rush was still building. Farmers, woodchoppers, and roustabouts rented cots. Clerks and professional men filled the staterooms. A few big planters and rich businessmen peopled the suites upstairs. Pearl-hunting appealed to all classes.

Carol Anne ordered stock for the store with pearl-hunters in mind. She sold knives suited to opening mussels, and all kinds of camp gear. She couldn't keep mosquito bars in stock.

"Keep some sandalwood oil on hand, if you can," Billy suggested. "It keeps the pearls from drying out and improves their luster."

Between cooking meals at the inn, Billy drove a well-stocked supply wagon to the South Shore pearling camps, which now extended from Annie Glade Bluff, past Taylor Island, to old Esau's place on Goose Prairie Cove. He sold almost everything in the wagon on each trip and took orders for more goods.

He often crossed paths with the open-topped coach from Joe Peavy's livery barn. It made a constant circuit through the camps and past the mussel beds, shuttling pearl-hunters to and from town. Passengers commonly paid their fees in seed pearls.

Peavy had also established a twice-weekly stagecoach service that ran south to Marshall, where he would pick up pearl-hunters who had ridden the rails in from Louisiana. The stagecoach stopped right in front of the Treat Inn, and turned around at the wharf, swinging past the jailhouse.

In his kitchen at night, Billy made projections based on the gross profits the inn and the store had made so far. He estimated that he and Carol Anne would be out of debt by the time the lake level rose and the riverboats came back. Then they would start recouping their investments.

Pearling would drop off severely when the water got too cool to make wading comfortable. Some pearlers would try to use George Blank's mussel rakes through the winter, but Billy knew few of them would stick with it. That kind of pearl-hunting was hard work, compared to the pleasures of summer wading. The pearl rush would lie virtually dormant until next spring, but the riverboats would be running, and that would sustain some measure of prosperity until the waters warmed.

He was being conservative when he judged that he and his partner would turn their first profit about July, next summer. Then he would ask her to marry him. They would have known each other over a year by then. He would have gotten around to kissing her by then, too, probably around Christmastime. Maybe under some mistletoe. He would marry her, and then it wouldn't matter if the Caddo Lake pearl industry went belly-up like a dead fish, or if the railroads forced riverboats into obsolescence, or if Port Caddo died and sank into the bayou. He would have Carol Anne for life. They could go somewhere else and start over.

For the first time in years, he was planning his future. He had once been an inordinate planner, but he was going to try to control that now that he was finally through grieving over his catastrophe in the South Pacific. Maybe what had happened there was his fault, and maybe it wasn't, but he couldn't punish himself forever.

Don't try to plan the lives of everyone in town, he thought. Just mind your own business, and give your advice when asked. That way, if something goes wrong, you won't have to blame yourself. You don't have to save this town for these people. Let them do it themselves.

It was strange that he had found the pearl here. He of all people. There was more to it than just chance. It was as if the weeping angels and the gods who rode the rainbows were trying to tell him something. He had suffered enough. It was time to live again. He was in love with Carol Anne.

11

TREVOR BRIGGINSHAW HELD A GLASS OF WHISKEY IN ONE HAND, A CIGAR
in the other. His satchel full of pearls and money rested between his
feet. He was on a Saturday-night tear at Esau's pearl camp and saloon.
Someone had started him talking about pearling in the South Sea islands.

"I had my own vessel then. A sloop I called the *Wicked Whistler*.
Just forty feet she was, but full-rigged and quick as a hungry shark."
The more he drank, the thicker his Aussie brogue became.

Esau's saloon was just a shack with some tables and chairs scattered
around inside and out. At night, the men liked to come inside and
smoke the place up with cigars and pipes to keep the mosquitoes out.
There was no bar to lean against, but there was whiskey—some of it
store-bought and labeled, some of it cooked in Esau's moonshine still
that was hidden in the swamps.

"I had a four-pounder swivel gun mounted on the foredeck to dis-
courage pirates," Trevor continued, "and my pearl-handled pistol." He
pulled back his white cotton jacket to reveal his weapon.

"Pirates?" Judd Kelso spouted. He had been matching the pearl-buyer drink for drink for about two hours. His bankroll had been shrinking all summer. He had lost most of it in card games with pearl-hunters. Now he was down to a few thin bills and was watching them go quickly into Esau's till. "I don't believe in no damn pirates!"

"Then you're either ignorant or a fool. There are thieves on the high seas as sure as you have them on land. What's the name of that outlaw gang about here, Esau?"

"Christmas Nelson's gang?" the old Indian said.

"Right! Bloody idiotic name, isn't it!"

"They say he was born on Christmas Day," Esau said.

Kelso shifted in a creaking chair. "Christmas Nelson's just a good ol' rebel Southern boy who don't know the war's over yet. He ain't no damn pirate."

"Of course he's not a pirate!" Trevor shouted. "He doesn't even have a boat! But there are pirates in the Southern Seas as sure as life. Common criminals is all. Ask Billy Treat. He narrowly escaped from them, he did."

"What about that Billy Treat?" a backwoods farmer drawled. "He 'pears to know a hell of a lot about pearls. Where'd he come from to know so much?"

"I found him in New York City. Looked me up, he did. Said he wanted to go pearling. He had found a freshwater pearl in a stream in New Jersey and all he talked about was pearls. The Romans, the Greeks, what all the ancient civilizations thought about them. He was a strapping Yankee lad, so I took him where he might find some pearls."

"You mean *damn* Yankee, don't you?" Kelso said.

The Australian's angry glare sliced toward the gator-eyed man.

"Where was it you took Billy to find pearls?" Esau asked, before Trevor's ire could reach its boiling point.

"Where? Bloody where did I not take him, mate! I was an independent buyer then. I fetched the best pearling waters of the Pacific every year, then sold my pearls in New York and London. Billy went 'round the Horn with me—this was sixty-one, I recall, because the war had started here—and he made a fair sailor. He had a look at Venezuela, Panama, Mexico. Didn't like what he saw until we got into the Pearl

Islands of the South Seas. That's where he became king of Mangareva, in the Gambier Islands."

"Where?" Judd Kelso said, laughing disparagingly as if the place didn't exist.

Trevor set the cigar between his teeth. "Mangareva, I say, man! In the Gambiers. Volcanic islands they are, and Mangareva's the best pearl island among them. Bloody beautiful tropical spot that is, gentlemen. Green mountains rising from the sea. The water there is so clear you can see pearl oysters on the reef five fathoms deep. And the women! Dark-skinned as Esau here, fair as angels, and bare as babes above the hips, every one!"

"You mean naked?" a pearl-hunter asked.

"And willing! That's where Billy Treat jumped the *Wicked Whistler*. He made Mangareva the richest pearl island in the South Seas. Wasn't easy, either. The natives don't like work there. They like to catch fish, chop coconuts, lay about under the palm trees, swim a bit, and make little natives, but they don't like work."

"How did Billy get them to work?" Esau asked, reaching for his flask.

"Not by my methods. I suggested he trade them rum for pearls. They like rum, they do. But he's against drink. You all know that. He wouldn't hear of it. So here's what he did. He became one of them! He bloody well did! He lived in a hut thatched with palm leaves, just like they did. He fished with them, chopped coconuts, learned everything they knew till he had their confidence.

"I left him there, and sailed to Sydney. When I came back to Mangareva several months later, he had the men, women, and children diving two hours a day, every one. And the pearls he had to trade looked like billiard balls compared to your little mussel pearls here.

"They loved Billy Treat on Mangareva. He had his pick from the whole lot of naked girls there, he did. I think he liked it there. Wouldn't you?"

"Damn right!" an old married pearl-hunter said, and laughter filled the smoky saloon.

"But wait!" Trevor said, after draining his glass and signaling Esau

for more. "The most peculiar thing about Billy in Mangareva was that
he would dive with them every day. Maybe that's the way he got them
to do it in the first place—by example. He could hold his breath almost
three minutes, he could. I clocked him one day. He would dive four
fathoms and come up with oysters broad as my hat!" He flourished his
panama at his listeners.

"By God, that's how he done it!" Junior Martin said. "I've heard
how he saved seven drownin' men when the *Glory of Caddo Lake* went
down. They say he stayed under three or four minutes getting John
Crowell's boy out."

"I was there," said George Blank, the blacksmith. "I swear I had
given him up for dead a full three minutes when he finally came up
for air."

Some of the pearl-hunters looked sideways at Judd Kelso when talk
of the *Glory* started, but Kelso just sat remorselessly in his chair. He even
snorted a little to show his disregard.

"That's how he learned pearls," Trevor said. "He used to tell me his
plans for preserving the oyster beds. He had everything scheduled to
the year and month. He would protect the oysters in certain localities
about Mangareva during certain years, to make sure the natives didn't
harvest them all. He wasn't happy just to dive for them, either. He
wanted to become the world's expert on pearls. He was going to spend
five years diving for them, the next five buying them, like me, and the
rest of his life acquiring and collecting them. I believe he would have
done it, too, if the bloody pirates hadn't come to Mangareva."

"Oh, hell," Kelso groaned. "Here come the pirates again."

"What about those pirates?" George Blank asked. "What happened?"

"Bloody pirates they were," the captain said, putting out his cigar
and sipping at his whiskey jar. "Outcasts from France, Spain, the East
Indies, and South America. Cutthroats. No other name for them. They
told Billy they wanted half the pearls the natives harvested or they
would kill everyone in the village. Billy got mad then, he did. He had
a pistol I had given him, and he put it against that pirate captain's head.
He went with them to their schooner, holding that gun on the captain.

Made them throw their cannon off the bloody deck. Two six-pounders! He told them never to come back and threaten him again or he would have the natives boil them alive!"

"But they came back anyway, I guess," Esau said.

"Aye, they came back, mate, and Billy knew they would. He was ready for them. He and his pearl-divers had brought those two six-pounders up from the harbor. He had learned how to shoot them, too, and borrowed some powder from the *Wicked Whistler.* They kept a watch up day and night, and when those pirate bastards sailed into the harbor with new cannon and fired on the village, he crippled them good. Blew the mizzen mast away and sent them limping for Tahiti!"

"So, he whipped 'em!" Junior Martin said.

Trevor shook his head sadly and nudged his satchel with his foot to make sure it was still there. "They came back yet again, they did. I was there at Mangareva in sixty-seven when it happened. The guards were posted about the harbor, and Billy was ready for another attack by sea. But the bloody cutthroats had anchored out of sight, around the coast, and they sneaked into the mountains above the village. At dawn, they came down. Every one of them had a revolver and the best rifle available. Billy had only a few old muskets and the pistol I had given him.

"We fought at first, we did. But it was suicide to stay. I used all my ammunition and jumped in my launch to reach the *Wicked Whistler.* I told Billy to come, but he wouldn't. He tried to organize the natives, but they were scattering all over the place running like scared dogs. The bloody pirates were killing them everywhere. My God, what a mess that was. Young children killed, women violated. Billy stood on the beach and shouted, trying to pull the villagers together, but they didn't know much about fighting pirates. He wouldn't leave, so I knocked him on the head with my pistol butt, threw him in the launch, and took him away by force."

"And you got away?" Junior Martin asked.

"Hell, he's here, ain't he?" George Jameson said, and the saloon shook with laughter.

"The pirates were shooting at the *Wicked Whistler*, but we were well out in the harbor. Once we got out around the reef, they had no chance of catching us."

"What happened to the village?" Esau asked.

"Destroyed. The whole thing burned. Billy went well-nigh crazy with guilt. He swore he had brought death and ruin to those simple natives. He said I should have let him stay on the beach and allowed the pirates to kill him, too. Bloody stupid move that would have been. It wouldn't have helped anything, but Billy tortured himself.

"I had saved the Mangareva pearls in my launch when the Frenchmen attacked. When Billy found those pearls aboard the *Wicked Whistler*, he went screaming about the deck, throwing them in the ocean like a madman. I put him ashore in San Francisco. Never thought I'd see him again."

The saloon fell silent, and Captain Brigginshaw took a swallow of Esau's moonshine.

"Well, I lost the *Wicked Whistler* last year in a bloody, wretched hurricane on Jamaica, so I've been buying pearls for International Gemstones to earn enough in commission to buy a new vessel." He sneered a little when he mentioned his company's name. "I was in New York when Billy's letter came from here. He's not the same old Billy yet, gentlemen. Coming around a bit, but he's still got Mangareva on his conscience. Won't bother with pearls, either. Says they brought evil last time he fooled with them.

"Anyway, that's the story of Billy Treat. He knows pearls, he does. And a few other things as well." He drained his jar and handed it to Esau for a refill.

Kelso had finished his drink, too, and got up to buy another. He smirked and shifted his ugly gator eyes as he crossed the smoky room. "So that's the story of Billy Treat. Hell, it all makes sense now. I see why he gets on so good with Pearl Cobb." He stood beside Brigginshaw and held his glass up to Esau. "They belong together. Him a coward and her a whore."

The blow came without the slightest warning. Kelso's eyes stood level with the big Australian's shoulder, so the fist angled down on him, backhanding him to the floor. Esau moved gracefully aside. The saloon customers gasped, then sat still and quiet.

Kelso jumped up but, dizzied by the sudden stroke, stumbled back against a table whose legs rattled across the wooden floor like the hooves of a startled horse. He shook his head, touched his brow to check for blood, gathered himself, and rushed the pearl-buyer with grunts and gritting teeth.

Trevor doubled over and latched one big hand around the handle of his money satchel. Kelso's fist against his temple staggered him a single step, but he slung the smaller man aside with his free arm, sprawling him across a cracker barrel.

Some of the men left the saloon quickly, others merely stood and moved out of the way. A few smiled with excited eyes, and one shouted, "Get him, Captain!"

Trevor drew himself to his full height, holding the satchel in his left hand. He waved Kelso in with his right hand, then made a fist of it. "Come ahead, mate," he said, his teeth showing a smile in the middle of his beard. "You're a little man, so I'll just use my one fist. I fight fair, you know." He cocked his arm like a pugilist, elbow down, slightly bent, his fingers curling up and in toward himself.

Kelso stood and got both fists up. His eyes narrowed with anger. He moved in cautiously, staying out of reach, circling to the Australian's right. The moment he made his move, Trevor came around with the heavy satchel, catching Kelso in the head and bowling him into a shelf filled with jars and glasses.

The roaring laughter of the pearl-buyer followed the tinkling of shattered glass. He dropped his guard and looked around at the men in the saloon. "Never trust a drunken sailor to fight fair, mates! It isn't in him!"

Kelso chose the moment to spring from the shattered glass and throw a wild blow at Brigginshaw's head. The captain's beard absorbed the punch as his knee came up and caught Kelso in the ribs. He made playful jabs at Kelso's nose and ears, backing him up until he knocked him over the stove. There was no fire, but the stovepipe fell out and a black cloud of soot dropped into the saloon.

When Kelso got to his feet, the leather satchel swung again, knocking him all the way through the door and into the woodpile outside. Trevor began shaking with laughter, and the customers remaining in the saloon joined him. Even Esau smiled, though he was shaking his head and surveying the devastation around him.

"Not to worry," Brigginshaw said. "International bloody Gemstones pays all my expenses." He put the leather satchel on a table and began unbuckling it. "Including damages incurred in protecting my pearls."

As he peered into his leather case, Trevor sensed a sudden change in the mood of the crowd. He pulled back the tail of his jacket, found the grip of his revolver, and drew it. As he turned, he cocked it, and found Judd Kelso in the sights as the burly little man came through the door, an ax above his head.

Kelso stopped so suddenly that his shoes slid across the dirty wooden floor. He was still quivering with rage, but he knew better than to rush the big man now. He stood as if in leg irons, the ax handle at his shoulder, the broad steel blade above his head.

"Drop that weapon," Trevor said.

Kelso's face writhed with flexing muscles.

Trevor raised his aim a few inches and sent a bullet glancing off the ax head, humming through the wall, and sailing out over the lake. The weapon jerked in Kelso's hand. A couple of customers bolted for the door, and others dove under tables or behind barrels.

"Drop it!" Brigginshaw repeated.

Kelso threw the ax aside.

The big Australian laughed again, but in a distinctly devious tone. "You'll wish you hadn't raised a weapon to Trevor Brigginshaw when I'm finished with you, mate."

Esau shuffled through the broken glass. "Captain, let him go," he said. "There's been enough trouble. The constable may have heard you shoot."

"Not until we finish our fight," Trevor said, easing the hammer down on the pistol and returning it to his belt.

"I ain't fightin' you with that gun on!" Kelso said.

"Then you will be shot," Trevor said, bringing both fists up and assuming his boxing pose. "The choice is yours."

"There's been enough damage done, Captain," Esau said.

"There's been too much bloody damage done," Trevor answered. "And no one will leave this room until some of it's been accounted for." He bent his head forward and moved toward Kelso.

"I don't want to fight no more," Kelso said, taking a step back. "I give."

"Run, and a bullet will stop you, mate. Put your fists up and fight like a man!"

Reluctantly, Kelso put his fists in front of his face and circled away, backing around chairs and tables clumsily. "Goddam, Esau! Stop the crazy son of a bitch!"

Esau did nothing.

Trevor continued to stalk the retreating man until he got him trapped in a corner. When Kelso crossed his arms in front of his face, a flurry of crushing blows arrived, coming with incredible rapidity from a man of such size. Kelso doubled over until a punch to his chin stood him straight. Another snapped his head against the wall. His knees buckled and he slid unconscious to the floor.

Trevor, as if he had failed to see his opponent fall, continued to belabor the wall until a board came loose, letting all the lake's animal croaks and chirps into the saloon.

Still fuming, he turned to glower at the men left inside the saloon. He saw his leather satchel open on a table. He saw the ax on the floor. He stalked across the room, picked them both up, and went outside.

Esau breathed a sigh of relief when he heard the ax splitting wood. He motioned to a couple of customers. "Drag Kelso out through the back," he said. "Don't let the captain see him." He mopped his sleeve across his forehead and reached for the flask in his pocket. "That Australian sure gets mean when he drinks."

12

I GOT SOOT IN MY EYE WHEN THE STOVEPIPE FELL OUT OF THE CEILING. Adam Owens and I had sneaked down to Esau's place after dark to watch through the knotholes in the wall. We were hoping to see a fight, but hadn't bargained on guns and axes. Adam ran for home as soon as the pistol slug glanced off the ax and ripped through the wall.

I was more curious and less cautious. I stayed until the bloody end, and even watched Captain Brigginshaw chop wood until he was so tired he could hardly stand up. I watched from a distance, because it was frightening to listen to him heave and grunt, and to look at his crazed face. He must have split enough wood to last a week.

While Brigginshaw was chopping, I was wrestling with my conscience. It wasn't the fight that was on my mind, but the story the pearl-buyer had told of Billy on the island of Mangareva. It had given me an unforgivably wicked idea. I knew it was wrong, but I couldn't help myself from thinking about it. I was fourteen and in love with the most seductive woman in creation.

Before Billy Treat, there had been a far-fetched hope that Carol Anne would share her body, if not her heart and soul, with me someday.

But since they had gone into business together, and started socializing around town, arm in arm, there was no hope of anything. Billy would have her all—heart, soul, and body.

Billy had saved me from the sinking riverboat. He was the first adult to treat me as a man. He had started me in the lucrative catfish and drinking-water enterprises. He was my hero, and a hero of the entire town. I idolized him. It was difficult to think of stabbing him in the back, but I was a desperate whirlwind of surging confusion.

My crush on Carol Anne had become an obsession. She was everything to me. Visions of her consumed me, day and night, only to be intruded upon by visions of Billy Treat.

Until that night at Esau's place, I had thought Billy invincible. There had been no chance of weakening his hold on Carol Anne. I was doomed to watch him take her. Then I heard the story of Mangareva. I knew why Billy seldom smiled. I knew why he suffered. There was no greater shame for a man than to be labeled a coward, and Billy had so labeled himself for not dying with his island friends. I saw a weakness in the invincible Billy Treat.

It was wrong to even think of it. I knew very well it was wrong. I personally didn't think of him as a coward, even if he thought of himself that way. I knew what kind of mettle he was made of. I owed the man my life.

But I was fourteen and driven by motives I could not control. I couldn't win. Either I would lose my slim chance with Carol Anne, or I would lose the respect and friendship of Billy. According to the stuff that was coursing through me, there was no choice to make. I could do without Billy.

I waited until the next morning after breakfast, when Billy drove the store wagon to the pearling camps. I sauntered into Carol Anne's store, already ashamed of what I had not even done yet, and waited until she and I were the only ones in the room.

She looked at me and smiled. She had taken to smiling more since she and Billy had started their business. She was wearing the Treat Pearl, the one I should have found. Lord, she was a sight to make a boy yearn. I knew then that I would betray a hundred Billy Treats for a thousand-to-one chance at knowing the pleasures of her flesh.

"Hi, Ben," she said. She was dusting the tops of some canned goods and she couldn't prevent herself from moving provocatively all over, though she was only using a feather duster. She didn't do it on purpose. She was just put together that way.

"Mornin'," I replied. "Have you heard?"

"Heard what?" she asked.

"Captain Brigginshaw got drunk last night at old Esau's place."

"Oh, yes. I think I even heard the gunshot last night. I know I heard something."

"I was there."

"Ben!" She propped her fists on her hips and stared at me, half amused and half concerned. "What's a boy like you doing around there? You should have been home in bed!"

That hurt, but I only shrugged. "You know what the fight was about?"

"From what Billy says, Captain Brigginshaw doesn't need much of a reason to fight when he gets drunk." She was not really very interested.

"Judd Kelso said Billy was a coward."

She stopped in a shaft of morning light that was streaming through the store window. Tiny particles of dust swarmed around her like the fancies of a young boy, wanting to be near, but afraid to touch her. She suddenly seemed to realize that I had come to tell her something important. "That was a stupid thing for him to say. Why would he even think such a thing?"

"Captain Brigginshaw told everybody at Esau's a story about Billy, and Judd Kelso said it made Billy a coward." I didn't tell her that Kelso had also called her a whore. I wasn't trying to destroy her image of herself, just her image of Billy. It was a sneaky, cowardly thing for me to do, but I was beyond honor. I was fourteen.

She asked me to sit down with her behind the counter, and I repeated the story as Captain Brigginshaw had told it, trying to remember his every word, wishing I could borrow his accent. In my version, Billy put up a little less of a fight as Captain Brigginshaw thumped him on the head, deserted the island village a little easier, and went a little crazier with shame aboard the *Wicked Whistler*.

It was sad to watch Carol Anne's face as I talked. The story hurt her. I thought it might be breaking her heart. By the end of the tale, her fingers had fallen from the Treat Pearl and lay clasped in her lap. She wasn't smiling now.

"So that's it," she said. "I knew there was something. I could tell." She got up and walked aimlessly out into the middle of the store, holding her fingers to her lips. "That's why he never talks about the South Seas. I knew something had happened there."

I barely enjoyed ogling her. The story had taken the luster off her smile. "Well, I thought I'd better tell you," I said.

She turned and looked at me. Her eyes were glistening with tears that wouldn't quite roll down her cheeks. Suddenly she came toward me. I jumped from the stool I had been sitting on just as she reached me. She put a warm hand on each side of my face. I felt electricity in her touch.

"Thank you, Ben. I'm so glad I heard it from you instead of from some gossip."

She leaned toward me and kissed me square on the forehead. I went almost as blank as Judd Kelso had the night before. Fire started on the spot where her lips had touched me, and sent a wave of crimson across the rest of my face. It was happening fast. Too fast for me to handle.

I pulled her hands away from my face and took a step back. "I gotta go now," I said. I tried to regain some semblance of composure. "I have to haul some water to the pearl camps. Those folks won't have any water if I don't." I figured that while I was tearing Billy down, I might as well build myself up. I must have been cardinal-red when I left.

I walked to Esau's camp in a trance. She had kissed me. My betrayal of Billy had worked quicker than I could have imagined. It was only a kiss on the forehead, but I never expected her to kiss me on the lips the first time.

I was virtually worthless hauling water with Cecil and Adam that afternoon. Cecil kept trying to get me to tell him about the fight at Esau's the night before because Adam had a poor memory for details, and had left before it was over, but I was so wrapped up in Carol Anne's lips that I couldn't concentrate on anything.

"Well, Ben?" Cecil said. "Ben!"

"Huh?"

"Well, what happened then? What's wrong with you? Didn't you hear me? What happened after Judd Kelso came in with the ax? When did Captain Brigginshaw shoot?"

Poor Billy Treat. I had ruined him. It was a sorry reward for his saving my life. It hadn't been fun destroying him, only necessary. Anyway, I didn't have a lot of room left in me for pity. I was too full of wonder. My skin still tingled where she had kissed me.

"Ben. Ben!" Cecil shouted.

"What?"

"Why haven't you got the danged mussels opened yet? We're almost to the trotline, boy. Hurry up. Haven't you been listening to me? You must be sick or something."

"He don't look too good," Adam said. "I think he's feelin' peaked."

I avoided my usual haunts that evening after supper. I didn't want Cecil or Adam intruding on my thoughts of Carol Anne. I had plans to make. Tonight was the night Carol Anne was going to tell Billy she didn't want to wear his pearl any longer. It was a vicious thing, but I wanted to see Billy get rejected. Not because I would get any pleasure from it, but because I wanted to make sure he was really out of my way.

Well, maybe I would get a little pleasure from it, and that was the disturbing part. Until that moment, I truly believed that I wasn't doing anything to spite Billy. I could have sworn that I was only filling my own instinctive needs. It was primal, like a coyote howling for a mate. But I had to admit I was going to get some kind of kick out of knocking Billy down a peg, and that vicious feeling gave me no pride. My shame began to build, but there still wasn't much room for it next to the hope I had been breathing in all day.

I was naive beyond imagination. I truly believed that just because Judd Kelso had called Billy a coward and I had repeated it to Carol Anne, she would think of him in that way. That little peck she had given me on the forehead must have soaked through my skull and addled my brain. Can you believe that I actually had some kind of hope that she was going to shun Billy and take up with me?

Of course my plan backfired. I'll tell you how I found out. I wandered around to the Treat Inn that evening to flirt with Carol Anne. I was approaching the building when I saw Billy knocking on the door to Carol Anne's room. Unseen, I stepped into the shadows to watch. Carol Anne came to the door. I couldn't see her face, but I figured she was telling Billy to get lost because word was all over town that he was a coward, and she didn't want to be seen with him anymore.

Poor Billy Treat, I thought. He had taken some hard knocks. First Mangareva, now this. He would never kiss Carol Anne. She wouldn't want to wear the pearl of a coward. He would probably leave town. It would be a relief to see him go, but it would make me a little sad, too. I was going to miss him. I admired him and I knew he was no coward, but he was standing between me and Carol Anne, and that was justification enough for my treachery.

"Sorry, Billy," I whispered as I watched from a distance. "But I was here before you."

Then it happened. I saw Carol Anne step from her room. Her hand reached behind Billy's neck, and she kissed him. I don't mean on the forehead like that little smack she had given me earlier that day. She kissed him full on the mouth, and pressed herself against him in the most aggravating way. I turned and walked away then, because I couldn't take it anymore.

The hope that had been filling me all day fled. I felt sick and helpless. My heart was tender and it fell into halves, as if some pearl-hunter had pried it open with his mussel knife and, finding no gem there—for my treacherous heart was destitute of anything that worthy—had thrown it back into the murky waters.

My pain and shame deepened. Confusion mounted. Anger surged. The hollow where my heart had been froze. It was awful.

It took me years to understand, but one morning I woke up thinking about the summer of pearls and realized what had happened. No honorable man wants to be a coward. He can think of nothing worse. Billy Treat was a brave man, but he blamed himself for what had happened on Mangareva. The fact that he had not stood and fought to the death made him feel like a coward, whether he was or not. It wasn't as if he had had a choice in the matter. Trevor Brigginshaw had knocked him on the head and dragged him away. Still, Billy blamed himself.

No honorable woman wants to be a whore. She can conceive of nothing lower. Carol Anne wasn't a whore, but she had thought of herself that way. She had allowed herself no excuses. It didn't matter that she had grown up watching her mother take strange men into her bedroom. The fact that Carol Anne had been seduced with a pearl excused her from nothing. She had punished herself by secretly, privately, calling herself a whore of the lowest order—that is, until Billy convinced her otherwise.

Billy had given her honor, and she was only too happy to return the favor. A woman can restore a man's self-respect even if he has given up finding it himself. I'm sure Carol Anne knew ways I will never fathom. She knew how Billy suffered under the weight of his own useless shame. She knew how to relieve him, renew him, replenish his dignity, his honor. A good woman can do that. Those two needed each other more desperately than the earth needs the sun.

Of course none of that occurred to me as I walked away from the Treat Inn that night. All I knew then was that I had betrayed Billy and lost Carol Anne in the same day. I was shamefaced, guilt-ridden, and heartbroken. I knew how Billy Treat must have felt after Mangareva. I deserved it. I had gone behind his back—like a coward.

I made up my mind about one thing right then and there. Maybe I would never have Carol Anne, but I was going to earn my self-respect back somehow, because I felt too terrible to live. I was through passing gossip. I was not cut out for intrigue. Never again would I attempt to hurt someone else to better my own lot.

Strange it is that often from the worst of burdens, a person's character can find the way to its greatest worth. Such is the way of the pearl. It begins as something that galls and hurts. It results in something fine and beautiful to behold. But no pearl emerges overnight. It takes time. It takes a long, long time.

13

I WAS USELESS FOR DAYS. ADAM AND CECIL MIGHT AS WELL HAVE RUN THE trotline and hauled the water without me. I didn't care about making money anymore. All I knew was an empty void. I stayed at home and sulked at night, instead of prowling around spying on girls.

"What's that boy been so crotchety about?" my pop asked my mother one night when they thought I was asleep.

"Leave him alone, John," she said. "He's in love."

Women are peculiar creatures. Especially mothers. I don't know how Mama knew, but it actually helped a little to hear someone acknowledge it. Yes, I was in love. I would always be in love with Carol Anne Cobb.

Luckily for me, always doesn't last too long when you're fourteen. The summer wore on and I got bored silly feeling sorry for myself. The pearl boom was attracting more fortune-hunters all the time. Families were coming down from the hills and crowding the lakeshore all the way to Harrison Bayou. Some of them brought daughters, of course, and I hated to admit it to myself, but more than a few of them made my eyes swivel in their sockets.

I stuck my hand into my pocket one day and discovered a lot of money there. I hadn't spent a dime since my heart got broke, but all of a sudden I figured that maybe what I needed to get over Carol Anne once and for all was to buy something. Something big. Something that had beautiful curves and was fun to ride. I wanted an Ashenback bateau.

The bateau was sort of the official boat of Caddo Lake back then. It's something like a canoe, but wider and flatter across the bottom, and it pitches up more in the front and back, and has prettier flares all around. It's made for paddling sluggish bayou waters.

Charlie Ashenback made the finest bateaux ever to float the lake. I set my mind to saving enough money to buy one of his works, with mulberry stems, red cypress planking, a live well in the middle, and a minnow box within easy reach of the seat. I learned a trick that summer that still works for me: If you want to get your mind off of women, think of money and boats.

We had picked up the game of baseball from somewhere that summer. Cecil Peavy and I wound a bunch of old trotline cord into a ball and Adam Owens found a pine limb that made a pretty good bat. We would get some farm boys together on the lakeshore at Goose Prairie and teach them the rules and we would have some pretty good games and arguments and fistfights. The girls stood around, watched, and giggled at us.

Well, one day I was playing third base when I saw Billy approaching. He had been stepping a lot livelier since sharing Carol Anne's dark room with her. I guess I would have, too. Trevor Brigginshaw had been heard to remark that Carol Anne had uncovered the old Billy Treat. Billy smiled and joked more than he had since coming to Port Caddo. When he drove his supply wagon down to the pearling camps, he attracted a regular crowd.

I still hadn't spoken to him since that night. Half out of shame, and half out of anger. I really didn't want to have anything to do with him, but as he approached our baseball field, he headed straight for third base.

"Morning, Ben," he said. "Who's winning?"

"Who's keepin' score?" I said. "We just play till the fight breaks out."

He laughed. I couldn't believe it. I made Billy laugh.

"Well, when the game is over, I have an idea for you and your partners. That is, if you want to make some more money."

I would have said I wasn't interested, but he had engaged my interest with talk of profits, and I got a sudden vision of the Ashenback I was going to buy. Maybe Billy could take Carol Anne away from me, but he would never take my bateau once I had saved the money to buy it.

"What kind of idea?" I asked, concentrating harder than usual on the batter, so I wouldn't have to look into Billy's eyes.

"I've been thinking about all these dead mussels the pearl-hunters have been throwing in piles around here. It's not sanitary."

"They stink somethin' fierce," I said.

"Yes, they do. And that's the problem. Some of them are regular maggot ranches."

"So where's the money in it?" I asked.

He paused for a moment while the batter swung at a wild pitch. "You're starting to sound like your friend, the Peavy kid. I'm talking about doing something that will benefit the whole camp, and all you can think of is money."

I smirked at him pretty severely. "You're the one got me started makin' money this summer. What's wrong with that?"

"Nothing, as long as you do a good job and enjoy the work. But when somebody offers you a deal, find out what's involved first. Then, if you're still interested, ask about the pay. Otherwise, you'll end up in some kind of job you don't like just to make money."

"What's involved?" I asked.

"It was Esau's idea. He said that if somebody would build a hog pen near the camp, the hogs could fatten on the mussels and keep this place smelling better."

The kid who had been batting either struck out or got tired of swinging and threw the bat down.

"I don't have any hogs," I said.

"Esau has some wild ones running back in the woods along Harrison Bayou that he doesn't want to fool with anymore. He said that if you and your partners can trap them, you can have them, and fatten them on mussels. Then you can sell them in the fall at pure profit."

"What do hogs sell for?"

"Read your father's paper. He prints farm and stock prices twice a week." He turned and walked back toward his supply wagon.

"If you know, why don't you just tell me?" I shouted.

He stopped and flashed a smile at me. "When I was your age, nobody told me about pearls. I learned about them on my own. If you want to know what hogs sell for, find out yourself."

I stared at the back of his head as he walked away. Just then a thump came from home base and that ball of trotline sang right past me like a cannon shot. Some kid at second base told me to keep my mind on the game. I told him to shut up, and the fight commenced.

Cecil carried Esau's ax, Adam hauled a sack of shelled corn he had snuck out of his daddy's barn, and I brought a black eye from the ball game. We paddled a skiff back into Harrison Bayou and found a place not far from the water where hogs had been rooting for bugs and worms.

Cecil got me and Adam to do most of the chopping and dragging of logs while he chose the site for the trap. We knew as well as he did there was no trick to choosing a site, but he pretended to be busy at it long enough for us to do most of the hard work. Cecil was like that. He was always afraid hard work was going to sap strength from his brain.

"I hear some of these old pine-rooters get big tushes on them," he said as he marked off a square in the forest litter with his bare toe.

Adam laughed. "You're scared! Ain't you never caught a hog before?"

"I'm not scared. I just said they had big tushes."

"Well, don't worry," Adam said. "I'll bring old Buttermilk. He'll get 'em by the ear so we can gather their back legs and tie 'em up."

"I'm *not* worried," Cecil replied.

No, he wasn't any more worried than I was. Cecil and I had both heard wild hogs pop their tushes together before, and knew they meant business. We were both wondering how we would move those trapped hogs out of our pen without getting a couple of fingers snapped off. Adam mentioning old Buttermilk made me feel a little better. According to Adam, Buttermilk was the best hog-rasslin' dog on the South Shore.

We built our trap by laying up limbs sort of like a log cabin. We had brought some rope to tie the limbs together at the corners so the hogs wouldn't push the walls down. On one side of the square trap, we left a hole for a door that we had already built out of some old planks Esau let us have. We rigged that door to slide up and down in the hole.

That's when Cecil surprised me. It seemed he really had chosen the trap site for a good reason. There was a pine limb growing right over the sliding door. We tied a rope to the door and ran the rope over the limb. Adam cut a stake and drove it into the ground at an angle in the middle of the trap. Then we tied a loop in the end of the rope and hooked it over the stake. That held the sliding door up so the hogs could get in.

We fooled around with the stake and the rope for a while, adjusting them so a nudge would make the rope slip off the stake, letting the door fall shut. Finally we tied an ear of corn to the rope and hooked it over the stake, setting our trap. The hogs would come in, yank on that free ear of corn and pull the loop off the stake, letting the sliding door fall. Before we left, Adam made a few trails of shelled corn on the ground, all of them leading to the trapdoor.

Adam and I stood back for a moment and admired the ugly little log pen. He took as much pride in building it as I did. Both of us liked to do things with our hands, unlike Cecil.

"Well, come on. We better run the trotline before it gets dark."

"Yassuh, Marse Cecil!" Adam sang.

I almost hurt myself laughing. Adam didn't come up with many jokes, but when he did, they usually tickled me something fierce with their suddenness. It felt good to laugh after sulking for so many days about Carol Anne. Maybe I was going to get over her after all.

•   •   •

They say dogs sometimes get to looking and acting like the people who own them, and Buttermilk was a good argument for it. He was a canine Adam Owens—lean, strong, not too bright, and utterly unafraid of any wild animal. He was the color of buttermilk, medium-sized, with perky ears, and a crooked tail he always carried high.

"Why doesn't he ever let his tail down and cover his asshole?" Cecil asked as we paddled back up Harrison Bayou to check our hog trap the next day.

"He's daring you to sniff it," I said.

Buttermilk had been jumping all around the skiff, looking for critters in the water and getting in Cecil's way. As we got closer to the trap, he started quivering with excitement, as if Adam had told him he would get to tackle a hog this morning.

We could see from the skiff that the door had fallen on the trap. When we pulled the boat up on the muddy bank, the trapped hog heard us and tried to knock the pen down, but the log walls held. I thought Buttermilk was going to bust with hysterics, but Adam had trained him well and he didn't dare take off after anything without permission.

I was nervous about meeting Mr. Pig, but Adam looked like he was taking a Sunday stroll. He sauntered up to the trap and watched the hog smack its snout a couple of times on the log walls. From his pocket he removed a length of cord that had a loop in it like a snare. "You ready, Buttermilk?" he said, and the dog crouched. "Git him!"

Buttermilk skipped off the top of the log wall and leaped blindly into the pen with the wild pig. Now, this pine-rooter wasn't like any barnyard slop-eater you ever saw. When pigs go wild, they get long-legged and lean, and grow teeth that can cut like scissors. They get so strong that they can root up pine saplings with their snouts, looking for worms and stuff to eat. When Buttermilk lit alongside the two-year-old boar in our trap, he had a fight in front of him.

The hog jumped to one side with a grunt and backed into a corner to get a look at Buttermilk. The dog barked a couple of times and the pig lunged backward against the logs until it figured out it had nowhere to go but forward. Then it put its head down and ran at Buttermilk like a cow protecting her calf. The scissor teeth snapped at air as Buttermilk sprang on all fours, humped his back, and bit down on the end of the boar's right ear.

Grunts, squeals, and growls filled the woods for several seconds, and our little log trap shook like a boxcar on a downhill run. Buttermilk tried to get a better bite, lost his hold and went flying against the inside of the pen. When the boar rushed him, he leaped out of the pen, nimble as a cat, but I think he started jumping back in even before he hit the ground between me and Cecil. He must have been taking lessons from the fleas he hosted, because he looked like one of them springing back into the pen.

He came down on the hog like an eagle and this time got a firm bite on the base of the ear. The piercing squeal lasted about two seconds, then the pig went to its knees.

Adam bounded over the log partition in a blink and jerked the hind hooves off the ground as Buttermilk clenched the ear to the dirt. Adam tied the hind legs together first, then produced another length of cord from his pocket to lash the front ones. He tied them quick as a rodeo cowboy. "Git out!" he said to his dog, and Buttermilk sprang over the logs like a deer. When he lit, he went prancing around the pen, wagging his tail.

The pig soon stopped squealing and trembled as if it had taken the palsy. We ran a long green limb in between its legs where they had been tied together, and carried it out of the pen to the skiff. We set the trap again and spread more corn before we left, having gotten off to a good start in the hog business.

Buttermilk perched in the bow and wagged his tail in broad, proud sweeps as we paddled back to Goose Prairie Cove. We grinned over our success and poked a lot of fun at each other. The sticky swelter of the bayou summer caressed us and made us carefree as we wove among the cypress knees. The hog lay between the bulkheads and rolled its eyes in fear. It looked dumb as a boated catfish tied up there.

The moss in the cypress limbs strained the sunlight like lace as we paddled through air pockets of different temperatures; here as moist and warm as a woman's breath, and there as cool as the draft she leaves when she's gone in the night. Caddo Lake was mysterious like a woman. Like life.

I had been lost in Harrison Bayou before, but I knew where I was going this morning. I wished I could say the same about my future. My heart still hurt a little when I thought of Carol Anne, but I knew I would get over her. Then what? Pigs and catfish the rest of my days? I wasn't worried about it, just curious for the first time. It was a mystery and it intrigued me.

That was the summer of pearls. Mystery and discovery. Love and heartbreak. Wealth and poverty. Pigs and catfish. I was a boy, learning. I stabbed my paddle deep into the inky waters and stroked with undaunted strength. I had things to do.

I GAVE CHARLIE ASHENBACK EVERY PENNY I OWNED AND TOLD HIM I would have the rest of the money by the time he finished building my bateau. It would take him a week or so to get around to it, but only a day or two to build. Charlie could slap a boat together in his sleep, but he had a lot of orders from pearl-hunters ahead of me.

I fell into a daily routine again after I swore off thinking of Carol Anne. All the desire I had once held for her I now directed toward my bateau, my work, and my earnings. I took the risk of becoming like Cecil Peavy, always thinking of money, but it eased my heartache to have my brain occupied.

I rose at dawn every day and met my friends at Goose Prairie. We took Buttermilk with us everywhere now, and he loved watching Adam pull big catfish up on the trotline. He would bark at them as they splashed in the water. After selling the fish, or throwing them in the holding tank, we would paddle to our hog trap and let Buttermilk do his job. We had barely enough time before lunch to make the morning water run to Ames Spring, across the lake.

In the afternoons, we shoveled dead mussels into a wheelbarrow and hauled them to our hog pen. The pearl-hunters helped us by throwing the mussels in designated piles. They didn't mind, because we kept the lakeshore clean and smelling tolerable. They also threw garbage in with the mussels—any kind of refuse a hog would eat, and that covers about everything that will rot and stink.

We built the hog pen of rails about halfway between the lake and our catfish holding tank. Once they had gorged on mussels for a couple of days, our hogs calmed down pretty well and started acting domestic. After catching eight hogs in ten days, we abandoned the trap on Harrison Bayou.

After slopping the hogs, we would take it easy for an hour or so and wade for mussels. I had given up on finding a pearl, and just sold any mussels we didn't need for the trotline to rich tourist pearl-hunters who didn't want to get in the water.

On some days we would go out on the islands and cut hay to sell. Grass grew eight feet high on some of the islands where no stock ever grazed. With all the horses and mules in camp, we had little trouble selling hay, or trading it for seed pearls. A few campers had even brought milk cows with them, and they needed hay, too.

Toward late afternoon, we would paddle to Ames Spring on the second daily water run. That left us just enough time before sundown to make the evening run to the trotline.

My arms became hard as hickory from paddling all over the lake. My pockets began to fill back up with money earmarked for the Ashenback bateau. My parents glowed with pride.

"You've earned that Ashenback," my pop said to me one evening. "Billy Treat told me yesterday what a fine job you and your friends have done keeping the camp clean and supplied with hay and water. I'm proud of you, son."

Things seemed to be getting simple again, and I was hoping that my love affair that never happened with Carol Anne was just an aberration in life that would never recur. Once again I could look into an uncomplicated future. I saw myself working, making money, buying boats, and spending time with my friends. Only one thing could have plunged me back into wonderful chaos, and when it happened, it was like this.

One day Adam was shoveling mussels into the wheelbarrow I had been pushing along the lakeshore, when Cecil, who hadn't bent his back to do a lick of work all afternoon, said, "Hey, look, Ben, that girl over there's smiling at me."

I glanced toward a neatly kept camp and saw a blonde-haired farm girl sitting under a wagon-sheet shade cloth. What surprised me was not only how pretty she was, but that she was smiling at me instead of at Cecil. Cecil's eyes never did see the truth very well where women were concerned. He went through three wives before he finally just gave up, hired a housekeeper, and patronized the whorehouse twice a week. He was always much happier with the women he paid than he was with the ones he married.

But anyway, when I saw that blonde country girl smiling at me, I felt the hot flush and got the same silly quivering feeling Carol Anne used to give me. I would have groaned in disgust if it hadn't felt so good. I should have realized then that the world was too full of women for things to remain uncomplicated for long.

"She's not smilin' at you, Cecil," Adam Owens said. "She's smilin' at me." Adam was even less realistic about women than Cecil was. Maybe that's why he died a bachelor.

Cecil went after her like a business deal, but Adam and I didn't have the nerve to enter her camp. We just continued collecting garbage and dead mussels. While we were slopping the pigs, Cecil came trudging up to the hog pen, looking dejected.

"What's wrong with you?" I asked.

"She said she wasn't smiling at me," Cecil grumbled.

"I told you it was me!" Adam shouted so loud that he scared the pigs.

"Oh, hell, why would she be smiling at you, Adam? It was Ben she wanted to know about."

They looked at me as if they would throw me to the hogs.

"Me?"

"Yes, you. Her name's Cindy. Said her old man brought the family all the way from Longview to hunt pearls. If you want to know anything else about her, you can find it out yourself." He stalked away, obviously mad at me for getting smiled at in his stead.

"Dang, what's he so mad at?" I said.

Adam frowned and shoveled some more slop to the hogs. He wasn't feeling real friendly toward me, either. This was a new experience. My friends and I harassed each other daily, and often got mad enough to fight. But this was a silent anger I was feeling from them now. It was the same treatment I had given Billy after that night the lantern went out in Carol Anne's room.

I had to admit that Cecil and Adam were the last of my worries. What concerned me was how to approach that pretty blonde girl named Cindy. In the next few days I suffered brief moments of rationality during which I told myself it would be better to leave her alone than to risk getting my heart wrenched out of my chest again. Then I would see her smiling at me as I carried a load of catfish or a barrel of water, and knew I would have to find the nerve to speak to her.

As it turned out, she came to me one afternoon as I ate my lunch under the mulberry tree at Esau's place. She snuck up behind me and said, "Are you the boy with the hogs?"

I turned like a startled deer and almost choked on a biscuit when I looked into her blue eyes. My mama had taught me better than to talk with my mouth full, so I just had to nod and turn red while I chewed.

She smiled. "My daddy wants to see you." She had such a beautiful, twangy, piney-woods voice that I knew she had to be exaggerating it some for my sake. "Come on," she said tossing her head toward her camp.

I was afraid her daddy might want to fill my britches with rock salt for being there for his daughter to smile at, but I wasn't about to refuse to follow her. "What's he want?" I managed to say, wiping crumbs from my face with my sleeve.

"He wants to buy a couple of them hogs of yours."

"What for?"

"He found a pearl. Got a hundred and sixty-five dollars for it. We're gonna celebrate tonight."

"You inviting the hogs?" I said, trying to be clever.

"No, silly. We're gonna cook 'em."

"Oh."

We walked on in excruciating silence for seconds that seemed like hours. I couldn't think of anything to talk about but catfish, and I knew she wasn't interested in that. She smiled at me a couple of times as we headed toward her camp. The silence didn't seem to bother her, but then, she didn't need to talk, and she probably knew it, as females know things.

"I'm gonna buy a boat," I blurted at last.

She seemed impressed. "What kind?"

"An Ashenback bateau."

She wrinkled her pretty little freckled nose. "I don't know much about boats."

"That's the best kind there is." We were approaching her camp.

"When you gonna buy it?"

"I guess after your pop buys those hogs from me. I should have enough money then."

"Maybe . . ." she said, glancing toward her camp and lowering her voice. "Maybe you can take me for a ride in it."

A light of pure joy filled the air around me until the shadow of Cindy's father blocked it out. I almost ran into him as he came around the back of the wagon. "Cindy!" he shouted, making me flinch. "Oh, there you are. Is this the boy?"

"Yes, sir," Cindy said.

"What's your name, boy?" He looked big to me, but was probably average-sized, made of good solid country stock. He had stubble on his face, a battered straw hat on his head. "I say, what's your name?"

"B-B-Ben Crowell," I answered.

"You the boy owns them hogs?"

"Yes, sir."

"Want to sell a couple?"

I glanced at Cindy. "Sure, I guess."

He offered me a price on two head of swine and I took it without attempting to negotiate or confer with my partners. I figured my third of the sale price quickly in my head, and it was enough to pay Charlie Ashenback the rest of what I owed him for the bateau. And Cindy wanted a ride! I was happy as a drunken possum when her pop put the money in my hand.

"We'll come up to the pen and get them hogs this evenin'," he said.

"Just pick whatever pair you want."

He nodded and shook my hand, then disappeared behind the wagon.

Cindy walked me to the edge of her camp. "Don't forget about that boat ride, Ben," she said.

It was over two miles to Charlie Ashenback's boatyard in Port Caddo, but I ran every step without stopping to rest. He had my bateau on a pair of sawhorses. "Sure, you can take it now," he said. He was a friendly old man with sawdust in his white hair. "Paint's dry."

It was so beautiful I was nearly afraid to touch it. It almost looked alive, arching its back as if diving into the water. It wanted a bayou under it. "Will you help me carry it to the water?" I asked.

"Sure." He picked up the bow and we lifted the boat and headed for the bank of Big Cypress Bayou. "Don't fret if she leaks a little at first. Just leave her in the water and those planks will swell and close the cracks. Then she'll be tight as a virgin with her legs crossed." He turned his face up and laughed as he waddled along with his end of my boat.

When we put the bateau in the dark bayou water, I swore I felt her trying to swim. It was at that moment I realized I didn't own a paddle. Old Charlie had some for sale, but they were above my means. The bateau had just about cleaned me out.

However, I had Cecil and Adam's share of the hog money in my pocket. I knew one of them would lend me enough to buy a paddle, so I went ahead and paid Charlie for one of his. I was dying to get that boat between me and water.

Bayou water is flat, but the Ashenback seemed to go downhill everywhere it went. It was like flying compared to the way Esau's cumbersome skiffs plowed through the water. I wasn't sure if maybe I hadn't wasted my money, as well as Cecil and Adam's, on the paddle. It seemed my bateau would go all the way across the lake with one push.

I had never known a happier moment. I had earned that boat. As I slipped effortlessly past the mouth of Pine Island Slough, I thought of how Cindy would look in the bow. I imagined Carol Anne there, too, but only briefly. Cindy was my age. She belonged in my bateau. Carol Anne belonged to Billy Treat.

I took a shortcut through Mossy Brake, to see how my vessel would handle among the trees. She went like a snake, twining her way around the cypress knees. The air was dark and still back in the brake, but my bateau brought me through to Taylor Island before I could even worry about getting turned around. I passed right by our trotline, but didn't even glance at it. I was having too much fun to think of work.

I used all my strength on the last stretch to Goose Prairie Cove. I wished the steamboats were running, so I could have showed off to the passengers. I passed the first of the pearl camps and noticed some of the waders admiring my speed, which gave me strength to stroke even harder. I was dying to show Adam and Cecil. I could give them their share of the hog money, then we could celebrate with Cindy's family. It was going to be a great day.

When I slipped into Goose Prairie Cove, I didn't see my friends anywhere. I raced past Captain Brigginshaw in his Ashenback rowboat so fast that he said to his oarsman, "Giff, why don't you row as fast as Billy Treat's young friend, there?" Wading pearl-hunters turned their heads to watch me streak by.

Esau greeted me as I beached my bateau near his saloon. "That yours?" he asked.

"Yep. Just bought it."

He slipped his flask into his back pocket. "That's an Ashenback, ain't it? I can tell by the way he angles the planks on the bottom."

"Yep. Where's Cecil and Adam? I want to show them."

"They were here looking for you a while ago. They said they would wait for you at the hog pen."

"Thanks, Esau." I started up the lakeshore.

"That's a good boat," he said, stopping me. "You work hard, and stay away from whiskey, and you earn a lot of good things like that."

I paused before continuing up the shore. Esau had never lectured me or given me advice before.

"Ben," he said, stopping me again. He grinned. "They looked mad."

"Who?"

"Your friends."

"Mad? About what?"

Esau shrugged. "Somethin' about the hogs." He reached for his flask again as I turned away.

15

I SAW THEM SITTING ON THE RAILS OF THE HOG PEN, SCOWLING AND FUMING. They had been a little edgy toward me lately, because of the way Cindy flirted with me all the time instead of with them. But I couldn't think of what I had done to make them this mad. I reasoned it was probably Cecil's doing for the most part. Adam usually didn't get mad unless somebody told him to.

Cecil jumped down from the fence when I got close, and Adam quickly followed. Buttermilk stood between them, wagging his tail. They ground their teeth and glowered at me until I was near enough for them to holler at.

"What the hell's going on?" Cecil demanded.

"That's what I want to know!" Adam added.

"What are you talking about?" I said.

"Your girlfriend's daddy came up here and took two of our hogs. Said you told him he could do it."

"She's not my girlfriend."

"Well, whoever the hell she is, her daddy came up here and took our hogs. What did you do, trade him a couple of hogs to feel on her or something?"

I was still in good spirits from buying my bateau, but that sort of talk was going to make me mad quick. "I sold him those hogs," I said.

Cecil took off his hat and threw it on the ground. "You what?" Buttermilk grabbed the hat, thinking Cecil wanted to play. "Who gives you the right to sell our hogs without asking us? I thought we decided to fatten those hogs till fall. Now you've sold them cheap and run off with the money without even asking us."

"Yeah!" Adam said.

"I didn't run off with the money. I just went to buy my new bateau from Charlie Ashenback. Come on down to the lake and look at it."

Both of them fumed. Adam threw *his* hat on the ground.

"You used our money to buy your bateau?" Cecil shouted.

"No! I just used my own money for the bateau. I've got your money in my pocket."

"Well, let's have it. I want to see what you sold those hogs for. And I'm going to ask that little bitch from Longview what her daddy paid, too, so don't try to short me."

Now we were all about equally mad. "You don't have to talk about her like that, Cecil. She hasn't done anything to you."

"I'll bet she hasn't done anything to you, either, and if she did, you wouldn't know how to do it, anyway. Now, give us our money!"

I looked at Adam as I scooped the money out of my pocket. "Here's your cut," I said, getting ready to count out his share. "Oh," I added, after putting the first coin in his hand, "would you loan me enough to buy a paddle?"

"Hell, no, he's not going to loan you any money!" Cecil shouted.

"Hell, no, I'm not going to loan you any money!" Adam echoed.

He probably would have if Cecil hadn't said anything. There wasn't a greedy bone in Adam's body. I counted the rest of his share into his palm as Cecil watched.

"Is that all you sold those hogs for? Is that our whole share? Damn, Ben, that farmer took your shirt!" He held his hand open.

"Cecil," I said, before giving him his share, "I don't suppose *you* would loan me the money for the paddle?"

He answered by thrusting his open palm at me. I put the money in his hand in one lump sum, but I knew he was going to count it.

"Wait a minute," he said. "Wait just a damn minute. How come Adam got more than me?"

"Well," I said, "the truth is I already bought that paddle. I thought one of you would be my friend enough to loan me the money."

"That does it!" Cecil said. He kicked his hat toward the hog pen, and Buttermilk went after it again. "I'm about to kick your ass, Ben!"

"Oh, settle down," I said. Then Cecil's fist hit me right in the forehead and knocked me to the ground. When I looked up, he was standing over me with his fists waving in front of him. Buttermilk was jumping around with excitement, wagging his tail.

"All right, Cecil," I said. "If that's the way you want it."

He rushed me when I got up, but I ducked his wild punch and hit him in the lip with the top of my head. I pushed him away and got my fists up. His lip was bleeding.

"Damn you, Ben, I'm really gonna kick your ass now!"

"That's right, Cecil," Adam said. "You show him!" Adam loved a good fight, even if he wasn't in it.

Cecil rushed me and I slipped in a quick punch to his nose that buckled his knees and landed him on his rear end.

"Cecil!" Adam yelled. "What are you doin', boy? Git off your ass and *git him!*"

Now, old Buttermilk didn't know too much English, but *git him* was his favorite phrase. He took two springs toward the pen and landed among the hogs before Adam even realized what he had said. A great surge of pork crashed against one side of the fence, and logs flew as if they had been blasted. I tried to jump in the way of the last two hogs left in the pen, but with Buttermilk behind them, they thought little of running over me, their scissorlike teeth gnashing in my face.

"Damn it, Adam!" Cecil yelled as he got up. "Don't ever say *git him* when Buttermilk's around!"

The dog had caught one of the pigs by the ear and had it almost immobilized.

"Ben, fix the hog pen! Adam, go catch that hog!"

Adam sprinted for the pig Buttermilk had caught and I started stacking the logs back. By the time we got the single hog back in the pen, the mayhem had started down at the pearling camps. All five remaining pine-rooters had stampeded the tent city. We could hear pots and pans clanging, women screaming with terror, children shrieking with joy, men swearing, dogs barking.

If not for Buttermilk, we never would have recaptured any of them. The steady diet of mussels and garbage had slowed the hogs down a little and made them easy for the dog to catch. People tried to herd them, shoo them, and tackle them, but Buttermilk was the only successful hog-rassler. With his help, we managed to catch three, but two escaped to the woods.

There was a big panic for the first few minutes of the hog scramble, then everyone in camp pulled together to catch the strays. Many grown men ran from popping tushes while their wives stood their ground with shovels or frying pans. Nobody blamed us boys. I guess we and our hogs had done the camp more good than harm over the long haul.

When all the hogs had been tied or run into the woods, a group of men helped us carry the caught ones back up to the pen. Billy Treat was among them. He had pulled his supply wagon up at the pearling camp about the time the stampede broke out.

"Hey, no hard feelings," I said to Cecil when we got the last tush hog in. "I'll pay you back for the paddle."

He had dried blood all over his mouth and chin. He smirked and waved at me in a peculiar way as he walked off.

"What was all that about?" Billy asked, coming up behind me.

"Nothin'," I said.

"I thought you two were friends."

"I thought so, too."

Billy grunted. "What was the fight over? Girls or money?"

The men were returning to their camps, leaving Billy and me alone at the pens. When I looked at him, I couldn't help grinning a little. He was sharp, that Billy Treat. You had to like a guy like that. "A little of both," I said.

He grimaced. "Well, don't worry, he'll get over it."

We stood there together for a few quiet seconds, looking out over the camps and the boats and the lake.

"I heard you bought an Ashenback."

I nodded.

"Well, where is it? Let's see it."

I felt better almost instantly. I was dying to show off my bateau. "Come on, I'll show you," I said. I forgot all my troubles as I walked with Billy toward Esau's place. My partners and I had lost two hogs, but they hadn't cost us anything but time and a little sweat. Now that I had the Ashenback, I wasn't worried much about money. I had my mind on my bateau, and that girl, Cindy, from Longview.

To make conversation, I asked Billy how the business was going, and he told me all about it. He mentioned Carol Anne's name several times, but it barely fazed me. It seemed as if I hadn't been in love with her in a long time.

"I bet she moves like a skipping stone," Billy said, examining my bateau.

"Yeah, you want to try her?" I asked.

But before he could answer, I heard a voice as sweet and smooth as wild honey call my name.

"Hi, Ben," Cindy said, strolling by on the lakeshore.

I felt myself blush. "Oh, hi," I replied.

"That your boat?"

I nodded.

"I still want that ride." She stopped and flipped one side of a mussel shell over with her bare toe. "See you at our party tonight."

I watched her walk down the shoreline until I heard Billy whistle quietly.

"That's who the fight was over?"

"Yeah," I said, groaning with embarrassment.

"I'd fight you for her myself if I was fifteen years younger."

I scoffed, because I knew Cindy had nothing on Carol Anne.

"My God, Ben, why are you turning so red?"

"I don't know." I cringed and waded into the water next to my bateau. "Shoot, I don't know anything about girls," I said.

"Yeah, neither do I. I guess that's what gets us so all-fired interested in them. They're a mystery, and no man can resist that."

I glanced up at him and caught that sparkle in his eye, like when he talked about pearls. "You must know something about them," I said, a little accusingly. "You sure got you one."

He was looking at the sky. "All I know is to behave like a gentleman. That's all there is to it, Ben." He smiled, still looking skyward. "That throws them. They don't encounter much of that."

I looked to the north to see what he was staring at, but found nothing in the sky where his eyes led.

"It's a rare thing, Ben."

"What is?"

"True love. Rare as a pearl."

I felt awkward listening to him philosophize. Fourteen-year-old bayou boys don't have much use for that kind of talk. But nobody was listening, and he had complimented my bateau, and besides, I idolized Billy. I decided to humor him a little. "How rare *is* that?" I said.

He looked at me suddenly, as if stunned to think he might have gotten through to me or something. Then he stroked his chin and dredged deep into his reservoir of philosophies. "Have you ever seen the moon through a rainbow?"

I wrinkled my face. He was looking at that place in the sky again.

"Rainbows don't come out at night," I said.

"No, but sometimes you'll see the moon in the daytime."

"But if there's a rainbow, that means it's been raining, so there are probably some clouds in the sky. They would cover up the moon." It was a strange conversation, because I didn't really even know what we were talking about.

"True. But a rainbow also means there's some sun shining. That means clouds are clearing. Conditions would have to be just right, Ben, but it could happen." His gaze fell from the sky and landed on me. "It might happen one day out of ten thousand. That's how rare a pearl is. That's how rare true love is. It's one in ten thousand. Like the moon through a rainbow."

Suddenly I wasn't embarrassed anymore. I was thinking higher thoughts with Billy Treat. I was imagining the full moon through a rainbow. It *was* like a pearl! I turned to that place in the sky over the lake. I could almost see it there, perfectly round and shimmering through the bands of light-borne color. When I looked back at Billy, he was walking toward his wagon.

"Just remember you're a gentleman," he said, looking over his shoulder and shaking a warning finger at me.

But Billy had misjudged me. I was no gentleman.

The party drew almost everybody in the tent city to the camp of Cindy's parents. The hogs were roasted and carved on spits over banks of orange coals. Catfish fried in huge iron kettles. The fiddlers and banjo-pluckers circled the campfires. Pots of brewing coffee filled the air with a fine, rich aroma. With all the campfire and tobacco smoke, the mosquitoes found few opportunities to probe for blood, preying mainly on the men who went to sip whiskey in the dark.

Cecil and Adam avoided me, still mad about the hogs, envious of my bateau, and jealous over Cindy. Most of the other Port Caddo kids went home after dark, so I was left to shift for myself. After I ate some pork and cornbread, I didn't have much to do, but I kept wandering around, hoping to bump into Cindy, and yet avoiding her wagon for fear I would bump into her. I was about ready to give up and go home when it finally happened.

When I saw her coming, I fought an urge to turn and run. I could face Cecil Peavy in a fistfight every day of the week, but I was sure scared of girls.

"Hi, Ben," she said in her cheerful, self-assured drawl.

I returned the greeting and looked away, nervously only risking glances at her. Our conversation consisted mainly of her asking me questions and me grunting affirmative or negative.

"Daddy said to tell you those hogs was good eatin'."

I shrugged modestly. "A little tough. We should have fattened them longer." I was wondering when she wanted her boat ride, but I wasn't about to just come out and ask her. That seemed so forward I was afraid she might slap me.

"When are you going to give me that ride in your boat?" she asked, as if reading my mind.

"How about tomorrow?"

"Why not right now?"

Now? In the dark? Alone on the lake with Cindy? I was dumb-founded. It wasn't a bad idea, though. It was a very dark night. I wouldn't have to worry about looking stupid if she couldn't see me. Not a bad idea at all.

"Well?"

"All right," I said. "Come on."

That Cindy was a natural talker, which was lucky for me because my brain could hardly form a single word. She talked about everything from pearls to watermelons as we walked to my bateau on the lakeshore. She waded in ankle-deep and got in the bow, holding my arm to steady herself as she stepped in. I waded deeper and climbed over the gunnel to my seat in the stern.

"Where do you want to go?" I asked.

"Oh, I don't care. Just paddle around."

I slid my bateau out onto the lake with a powerful stroke of the paddle. Cindy's voice flowed like running water—a strange and beautiful sound to a boy from the bayou. The lights from the party came at us like skipping stones, leaving long trails as they clipped the wave tops. The sounds of the people droned with the singing bullfrogs. Out on the water, a warm breeze blew just stiff enough to keep the mosquitoes off of us. I didn't know how much Cindy knew about boats, so I stayed in water shallow enough to wade in. I didn't want her falling out and drowning.

"Do you like me, Ben?" she asked suddenly, in the middle of a soliloquy on something unrelated.

"Yeah," I said.

"Do you think I talk too much?"

"No."

"My brother says I talk too much. Sometimes my daddy says I talk too much, too. I like you, too."

I made a big circle in Goose Prairie Cove and let Cindy talk all she wanted. When I figured she had had enough of a ride, I took her back to the shore near Esau's place and helped her out.

"That was fun," she said. "You can take me again some time, if you want to. Do you want to?"

"Sure," I said, pushing the bateau onto the shore.

She held my hand as we waded to dry land and I felt a delirium I had never experienced. I wanted to grab her right there and put my hands all over her just to see what she was made of, but I remembered what Billy had said.

We stopped together a few steps from the water and turned toward each other. "Do you want to kiss me?" she asked, smooth as honey. I didn't get to answer, because the next thing I knew, her lips were on mine.

I never have put much stock in beginner's luck. That Cindy from Longview had done some kissing before. I know girls come by some seductions naturally, but she had practiced on somebody else before me.

I remember thinking how foolish I had been to misinterpret that peck Carol Anne had given me on the forehead weeks before. That was nothing compared to what Cindy was doing to me now. Even when I closed my eyes, I saw stars. But like everything else in the summer of pearls, it was too good to last long.

"Ciiindyyy!"

I heard her mother's long, siren call from the camp party. Cindy's lips broke from mine. She had both hands on my face, but my arms were paralyzed against my sides. I was afraid to move them, thinking that if I went to grabbing at her, I might not be able to stop.

"I have to go," she said. "Mama's callin'." She turned and ran like a sprite toward the camp lights. "See you tomorrow!"

It was all very overwhelming. She wanted to see me again. Tomorrow. I hadn't done anything stupid. I hadn't scared her off or made her mad. Maybe Billy had something. Maybe I really could learn to be a gentleman after all.

I left a good portion of who and what I was right there on the lakeshore that night. I can still show you the spot where it happened, and I can almost recall the feeling that numbed me for days and nights afterward.

There are moments you anticipate in life. Many of them disappoint you when they finally come. Others exceed your most fanciful expectations. That first kiss of mine at Goose Prairie Cove changed me. It confused and enlightened me. It fulfilled me, yet left me desperately longing.

Life was going to get complicated again, but I knew one thing for certain after that night. Ben Crowell was going to become a gentleman. He wouldn't be fourteen forever.

16

HENRY COLTON GOT HIS FIRST LOOK AT THE GOOSE PRAIRIE PEARL CAMPS
from Port Caddo Road. It was midmorning and getting hot. He stopped
in the shade of a pine and mopped his neck with a handkerchief as a
few hopeful tourist pearl-hunters walked past. He thought Chicago had
been hot when he left, but this place was suffocating. He suddenly understood more clearly the lure of a hunt that drew its participants into
the water.

He sat at the base of the tall loblolly pine to observe the activities
down at the lake. He knew virtually nothing about pearl-hunting. Doz-
ens of wagons and scores of tents dotted the lakeshore for as many miles
as he could see. Hundreds of campers milled about on the shore, and
hundreds more appeared as heads bobbing on the lake surface.

The coach from town rattled by him. It made a constant circuit of
the pearl camps for those who didn't want to walk to or from Port
Caddo. He shook his head in amazement. He had seen people get this
excited over gold and silver, but never over pearls. He checked his
pocket, as he had done a hundred times each day since leaving Chicago,

to make sure the little coin purse was still there. It was.

After watching for a while, he figured out that no one mode of pearl-hunting predominated. There were almost as many methods as pearl-hunters. That was a relief. It would be easy to fit in. This job was going to be a regular holiday.

Colton finally got up and sauntered down to the lake. He sat down on a drifted log and continued his observations. The men and boys who came out of the water had mud between their toes and under their toenails, so he knew the waders were feeling for the mussels with their feet. A pair of men about fifty yards out in the cove were throwing their mussels into a skiff. Another fellow, without a boat, opened his with a knife as he found them.

Colton caught some familiar motion in the corner of his eye. Looking to his right, he saw a dark-skinned man—the man whose movements had attracted his attention—loafing in the shade of a mulberry with a couple of companions. The man looked to be Indian, but had short hair. There was a shack there. Something familiar about it, too. No, he had never been to Caddo Lake before, but that shack represented something he knew well. What was it?

Turning back to the cove, he observed a man lying on his stomach in a skiff. To keep the sun from scorching, the skiff had a wagon sheet fixed to it on bows, like a prairie schooner. The man propelled himself through the shallow water with his hands. Occasionally he scooped a mussel shell from the mud and threw it over his shoulder into the covered skiff.

Colton shook his head. These pearl-hunters were a strange bunch of—

There was that distinct motion again! This time he glanced quick enough to see the old Indian reaching for the flask in his pocket. Ah, now he recognized the shack. Saloon. He had enjoyed better from Denver to San Francisco, but he had survived far worse in a hundred cow towns and mining camps.

A right handy saloon would make this vacation all the more endurable. Besides, he had to blend in. If the pearl-hunters were drinkers, well, he had better take an occasional snort, too. His bosses had told him to curb his vices or find other employment, but they didn't understand how it was in the field.

He licked his lips. True, it was early. If he started now, he'd stay drunk all day. The old Indian reached for the pocket flask again, as if to goad him. Better watch that muscular fellow next to the Indian. Those beady little squint-eyes meant trouble. Seen that look before. Pure meanness.

A trio of boys beached a skiff and began lugging kegs up to the saloon. Whiskey? No, drinking water. The kegs were heavy, but the boys handled them well. It was routine to them. He remembered being adrift at their age—Illinois to California. It was a wonder he had survived those years.

He found himself surveying the saloon again. After all, there was no hurry. The pearl-buyer wasn't even around. He had a description of Brigginshaw. A man that size would be hard to miss. Get acquainted with the drinkers first. Might learn something. He got up and sauntered casually toward the shack.

By noon, Henry Colton was somewhat drunk and very hungry. "Where's a man eat around here?" he asked.

"We'll fry some fish directly," Esau said. He heard Billy's buckboard rattling down Port Caddo Road. "Or you can buy some cold meats and stuff from the wagon." He pointed his thumb over his shoulder without looking.

"That sounds good," Colton said. He checked the purse in his pocket as he rose. He noticed the beady-eyed man sneering at the approaching wagon.

The wagon drew a crowd when it pulled up. Colton thought he recognized the driver from the Treat Inn. Popular fellow. Everybody had a smile for him, and a kind word or two.

"Aren't you the cook at the Treat Inn?" he asked as he paid Billy for his lunch.

"I am."

Colton congratulated himself. Drink, he believed, actually sharpened his mind for observations, even if it did slow his reflexes a little, and skew his judgments. Nothing to worry about on this job, though. Strictly routine. He retired to the shade of the mulberry with his food.

While eating his lunch, Colton saw a rowboat enter the cove from the main part of the lake. A black man pulled the oars, dwarfed by a huge bearded fellow who stood in the bow like George Washington crossing the Delaware. He had one hand on a pistol butt and the other wrapped around the handle of a satchel. That's where the money is, Colton thought. And the pearls.

The trace chains jerked on the supply wagon. Colton turned in time to see the driver wave. He followed the man's gaze out onto the lake. Brigginshaw removed the hand from his pistol grip and returned the salutation to the wagon driver. Friends. Interesting.

You're good, Colton. You don't miss anything.

"Pearl!" The cry came from the cove. "Over here, Captain!"

Brigginshaw's oarsman dipped the blades and wheeled the rowboat, propelling it easily toward the pearl-hunter in the water. As he chewed his cold ham and biscuits, Colton pulled his hat low over his eyes and watched the man in the white suit and panama. The oarsman held the boat beside the pearl-hunter, who handed Brigginshaw something over the gunnel. The buyer inspected the specimen and spoke to the hunter. Making an offer, Colton surmised. The hunter groused for a while, but finally nodded.

Colton narrowed his eyes against the glare and watched carefully. The Australian opened the satchel. He removed a small black case in which he placed the new pearl. Now the glint of a gold coin came from the satchel. Brigginshaw pressed it in the pearl-hunter's hand, inside the gunnels, so the hunter couldn't blame him if it fell into the water. Then the big man reached into the satchel again. He pulled out the notebook. Colton watched closely as the Australian made an entry with a pencil drawn from his jacket.

There it is, he thought. The entire procedure. This was going to be easy. Just figure out a way to separate Captain Brigginshaw from his satchel. Even for thirty seconds. How difficult could that be?

He finished his lunch and had Esau fill his jar with whiskey again. He watched as the buyer made two more purchases out in the cove.

Same routine. The pearl, the money, the entry in the ledger book. Finally the captain had his oarsman pull for the shore.

The muscular, beady-eyed man got up. "See you later, Esau," he said.

"Where you goin', Kelso?" the old Indian replied, smirking a little.

"To take a shit and name it Brigginshaw."

The Indian smiled and winked at Colton.

It was the slowest wink Colton had ever seen. "What was that all about?" he asked when Kelso got far enough away.

"Fight a few weeks ago. Captain Brigginshaw hurt him pretty bad."

Colton nodded and watched the big Australian consume the lakeshore in huge strides. He lifted his panama and smiled warmly as he approached the mulberry.

"Good day, my Choctaw friend. Gentlemen."

"Hello, Captain," Esau said.

"Mr. Kelso's not feeling sociable today?" The Australian's laughter shook the mulberry leaves.

Colton was thinking: Let's see how much this big man will stand for. "He said he was going to take a shit and name it after you."

"Did he, now? And who are you, mate?"

"Henry Colton. Just drifted down from Indian Territory. Heard about the pearl rush." He stood and offered Brigginshaw his hand. The Australian shook it and smiled. He was big and strong, with a heart to match. Good-natured, but be careful. As the Indian said, he hurt that Kelso fellow pretty bad. He hadn't loosed his hold on the satchel yet.

"Captain Trevor Price Brigginshaw. Pleased to meet you, Mr. Colton."

"Oh, don't 'mister' me. It's Henry to my friends."

"Thinking of doing some pearl-hunting, Henry?"

"I don't know. What are my chances of finding a pearl here?"

"In the bottom of a whiskey jar? Not good, mate." His laughter boomed into the pines. "Not good at all!"

Colton slapped his knee and laughed along. "Well, how much do you give for a pearl?"

"That depends on many things. Could be anywhere from twenty-five dollars an ounce for dust pearls to eight hundred dollars for a single specimen. I bought a fine drop pearl for three hundred this morning on the North Shore. Isn't that right, Giff?"

Brigginshaw's black oarsman had come up beside him after tending to the boat. "Whatever you say, Captain."

"How many have you bought in all?" Colton asked.

"Today?"

"No, I mean since the rush started."

"Good God! Thousands!"

"My goodness. How do you keep track of them all?"

The captain patted his satchel. "I carry my office everywhere I go. Pearls, money, and records." He hitched his coattail behind his pistol grip. "And security, as well."

"Mind if I look at your record book? See what pearls are selling for? Might help me make up my mind whether or not I want to hunt for 'em."

The Australian shook his head. "Sorry, Mr. Colton," he said firmly. "All sales must remain confidential."

"Now, don't 'mister' me, I told you. It's Henry to you, Captain."

"And Trevor to you, Henry. You might as well try your luck for a few days. You'll earn drinking money even if you don't get rich." He looked at his oarsman. "Take a rest, Giff. I'm going to walk through the camps."

"Yes, sir," Giff said, sitting on the ground against the trunk of the mulberry.

When Brigginshaw had walked beyond earshot, Colton looked at the black man and said, "Hey, boy. How about that fellow out there in the water? The one the captain bought the pearl from when you first rowed him into the cove. How much did he get?"

"Captain said that's nobody's business," Giff replied. "He said keep my mouth shut. He don't tell nobody what them pearls sell for."

"But you know."

Giff shrugged. "Sometimes I hear. Other times he don't even say out loud. Just write it down on paper and show the pearl-hunters and they say deal or no deal."

"But you can see the book when he writes in it."

"Can't read noways," Giff said.

Colton took a long draw from the whiskey jar and watched Brigginshaw deal for pearls at a camp a hundred yards away. "Does he really keep all those pearls in that leather case?"

"Safest place he knows," Esau said.

Colton whistled. "Is he crazy? I heard in the Indian Territory that some outlaw gang was hiding out down here. Christmas so-and-so."

"Christmas Nelson," Esau said. "The captain ain't scared of them. He sleeps with them pearls in his bed, he says. I'd hate to try to steal 'em from him."

"I'd hate it, too," Colton said, grinning. "I'd hate the hell out of it!"

He wandered through the pearling camps that afternoon, asking pearlhunters how much they had received for their finds. Their claims varied widely. He couldn't rely on them. The information would be of little use. He needed specifics. Checking the coin purse in his pocket, he drifted back to Esau's saloon to enjoy a few more drinks before returning to the Treat Inn for supper.

Near sundown, the mosquitoes began their forays, and Colton, now quite intoxicated, strode uncertainly back toward Port Caddo. As the afternoon wore on, he had thought more and more of the woman he had seen at the Treat Inn when he registered the night before. A real bayou belle. Maybe he would look her up tonight. He had thought it useless to approach her last night, sober. But now he had the cocksureness of a drunk. How could she resist him?

He arrived just as supper was being served, found an empty table in the corner, and sat down. Billy came out of the kitchen carrying four plates, which he delivered to another table. Colton caught his eye and waved.

"Be right with you," Billy said.

"No hurry," the guest replied, smiling. Then he saw her. The woman from last night had grown even more provocative. To Colton, it seemed she flirted a great deal with the male diners as she leaned over their shoulders to fill their glasses with water. He was sure he saw her pressing herself against them. Now he had her figured. She wanted company tonight, and he was just the man.

Billy came through the kitchen door with a plate of steaming food for the new diner. "Here you are, sir. Enjoy it." He smelled whiskey on the man's breath and remembered seeing him at Esau's place earlier. "Any luck pearling today?"

"Huh?" Colton said, tucking a napkin into the front of his shirt. "Oh! Hell, I didn't even get my feet wet. Maybe tomorrow."

Billy could read drunkenness in a man's eyes the way he could grade the luster of a pearl. But, unlike Trevor Brigginshaw, Colton didn't seem to be a mean drunk. He would probably go to bed after supper without causing any trouble. "Carol Anne will bring you some water in a minute," he said, heading back to the kitchen.

"How about something stronger?" Colton said, with his mouth full.

Billy stopped. "That'll be coffee," he replied, and left the man to his meal.

"Hello, darlin'," Colton said when Carol Anne came with the water pitcher. He mistook her suspicion for a look of interest.

"Good evening, Mr. . . ."

"Call me Henry, darlin'. Henry Colton. You remember me. You signed me in last night. Room number five."

"Oh, yes. Mr. Colton." She poured the water calmly.

"Now, don't 'mister' me. That's Henry to you, darlin'." He grabbed her wrist as she finished filling his glass. "That's room number five." He winked, now doubly drunk with desire on top of the whiskey. When he looked at her, he was sure he saw her wink back.

Carol Anne twisted her wrist from his grasp and turned for the kitchen. When she did, he reached for the roundest, softest part of her he could find and pinched it smartly between his thumb and forefinger.

The customers heard Carol Anne yelp, and looked up in time to see her empty her water pitcher in Colton's face.

"Goddamn, woman!" he said.

Billy was out of the kitchen in seconds and caught Carol Anne as she tried to rush by him. "What's going on?"

Her features were twisted in anger when she pointed. "He grabbed me!"

Billy marched to the table. "Get out!" he said to Colton.

"What? Are you gonna take the word of a water girl over a guest?"

"She's half-owner of this inn, mister, and I'm the other half. Get out before I throw you out."

"But, my dinner."

Billy yanked the wet napkin from Colton's collar, clenched a handful of his shirt, and lifted him to his wobbly legs. The chair fell over and slapped against the floor. The dishes rattled on the table as Colton kicked in surprise. One of the guests was quick enough to open the front door as Billy dragged the offender there and shoved him out.

"Goddamn!" Colton said as he lifted himself from the dirt. It had happened again. How many places had he been thrown out of now? Always drunk.

He looked up and saw the light of the open inn door wavering above him. He saw something coming. His suitcase and the rest of his belongings landed on top of him, knocking him back down. Reflexes slow. Damned whiskey. And this his last chance.

Where would he go now? He stood and staggered a few steps before he got his balance. Back to the pearl camps. Nowhere else to go. He stuffed his suitcase with his things, unable to keep his balance. He suddenly felt a great deal drunker than he had before.

Finally getting his belongings together, he began weaving toward the pearling camps in the dark. Halfway there, his stomach began to boil. He stumbled into the bushes to vomit.

He tried to stand again, but his stomach hurt. He felt better on the ground. Fumbling with his suitcase, he pulled out a pair of pants to use as a pillow. He squirmed under the pinpricks of thirsty mosquitoes. His head was aching now. He felt a chill, pulled another article of clothing over him.

Maybe he should check his pocket for the coin purse. To hell with it. Who really gave a shit, anyway?

This was a familiar misery. Too familiar. His only consolation was knowing that sleep would soon come—the insensible sleep of a drunk. He would go to sleep curled up on the pine needles like a stray dog. Yes, he would sleep. Just as soon as he got through puking again.

17

AFTER SEVERAL DAYS, HENRY COLTON HAD CAPTAIN BRIGGINSHAW pretty well patterned. The pearl-buyer arrived at the Goose Prairie camps about dinnertime every day and rowed out a couple of hours later for other mussel beds around the lake. Colton knew all he needed to know about the Australian now to put his plan into effect.

He was standing chest-deep in water, as he had done every morning for the past four days. He didn't think it would look good if he found his pearl too easily. But four days would have to suffice. Colton was not accustomed to bathing daily.

The morning after he got thrown out of the Treat Inn, he had sobered up and cleaned up, waited for Billy to take the wagon to the camps, then gone to see Carol Anne in the store. He carried his hat in his hand and kept his eyes on the floor.

"I was drunk and out of line," he said.

"Is that supposed to be an apology?" she asked, wishing Billy were there with her.

"The best I can manage," he admitted.

"All right, you're sorry. Now, get out before Billy finds you here."

He went to find Billy then. Henry Colton was a hard man to shame. He thought Billy might rough him up, but he could take a beating as well as any man. He went through the same routine. Hat in hand, eyes on the ground. "Drunk and out of line."

"That's no excuse."

"It won't happen again."

"Just stay away from our inn. You won't be welcomed there."

"If you say so."

He got drunk with Trevor Brigginshaw two nights later at Esau's place, and told the story of what had happened at the Treat Inn. Laughed about it, in fact. He found out then that the Australian was a mean drunk who didn't like strangers grabbing the lady friends of his old mate, Billy Treat. The fight didn't last long. Colton got in a few punches before the leather satchel laid him out.

When he came to, he thought it was remarkable that the pearl-buyer would not set his satchel aside even in a fistfight. It was going to be harder to get a look in there than he had at first thought. The beating had been worth it, though. He had learned quite a lot about Captain Brigginshaw.

Colton was not a man to hold a grudge. Even after the licking Trevor gave him, he became a friend and drinking partner of the pearl-buyer. For every wild tale the Australian told of the high seas, Colton had a match from the western territories. He had been everywhere. New Mexico, Montana, Oregon. Mining, cowboying, drifting, and gambling, he claimed.

He and Trevor both understood the debilitating pleasures of saloon life. Funny how many friendships he had started with fistfights over the years. Of course, the friendships never lasted long. He had to keep drifting in his line of work. He liked Trevor Brigginshaw; he truly did. After the fight and a few nights of drinking together, they got along well. But their friendship wouldn't last.

Now, wading in the murky waters of Goose Prairie Cove, Colton was planning the exact moment the friendship would end. The water he waded in did not feel the least bit cool. The long summer had warmed the shallows. Besides being warm, it was unusually muddy. For nearly three months, hundreds of pearl-hunters had been churning up the mud with their toes in search of mussels. When he came out of the water every day for lunch and drinks, Colton found layers of silt in his pockets, and his fingertips looked as wrinkled as prunes. He had enjoyed as much hunting as he could stand. It was time to find his pearl.

Giff Newton rowed the captain into the cove right on schedule. Colton reached into his right-hand pocket and found the little coin purse he had brought from Chicago. Carefully, he removed it from his pocket and opened it just wide enough to get his fingers in. He probed cautiously so as not to swish out the contents. In the bottom of the purse, the same thumb-and-forefinger grip that had pinched Carol Anne so smartly now delicately grasped the pearl he had been given in Chicago—a fine, round, freshwater gem of twenty-five grains. He let the purse sink and placed the pearl carefully in his left palm, closing his fist around it.

He drew in a breath and shouted "Pearl!" His voice cracked when he said it. He waved at the big Australian and saw the rowboat angle toward him.

"Henry!" The big man's voice came booming across the top of the water. "I have no time for bloody pranks!"

Colton held the fist above the water. "Prank, hell, Trev!" He put on his biggest grin. "You ain't gonna believe what I found."

The surrounding pearl-hunters stopped to watch the boat approach Colton in the water. Henry hooked the gunnel of the rowboat in the bend of his left elbow and slowly, carefully opened his hand. Brigginshaw stroked his beard, pushed his panama back on his forehead. His huge fingers delicately grasped the pearl and lifted it from Colton's lake-softened palm.

"This is what the fuss is all about, Henry? This?" His eyelids sagged disinterestedly. "Fifty dollars."

"Ha! Don't bullshit me, Trev. I didn't go into the pearling business half-cocked. I've talked to every successful hunter in camp, and read all the *Steam Whistle* articles from three weeks back, even before I came here. I know what a pearl is worth, and I won't take less than five hundred for that beauty!" He could feel the nearby pearl-hunters straining to hear.

Trevor rolled his eyes and looked at his oarsman. "Another overnight expert, Giff."

Giff played along, pursing his lips and shaking his head.

"With all due respect to my friend, John Crowell, his newspaper accounts are based on exaggerated hearsay. All pearl sales are confidential. I can offer no more than a hundred and fifty dollars for this slug."

"You're gettin' there," Henry said. "Pretty big jump, Trev, fifty to a hundred and fifty, but you've got a sight more jumpin' to do. That *slug*, as you call it, will go thirty-five grains, and I can't possibly take less than four-fifty."

The Australian's rich laughter skipped across the water. "What do you know about grading pearls, Henry?"

"When I was in the beef business, I could judge 'em on the hoof. When I was mining, I could assay a ton of ore with my eyes closed. Now I'm in pearls, and I know what's what with 'em. Get your scales out, Trev. I'll bet you four hundred fifty dollars that pearl weighs thirty-five grains."

The big man chuckled as he removed the pieces of his scale and put them together. He placed the pearl in the pan, and added weights to the tune of twenty-five grains.

"Bloody Hell!" Trevor said. "I had judged it at no more than fifteen grains. Its lack of luster makes it look smaller, Henry, but if it's twenty-five grains, I'll go as high as two hundred and fifty."

"Lack of luster, my ass, Trevor! That's the best pearl you've seen on Caddo Lake yet. Don't try hoodwinking Henry Colton!"

The captain smirked at Giff. The oarsman shook his head and looked at the sky.

"Three hundred," Trevor said.

"Four hundred."

"Three twenty-five, and that's the absolute ceiling."

"Three seventy-five."

Trevor looked at his oarsman. "What do you think, Giff?"

Giff shrugged. "Meet him in the middle, Captain."

Henry cupped his hand and splashed the oarsman. "Oh, hell, boy, you don't even know where the middle is!" he shouted.

The surrounding pearlers did not so much as ripple the surface. They were statues in the water, not looking, but listening to the negotiations and wishing they had ears like swamp rabbits.

"What Giff lacks in education, Henry, he makes up for with good common sense. His principle is a sound one, don't you think? If you won't take three-fifty, you might as well throw that pearl back to Goose Prairie Cove. I won't pay more, and I'm the only buyer on the lake. You could peddle it in New York, but your traveling expenses would consume everything over three hundred and fifty, if you could get more than that, and I doubt you could. Three-fifty, take it or leave it, mate."

Henry grinned. "Three-fifty and you buy the drinks tonight," he said.

"Bloody mercy, Henry! You drive a hard bargain. Done! Esau's saloon tonight at dark." He shook the grinning pearl-hunter's hand, pulled a velvet case from the satchel, and inserted the gem. "Now, what will it be? Gold, silver, or government notes?"

"Gold's the heaviest. I guess I ought to take some of that off your hands so's the next man to get hit with that money bag won't hurt so bad when he wakes up."

Trevor rocked the rowboat with his laughter. He counted out the gold coins, put them in Colton's hand, and reached for the ledger book. Opening the book, he held it above Colton's line of sight and flipped to the appropriate page. He reached into his coat pocket for his pencil and began writing in a careful, deliberate hand.

"What are you writing down in there, Trev?" Colton asked.

"White sphere . . ." he said slowly, speaking the words as the pencil spelled them. "Twenty . . . five . . . grains. Three . . . hundred . . . fifty . . . dollars. Henry . . . Colton."

"You sure you know how to spell three hundred fifty?" Colton said. "Ask Giff if you don't."

"I spell it 'three, five, zero,' you bleeding idiot." Brigginshaw laughed, slammed the book shut, and inserted it in the leather satchel. "To the camps, Giff. We've wasted enough time with Mr. Colton."

"Now, don't 'mister' me, Trev! I'll see you tonight at Esau's."

18

HENRY COLTON SAT IN HIS ROOM READING THE LATEST EDITION OF THE *Steam Whistle*. He had booked an upstairs suite on the north side of Widow Humphry's inn. Through the rain-streaked glass of his window, he could watch the movements around the Treat Inn and keep tabs on Trevor Brigginshaw. He still frequented Esau's saloon with the captain, too, and had learned that Trevor intended to take the first steamer to New Orleans, now that the rain had brought an early end to the pearling season.

September had come on wet. Day after day of rain and drizzle had dampened the spirits of the pearl-hunters and sent the farm families packing for their fields. After several days of rain, the Caddo Lake pearling camps had become little more than ash heaps and leftover wood piles.

The tourists left town as fast as Joe Peavy's stagecoach could carry them off. Many of them were concerned about getting back to Marshall before the road got too muddy. Wagons had been known to bog down between Port Caddo and Marshall.

In Port Caddo, however, morale remained high. These early rains would raise the lake level and bring the riverboat traffic back. It looked as if the town's run of luck would hold. The *Steam Whistle* predicted that the steamer season would begin early, supplementing the economic lift the pearls had brought to Caddo Lake during the summer.

That John Crowell is a hell of a booster, Colton thought as he turned a page. Hardly a dreary word to report in the whole newspaper. He glanced through the windowpane, then returned to the article Crowell had written about the steamer traffic.

The government snag boats had virtually finished removing the Great Raft from the Red River. Steamers would find a more navigable channel into Caddo Lake once the giant logjam was gone. True, Marshall was getting a railroad, but Jefferson, upstream on Big Cypress Bayou, had decided against the iron horse, preferring to stick with the familiar riverboat trade. Steamers would ply Caddo Lake for many years yet, according to the *Steam Whistle*.

Sentimental fools, Colton thought. Riverboats couldn't compete with railroads. They were slower, smaller, less reliable, and more expensive. Any town that chose steamboats over trains was signing its own death warrant.

The pearls, though—that was a different matter. Crowell's editorial headlined "Sustainable Pearl-Based Economy Challenge to Port Caddo" seemed to make sense, if the local folks would take it to heart.

"Our mussel beds," Crowell had written, "are more valuable than any deposits of gold or silver found elsewhere upon the continent. Our resource is a living, renewable one that if protected, will continue to produce fine gems for generations to come. . . ."

Crowell quoted extensively the two local pearl experts—Treat and Brigginshaw—and finally arrived at four laws recommended to protect the Caddo Lake mussel beds for future generations:

1. Divide the lake into four sections and allow pearling in just one section each year.
2. Establish limits regarding sizes of mussels to be opened and number of mussels allowed to each pearler.
3. Close the pearling season from January through May.

4. Prohibit destructive apparatus (such as George Blank's mussel rakes and tongs).

Maybe the pearl industry would last, Colton thought. But even if it did, Trevor Brigginshaw wouldn't be a part of it. His days as a pearl-buyer were numbered. If only he could get into the Australian's leather satchel. That was proving to be the toughest part of this assignment. The captain rarely let the thing get out of his grasp, much less his sight. Colton couldn't be sure of success until he got into that case, and the sooner the better.

This was his last chance. He had to see this job through, or find employment elsewhere.

He was about to doze off with the newspaper on his lap and the rain beating against the window, when the faint blast came. A single note from a faraway steam whistle. The pearl season was over and the steamer season had begun.

The boat was an ugly patchwork of unpainted lumber that had reached the age of ten in a rare case of longevity among light-draft steamers. She was called the *Slough Hopper*, and her pilot was an infamous old rake by the name of Emil Pipes, who had no objection to wiles such as price-gouging, smuggling, and graft, though he had never gotten rich off of any of them.

Unlike most Caddo Lake steamers, the *Slough Hopper* was a side-wheeler. Most people considered her unsafe because her paddle wheels were exposed. Huge fenders had once enclosed them, until Pipes decided to strip all unnecessary woodwork from the *Hopper* to lighten her and make more room for cargo. Now there was nothing to keep a man from falling into the churning machinery of the giant wheels that reached from the waterline to the texas. The exposed wheels presented danger to passengers and crew on the main deck, the boiler deck, and the hurricane deck.

If the *Glory of Caddo Lake* had once headed the list of favorite Port Caddo riverboats, the *Slough Hopper* anchored the other end. Her so-called "staterooms" were separated by moldy curtains. Her galley fare was barely edible. Her drab appearance was enough to drive a man to depravity, which was probably why the *Hopper* carried such a large stock of poor whiskey and hosted nightly poker games.

It was a sorry way to start the riverboat season, but it was a start nonetheless, and an early one at that.

The rain had let up some by the time the *Hopper* moored at the Port Caddo wharf. Townspeople started appearing on the street, easing toward the wharf to greet the first steamer of the season and to get the latest news from New Orleans.

Through his window, Henry Colton saw Trevor Brigginshaw and Billy Treat leave the Treat Inn and slog through the mud to the wharf. The captain had his leather case with him, of course. Colton folded his newspaper and left his room to join the throng.

A considerable commotion obscured his approach. People were talking and shouting to crew members on the steamer. Roustabouts sang a coonjine as they carried huge loads of firewood aboard. Colton reached the end of the cobblestones and slid down the muddy flood-bank between the Treat Inn and Constable Hayes' log jailhouse. Reaching the wharf, he eased up behind Billy and Trevor, who were looking at the *Slough Hopper* when he drew close enough to hear them speak.

"Why don't you wait for another boat, Trev? This thing's barely floating."

"The sooner I can get back to New York, the better."

"Why? What's your hurry?"

Trevor lifted his satchel and patted it. "Thanks to your little pearl rush, Billy, I've made enough in commission on this trip to buy a new sloop. The *Wicked Whistler Two*, I'll call her. I'll be back among the Pearl Islands next summer."

"You're not coming back here next year?"

"Afraid not, mate. I belong on the open seas, not in these bloody bayous."

Colton removed himself from the pair of friends and joined several Port Caddoans who were boarding the *Slough Hopper* to talk with the crew members. He had to jump between two wood-toting rousters to climb the mud-slick gangplank, which bounced under the weight of men and cordwood. He climbed the creaking stairs to the boiler deck and entered the saloon from the front of the passenger cabin.

Passing the whiskey bar and the dirty dining table, Colton came to the first of the berths enclosed by curtains. He pulled back the tattered cloth. He imagined Trevor lying in the berth, intoxicated. He might find his chance to open the leather satchel while aboard the *Slough Hopper*. He could reach in through the curtains and have a look-see while the Australian was sleeping off one of his violent drunks.

He left the saloon and climbed the next flight of stairs to the hurricane deck. He saw Emil Pipes smoking a cigar outside the grimy glass pilothouse standing above the texas.

"Afternoon, Captain," he said.

Pipes shook some ashes down on Colton, but didn't return the greeting.

"What's the schedule?" Colton queried.

"Ask the clerk." He turned into his pilothouse to avoid further interrogations.

Colton found the clerk on the bow taking note of some cargo the rousters were off-loading to the wharf. "What's the schedule?" he asked again.

The clerk was all of nineteen. "Take on wood and head upstream for Jefferson. We'll be back here, probably tomorrow night, for the downstream run to New Orleans."

Colton thought for a moment. "Can I take a berth upstream to Jefferson, then hold on to it for the downstream run to New Orleans, too?"

The clerk glanced from his ledger book. "Of course."

"I'll be back directly with my belongings."

Colton trotted back down to the wharf with his suitcase, but stopped before climbing the gangplank and veered toward Trevor and Billy. "It was a pleasure drinking and pearling with you, Captain, but it's time I headed back to my squaw in the Indian Territory."

Trevor was unusually formal because Billy was there, and Billy was still mad at Colton for having groped Carol Anne. "Very well, Mr. Colton."

"I've told you a dozen times, Trevor. Don't 'mister' me. It's Henry to my friends."

The shrill whistle of the *Slough Hopper* blew.

"So long, Captain. You, too, Mr. Treat."

Billy frowned, but tipped his hat.

19

HENRY COLTON STOOD ON THE BOW OF THE *SLOUGH HOPPER* AND WATCHED the dark bayou pass in the night. The rain had stopped while the boat was taking on cargo and a few passengers at Jefferson. Now the *Hopper* was steaming downstream for Port Caddo, New Orleans, and all points in between. The sky had cleared and stars were shining.

He would have seen them more clearly but for the burning pine knots. They flared and popped in a large iron basket that extended over the water from the bow, like a flaming figurehead. Coals fell into the bayou, but occasionally a spark blew back and landed on the deck.

It's a wonder this boat hasn't burned yet, he thought.

He was hurting pretty bad. He had pulled a good drunk in Jefferson. He had made unwise advances toward the girlfriend of a bully in a billiards hall. He could still feel the cue stick breaking over his head. That glorious drunk would have to stave him off until New Orleans. He would have to stay sober on the riverboat if he wanted to get a look into Trevor Brigginshaw's satchel.

He knew the captain was waiting to board at Port Caddo and ride to New Orleans. There was no other way the big Australian could get out of town. The roads were too badly bogged to get to Marshall.

A rouster came forward with a shovelful of fatwood chunks and threw them into the big iron basket to burn. A few sparks flew past the hogshead Colton was sitting on. "Watch it, boy!" he said.

The big black man didn't reply.

The trunks of huge cypress trees flickered strangely in the shadows, very near the boat in the narrow bayou. Emil Pipes rang the bell often. He used his side-wheels well to steer the *Hopper* through the crooked bayou, sometimes shutting down one wheel to take bends, or turning the wheels in opposite directions to make sharp turns in the channel.

"Good evenin', Mr. Colton," someone suddenly said over the pop and hiss of the steam engines.

Colton turned to see the *Hopper*'s young clerk smoking a pipe. "Howdy," he said. "Glad you happened along. I want to talk to you."

"What about?"

"When we get to Port Caddo, a big fellow named Brigginshaw is going to board for New Orleans. Wears a beard, talks with an Australian accent. You can't mistake him."

"And?"

"Well, I'd just as soon he didn't know I was on board. Personal matter. You understand."

"No, not really."

Colton took a gold coin from his pocket and flipped it into the air. "Well, if you could refrain from using my name out loud, and see that I get my meals behind the curtain in my berth, I would make it worth your while." He held the double eagle out for the clerk to take.

"I don't see any harm in that, Mr. Colton." The youth slipped the coin in his pocket.

"Now, don't 'mister' me, son. Just call me Henry."

He was watching from the shadows of the hurricane deck when the *Hopper* moored at the Port Caddo wharf. It was the middle of the night. He expected to see no one but Brigginshaw board. But as soon as the gangplank fell on the wharf, a burly man trotted from behind the jail-house, to the wharf, and sprinted up the gangplank.

Colton got only a glimpse in the dark, but recognized the new passenger as the man with the gator eyes. He had learned at Esau's that Kelso was suspected of blowing up the *Glory of Caddo Lake* three months before. And, he had a grudge against Brigginshaw. Colton sighed. He didn't care for complications at this point. What did Kelso have in mind?

Brigginshaw didn't leave the Treat Inn until the final whistle blew. Billy came out on the front porch and shook the big man's hand. Carol Anne hugged him. They were good friends to see him off past midnight.

As the captain boarded, Colton went quickly to his berth and pulled the curtain. He strapped on a shoulder holster holding a .44-caliber Smith & Wesson revolver. He pulled a light jacket on over the weapon and lay down on his berth to listen.

There was a card game going on in the forward part of the saloon, but he heard the Australian's long strides tramp across the floor, muting the swearing voices and clinking glasses.

"This will be your stateroom, here, Captain Brigginshaw," the clerk said.

"Stateroom, is it?" The deep laughter filled the long saloon.

Brigginshaw was across the saloon and three berths aft. Colton could lie behind his curtains and keep track of Trevor's comings and goings. He hoped Trevor was in a drinking mood. It had been three nights since the big Australian had tied one on. Colton had him pretty well patterned. Yes, the big pearl-buyer would be thirsty tonight.

But where was Judd Kelso? He hadn't come up to the boiler deck. Probably riding among the cargo on the main deck. The fares were lower down there. Every pearler in the Goose Prairie camps knew Kelso had run out of money two weeks ago. He had tried pearling for two days, then disappeared. Tonight was the first Colton had seen of him since then. What was he up to, sneaking aboard like that?

The *Slough Hopper* was backing into the Big Cypress Bayou channel when Colton heard Brigginshaw's boots pace forward to the whiskey bar. Someone was playing a harmonica, and playing it rather well, Colton thought. The steam engines were barking again. Still, he could hear Trevor's rich voice ordering a drink. The smell of the clerk's pipe tobacco hung in the stagnant air of the passenger cabin.

He found himself wishing for whiskey, though his stomach was still sore from retching this morning. Nothing to do now but wait. Wait for Trevor to get drunk, pick a fight, lay some poor devil out with the satchel, and retire to his berth. It would take till dawn.

He had been listening to Brigginshaw's loud talk and laughter for over an hour when the steam whistle blew.

"What's that about?" Brigginshaw asked.

"Someone wanting to board at Potter's Point, I guess," the clerk answered.

"You bloody guess!" The captain was beginning to feel belligerent. "I suppose I'll have to find out for myself."

Colton peeked through his curtains and saw the captain leave through the forward saloon door. He quickly left his berth and headed aft, climbing the stairs to the hurricane deck as soon as he left the saloon. Once above the passenger cabin, he snuck forward on the starboard side, passing between the texas and the exposed moving members of the huge paddle wheel.

Remaining in the shadows, he looked ahead and saw a lantern on the shore. He saw men and horses in the small circle of light. The bayou was wider here, the cypress trees fewer and farther away from the channel. Stepping momentarily into the light of the burning pine knots, he looked down on the boiler deck and saw Trevor standing directly under him, clutching the satchel, watching the men and horses at Potter's Point.

The *Slough Hopper* made for the lantern light and lowered the gangplank. Five men waited to board, with six saddled horses. Colton didn't think the extra horse unusual, except that it was saddled. Perhaps the men were taking the extra horse and saddle to a friend across the lake.

The clerk went down to the main deck to collect the fees for men and horses. The first four mounts clapped up the gangplank behind their owners as if they boarded riverboats every day. The fifth animal proceeded with much more caution, balking every few steps and craning its neck to see in the glare of the pine knots. The horse took the last step onto the main deck in a leap that knocked one of the horsemen down.

Colton heard Captain Brigginshaw chuckle.

The sixth horse at first refused to negotiate the gangplank. When finally persuaded to climb the narrow ramp, it got halfway up and jumped off, falling into the shallow water. Trevor stomped the boiler deck and roared with laughter.

One of the horsemen mounted the unwilling animal and rode up and down the dark lakeshore for two or three minutes, whipping and spurring the horse relentlessly. When the animal was well spent, it climbed the gangplank almost anxiously. Trevor laughed down on the entire episode from the boiler deck, and Colton looked down on Trevor from the shadows of the hurricane deck.

When the gangplank was raised and the *Hopper* under way again, the five horsemen climbed to the boiler deck where the Australian stood. Colton saw the buckle of a gun belt at one man's waist. Another carried a gunnysack, apparently stuffed with a change of clothes.

"Bloody fine entertainment!" the captain said as the men reached the top of the stairs.

"From up here, I reckon it was," the man with the gunnysack said.

"Come inside and let me buy you a drink for your trouble," Trevor said.

"Hell, partner, we don't want to drink that rotgut this old tub sells." He reached for a bottle in his gunnysack. "But you're welcome to drink some of our good whiskey with us."

Colton could barely hear their voices over the steam engines. The new passengers exchanged introductions, shook hands with Trevor, passed various bottles and flasks, talked and laughed loudly. The *Slough Hopper* was back in the channel, steaming forward, heading for the open water of Caddo Lake.

This might be just the break, Colton thought. These horsemen might be just what it takes to get Trevor drunk. He was thinking about sneaking back into his berth from the rear of the saloon when he heard a voice call from the boiler deck, below and aft:

"Hey, you ugly Australian son of a bitch!"

Colton recognized the voice as that of the gator-eyed man, Judd Kelso. He had almost forgotten Kelso was aboard. Now it looked as if he wouldn't be aboard for long. Brigginshaw was sure to throw him off.

"Who the hell is that?" one of the horsemen said.

"He must be talkin' to you, Captain. We're from Arkansas."

The horsemen laughed.

"Aye, he's talking to me, mates," Trevor said. "And he'll bloody answer to me as well."

The thin voice of the gator-eyed man rose again: "I owe you a ass-whippin', Brigginshaw. Come and get it."

From the deck above, Colton followed the footsteps and the jingling spurs aft, wondering what he should do, if anything. He knew Brigginshaw could handle Kelso. Maybe that's what concerned him. Kelso should have known it, too. Ol' Gator Eyes couldn't be stupid enough to think he'd fare any better against the big Aussie this time. Maybe he had a gun. Maybe he had murder on his mind.

"Hot-damn, boys," one of the horsemen said. "Looks like a fight."

When Colton came to the churning paddle wheel, the engine and machinery noises drowned out all the talk from the deck below. He strained to hear above the blasts of the exhaust valve and the rotations of the huge wheel. He didn't know for sure if he heard anything unusual, or if he saw a shadow move in a way it shouldn't have, or if he just plain smelled trouble. But suddenly he sensed that Trevor Brigginshaw needed help bad.

Colton stepped to the rail in front of the paddle wheel, leaned over, and looked below. The man with the gunnysack had put it over Brigginshaw's head from behind. Another man was pulling on the leather satchel in the Australian's right hand. A third held the pearl-buyer's left arm. A fourth had a leg. The man wearing the gun belt had drawn his pistol and was using it to beat Trevor about the head. Firing it would make too much noise, alert too many passengers. Instead, the men were trying to pistol-whip and push the big pearl-buyer headfirst into the turning paddle wheel. They were going to let the *Slough Hopper* do their murdering for them.

Trevor still had one leg free and was kicking heroically with it. With his outstretched arms against the structural members and hog chains, he was preventing the robbers from beheading him with the paddle wheel. But Colton knew that not even Brigginshaw could hold out long against six men. He drew his Smith & Wesson from the shoulder holster. No good. From his position above, he could barely see the bandit with the pistol, and that was the one he needed to shoot first.

He pulled himself back onto the hurricane deck and sprinted as lightly as he could to the forward stairs. He took the steps four or five at a time, leaping down to the boiler deck. He turned the corner of the passenger cabin and ran back toward the fight at the paddle wheel, leading with his Smith & Wesson.

Now he heard Kelso's voice: "Move, Christmas, and let me split his head open." The gator-eyed man wielded the *Hopper*'s iron capstan bar over his head.

The bandit with the pistol looked forward. Colton was proud to be sober. His aim was superb when he wasn't drunk.

The Smith & Wesson fired as the capstan bar came down on Brigginshaw's head. The bandit with the pistol fell, and the others scattered, leaving the Australian's body slumped inches from danger on the boiler deck, the sack still on his head. The robber tugging at the leather satchel came away with it and ran aft. Then Trevor's body fell over to one side, and Henry thought the paddle wheel would finish what the outlaws had started. The pearl-buyer's head came so close that the crushing wheel snagged the sack and yanked it off, exposing Trevor's bloody face.

Two of the bandits produced weapons and fired back at Colton. Coolly, he ignored the muzzle blasts and fired at the man carrying the satchel. The bandit fell, dropping the leather bag. Kelso jumped from the boiler deck, into the water. Two others swung over the railing, down to the main deck where the horses stood. The last outlaw ran down the aft stairs.

Colton heard the hooves drumming crazily on the main deck as he trotted aft. He kicked the revolver away from the first robber he had shot, for the man was still moving. He pulled Trevor away from the paddle wheel. He saw blood in the Australian's hair, but the huge chest was still heaving.

He continued aft and put his pistol to the head of the second bandit he had shot, but could tell that the man was dead when he rolled him over. The leather satchel was in the bandit's death grip. Colton grabbed it.

Horses were pounding the deck below, leaping into the lake. Colton looked over the rail and considered letting a few rounds go at a man on a swimming horse. No need. Let them go. Don't draw their fire now.

He looked forward and saw that Trevor Brigginshaw was still out cold. The leather pearl-and-money bag was in his own hand now. He had what he needed, and two outlaws, to boot. He felt his heart racing. He felt more alive than he had in months. Years!

Damn, Henry, he thought. Your luck's comin' back.

20

WHEN TREVOR BRIGGINSHAW CAME TO, HE SAW SEVERAL BLURRY MEN looking down on him. He heard voices and smelled tobacco smoke. He focused on the ceiling of the riverboat saloon and felt for his satchel with each hand.

"He's coming out of it, Mr. Colton," a voice said. "I mean, Henry." Trevor recognized the voice as that of the young riverboat clerk.

He tried to sit up, but his head hurt terribly, and the exertion made his stomach feel ill. He closed his eyes and remembered the smelly sack over his head and the horrible sounds of the paddle wheel, screeching inches from his ears. He remembered Judd Kelso, and a name: Christmas.

Opening his eyes again, he saw a familiar face. He grabbed Henry Colton by the collar. "My case."

"Easy, Trev. I've got it right here. I looked after it for you while you were out."

Trevor felt the familiar handle in his hand. He tried to sit up again, and succeeded with some help from the passengers. He found himself on the dining table of the *Slough Hopper*. "Henry, what in the bloody hell are you doing here?" He touched his head where the capstan bar had hit him.

"Saving your life, looks like," Colton said.

"The Christmas Nelson gang tried to rob you," the clerk added.

Trevor looked around at the passengers, then back at Colton. "I thought you were going back to the Indian Territory."

"That was just a story, Trev. Sorry I had to lie to you. Comes with the job."

"What bloody job?"

"Mr. Colton's a Pinkerton detective," the clerk said.

"That's right, Trev. I've been after that Christmas Nelson gang. Sorry you had to get between us."

The Australian saw two bloody men stretched out on the saloon floor. "Is that them?"

"Two of them," Colton replied. "One dead, one damn near dead. I don't know if either one of 'em is Christmas Nelson himself."

"Did they get anything?" He fumbled with the latches to his leather case.

"Not a thing, Trev." Colton put his hand on the big man's shoulder. "I stopped them before they could open it. Your goods are safe."

The pearl-buyer breathed a sigh of relief and stood, steadying himself with one hand on the table. "Where the hell are we, Henry? How long have I been out?"

Henry chuckled. "You've only been out a few minutes. That iron bar would have killed any other man on this boat. We're heading back to Port Caddo to put that live one in jail. Captain Pipes didn't hardly want to, but I told him the Pinkerton Agency would pay for the lost time."

Trevor motioned for a glass of whiskey that one of the passengers was holding. "Why are we going back to Port Caddo? They must have a better jail in Shreveport." He poured the contents of the glass over his wounded head, wincing as the whiskey stung him.

"Last thing I want to do is cross a state line with a prisoner. If that wounded one lives, I'll have all that extradition foolishness to deal with to get him back to Texas for trial."

Brigginshaw chuckled a little as he held his glass out for a refill. "You, Henry? A Pinkerton? I never would have guessed it in a million years." He poured the next jigger down his throat instead of over his head.

"That's the idea, Trev."

"How did you know the gang was going to try to rob me?"

"I didn't. If I'd have known that, I'd have warned you. I got a tip from an informant that they would board this boat tonight somewhere between Jefferson and Shreveport. And it looks like my informant was right."

"That it does," Brigginshaw said. "That it bloody does, and thank God for it. I owe you one, mate." He laughed, in spite of the condition his head was in. "Pinkerton detective!"

Colton went up to the pilothouse and asked Emil Pipes not to blow the whistle when the *Slough Hopper* returned to Port Caddo. "Last thing I need is a bunch of citizens around when I'm trying to put a man in jail."

"The son of a bitch is damn near dead," Pipes growled. "How much trouble could it be to get a near dead son of a bitch in a jailhouse?"

"It's standard procedure, Captain Pipes. I won't risk getting any civilians hurt if I can help it. For all we know, that Christmas Nelson gang might be on the way to Port Caddo to rescue their men. They could beat us there on horseback."

"Aw, the hell," Pipes growled.

"I've worked among outlaws for years, Captain. They'll surprise you."

The pilot growled and dismissed Colton with a wave of his hand. The Pinkerton man went back down to the saloon and pulled the clerk aside. "There's a constable in Port Caddo named Rayford Hayes. He lives three houses uphill from the livery barn. Do you know where that is?"

"Yes, sir."

"Good. As soon as we dock, I want you to run get him. Have him meet me at the jailhouse next to the wharf."

•   •   •

Henry Colton saw the *Slough Hopper*'s clerk leap to the wharf with his lantern before the rousters had the mooring lines fast.

He went back into the saloon and found the Aussie nursing his head wound and drinking whiskey. "Trevor, you said you owed me one. Now's your chance to make good."

"Name it, mate."

"You can carry that live one to the jailhouse for me. You're strong enough to do it on your own, and I'd just as soon keep as many people clear of the jail as possible. Never know who you can trust. I'll guard your leather bag while you carry the prisoner."

Trevor rose. "I've never trusted another living soul with this satchel." He smiled. "Until tonight, that is." He handed the leather bag to Colton and stooped over the outlaws laid out on the floor.

"Not that one, Trev," Henry said.

"What?"

"That's the dead one. Pick up the other one."

"By God, Henry! You're right!" The Australian put his hand to his head wound and filled the saloon with laughter.

Trevor was relieved to see Constable Hayes standing at the bottom of the gangplank with the *Hopper*'s clerk when he and Henry came down. The weight of the wounded outlaw in his arms burdened him little. It wasn't far to the jailhouse. He would deposit the outlaw there, get his pearls back from Henry, and be on his way at last.

"What's all this about, Captain Brigginshaw?" Hayes asked, yawning. He looked rather ridiculous with his gun belt strapped around his nightshirt, his black boots contrasting with his white legs.

"Ask Henry. He's the detective."

"Huh?" Constable Hayes looked at Colton.

"Give the constable your lantern," Colton said to the clerk, "and keep everybody on the boat."

"Yes, sir."

"Detective?" Hayes said, taking the lantern. "You?"

"Pinkerton Detective Agency," Colton said. "This wounded man is a member of the Christmas Nelson gang. There's a dead one on the boat. They tried to get Captain Brigginshaw's pearls."

"Christmas Nelson! Well, I'll be damned!" The constable trotted ahead of Trevor with the lantern to open the jailhouse door, his boots slipping in the mud as he ran.

Trevor had taken note of the Port Caddo jailhouse, wondering if he would ever land there drunk. It was a one-room log building with a door facing town and a tiny window facing the bayou. Both openings were covered by crossed iron bars, riveted together. The iron door swung on heavy hinges threaded deep into the logs. It was crude, but secure.

Rayford Hayes unlocked the door and opened it for Trevor. The big Australian had to duck to carry the wounded man into the cell. The iron grating of the jailhouse ceiling was barely over six feet high, and he didn't care to bump his already aching head on it.

"Just lay him out on the bunk," the constable said, holding the lantern inside the jailhouse.

When he lay the wounded outlaw in the cell, Trevor heard his satchel drop with a splash into the mud, and turned in time to see Colton shutting the iron door on him. Acting on reflex, he rushed to the door and put his foot in its path to keep it from slamming. Colton's Smith & Wesson appeared out of nowhere and leveled on Trevor.

"Colton, what the hell . . ." Constable Hayes said.

"Don't interfere, Hayes. Just give me the jail key so's I can lock him in. Trevor, back up."

The big Australian looked into the barrel of the revolver, his anger building. "Henry, what in the bloody hell are you doing now?"

"Look here, Colton!" Constable Hayes said, stepping forward with the lantern.

"I said don't interfere, Hayes. I'll explain everything just as soon as I get the good Captain Brigginshaw locked in your jailhouse. Now, give me the key. Trevor, move your foot and back up."

The Australian felt his face grow feverish with rage. He kept his foot against the iron door. He glanced at his leather satchel on the muddy ground outside of the jailhouse. "My pearls!" he said. "He's robbing me, Rayford!"

"Don't move, Hayes!" Colton warned. "I'm not robbing anybody. I'm a Pinkerton agent arresting Captain Trevor Brigginshaw."

"Arresting him for what?" Hayes said.

"Embezzlement."

"Embezzlement!" the Aussie roared. "Rayford, can't you see he's lying? He's after the pearls!"

"I'm tellin' the truth. Constable, pick up the pearl-bag. I'll let you hold on to it to prove I'm not after it. You can cover me with your pistol if you want. The evidence I need is in Trevor's ledger book."

Hayes put the lantern down on the muddy ground to keep his gun hand free. He moved carefully toward the leather bag and picked it up. Then he backed off a few steps. "Colton, put your gun away and we'll sort this out. You must have made some kind of mistake."

"No mistake. After I get Trevor locked behind this door, I'll surrender my weapon to you, Constable, and explain everything."

Trevor eased his right hand toward the mother-of-pearl grip of his Colt revolver.

"Your pistol won't do you any good, Trev. I took all the cartridges out while you were unconscious. Go ahead, check it."

Trevor carefully drew the pearl-handled Colt and spun the cylinder, finding the chambers empty. He was seething so with rancor that he felt on the verge of attacking the Pinkerton man, in spite of the cocked revolver aiming at him.

"Sorry I lied to you again, Trev, but like I said, it comes with the job. I wasn't after Christmas Nelson. I had no idea his gang would be on that boat tonight. I was after you."

Trevor felt a dark wave of guilt sicken his stomach, but tried to hold on to some kind of hope. "Don't trust him, Rayford. He'll lock me in and shoot us both dead for those pearls."

"Just give me a chance and I'll explain everything," Colton argued. "Like I said, Hayes, you can draw your pistol now and cover me if you want to."

For a moment, the only sounds were those of crickets and bullfrogs along the bayou.

"Let him say his piece, Captain," the constable finally suggested. "He could have shot you already if that's what he wanted to do. Maybe there's been a misunderstanding."

"No misunderstanding," Colton argued. "International Gemstones has suspected Trevor of raking off money for a year now. When he started out working for them, he was the best pearl-bargainer they had ever employed. Then he started losing his ability to get the lowest prices."

"I don't follow you," Hayes said. "No crime in that, is there?"

"Not in itself," the Pinkerton man answered. "But the company trusted his ability more than his honesty. They figured he was padding the prices he got and keeping the extra for himself."

"You're a lying little bandit!" Trevor bellowed. "You're no Pinkerton man! Look at him, Rayford! Does he look like a detective to you?"

Hayes looked as if he didn't know who to trust. "I still don't get it," he said. "You're not making sense to me, Colton."

"All right, listen and I'll explain it so's anybody can understand. I brought a pearl down here with me from the Chicago Pinkerton offices. International Gemstones sent me the pearl to use. I posed as a pearl-hunter for a couple of days, pretended to find the pearl I had in my pocket all along, and sold it to Trevor. He paid me three hundred and fifty dollars of his company's money for it."

"So what?" Hayes said. "That's the man's job, ain't it?"

"I'm not through yet, Hayes. When Trevor was knocked out cold on the boat tonight, I finally got a chance to look in that ledger book of his. According to the ledger, he paid me four hundred, not three-fifty. Now do you get it? He kept the extra fifty dollars for himself. Fifty dollars of his company's money. That's theft."

"For God's sake, Henry," the pearl-buyer shouted, straightening so quickly that he bumped his head on the jailhouse ceiling. "Did you stop to think I might have made a mistake and written four hundred accidentally?"

"Now, there you go," Hayes said. "That explains it, don't it, Colton?"

"I had you repeat the sum three times, Trev. I even tricked you into spelling it out to me as you were writing it in your ledger book. You couldn't have written four hundred unless you meant to."

"I don't know, Colton. It's just your word against the captain's. I don't feel right about locking him in jail just on your say-so."

"That colored boy, Giff Newton, was a witness. And some pearl-hunters were standing around listening. Besides, I'm sure I wasn't the only one whose price Trev doctored a little in his ledger book. He's probably done the same thing on every purchase he's made on Caddo Lake. Now, if you'll give me the key and let me lock him in overnight, we'll interview some local pearl-hunters tomorrow. See what they got for their pearls, and compare that to what Trevor's ledger book says. Then if you don't think we have enough evidence to prove what I'm sayin', you can let him out of your jailhouse and put me in there."

The jailhouse grew so quiet that Trevor could hear the shallow breathing of the wounded outlaw in the cell with him. He shifted his eyes from the leather satchel in Hayes' hand to the pistol in Colton's. How he longed to be aboard the *Wicked Whistler* now, far out to sea, where he made his own laws. Yes, he had skimmed a little off the top, but he had always planned to pay it back later. It was a loan, not a theft.

"Captain Brigginshaw," Hayes finally said. "I'm sorry, but I'll have to go on his word until we get this straightened out. I'll make sure you're comfortable in here tonight, and we'll sort it out first thing in the morning."

Colton grinned. "You heard him, Trev. Now, back up and let me close the door."

The Australian used every measure of control he possessed to cinch his temper in place. "Don't 'Trev' me, you lying little bastard. It's Captain Brigginshaw to you."

"Whatever. Back up."

Brigginshaw grit his teeth. He cast his eyes downward and sighed, as if in defeat. Slowly, deliberately, he slid his foot back from the doorway and took a half-step backward.

Colton pushed the door closed and aimed at Trevor through one of the squares in the iron grating. "The key," he said to Hayes.

The lone key jingled on its iron ring. Trevor watched Colton's eyes. Colton held his left hand open to take the key from the constable. The key came into view through the grating. Colton's hand closed around it. Trevor stood as if in resignation, but he was ready to explode.

The Pinkerton man's stare merely darted to the keyhole on the door, but it was enough to trigger Brigginshaw's attack. His huge leg kicked toward the iron door in a tremendous burst of angry desperation. Colton jerked his trigger, but the bullet clipped an iron bar and sang into the log wall above the wounded outlaw's body.

The heavy door swung open and caught Colton in the face. His head jerked back. The Pinkerton man flew backward as if blasted in the chest with a load of buckshot. The Smith & Wesson sailed into the darkness.

Trevor exploded from the jailhouse like a bear from its den. He glimpsed the astonishment on the constable's face, saw the lawman reaching for his side arm. He barreled into Hayes, knocking him over backward and wrenching the leather case from his hand at the same time. He struck Hayes in the jaw with his elbow—a blow he thought would surely knock the constable out cold. He began running for the *Slough Hopper*, unsure of what he would do when he reached her. Halfway to the boat, he heard a voice behind him.

"Stop, Captain!"

The words surprised him. The old constable could take a punch. The burning pine knots from the *Slough Hopper* cast a faint light across the muddy ground as he continued to run.

"Stop!" the constable yelled.

Trevor was almost to the riverboat when the bullet caught him in the leg. He fell, then tried to get back up. Another shot echoed across the bayou, and he dove into the mud. He tried to get up again, but the wounded leg slipped. A third shot missed him. He lay still. The shooting stopped. He should get up and run. But where? He was hit once already. The constable was a surprisingly good shot. He was caught. His head was still hurting. He clutched the leather satchel in his hand. Now how long would it be until he saw the high seas again?

There was a sickening silence about Port Caddo. The gunfire had quieted the bullfrogs. Then he heard Rayford Hayes' boots sucking at the mud. The constable moved cautiously in on him and took the leather satchel away.

"Go get in the jailhouse, Captain," he said.

Trevor tried to get up. "You've shot me, Rayford. I can't bloody walk."

"Then crawl, damn it. Get in the jail!"

Trevor saw the crew of the *Slough Hopper* watching him from the bow of the boat. He heard the door of the Treat Inn open. Looking back, he saw a guest peeking into the street. Thank God it wasn't Billy. Don't let Billy see you crawl. He managed to stand on his good leg and started hopping toward the jailhouse. He slipped once, and glanced up at Constable Hayes, the lawman's nightshirt caked with mud, looking so comical that Trevor almost laughed.

He hopped past the lantern on the ground and past Henry Colton, still stretched out motionless on his back. He ducked into the log jailhouse and collapsed on the floor.

Hayes covered the doorway with his pistol and went to get the jailhouse key from the mud beside Colton. When he came to the door, he said, "Back up, Captain. All the way across the floor."

Trevor obeyed and Hayes closed the door, locking the Australian in. Next, the constable went to check on Henry Colton, thinking to rouse him out of the mud. But he sighed as he put his pistol back in the holster.

"You've done it now, Captain. You've really done it good. Henry Colton's skull is split. He's dead."

21

I NEVER DID HAVE MUCH OF A MIND FOR LARCENY. WORRY IS WORK TO ME, and I get nervous just thinking about criminal activity. That's why I had such a hard time understanding Pop's explanation of what had happened to Trevor Brigginshaw. I could comprehend stealing something like a chicken or a watermelon—actually sneaking in to grab it and run. But to think of a man going to all that trouble with the pearls and the ledger book and his company's money was a little more than I could grasp.

The town was usually pretty quiet when I left for Goose Prairie at dawn each morning. But that day the streets were humming with excitement as soon as I stepped outside. Pop was coming in at about that time, and I could tell he had been up a while.

"What's goin' on?" I asked.

That's when he took me into the house and told me all about the death of Henry Colton and the jailing of Captain Brigginshaw. He had heard the gunshots in the night and had gone out to investigate. Light sleepers make good small-town newspaper reporters.

". . . and the outlaw from the Christmas Nelson gang died half an hour ago," Pop finally concluded. "They just carried him out. Constable Hayes sent a rider to Marshall to fetch the doctor. He let Brigginshaw take some laudanum to kill the pain. His leg is busted and swollen up pretty bad."

"What'll happen to him now?" I asked.

"He'll probably stand trial for stealing his company's money and for killing Colton."

"What'll happen to him then?"

My pop looked at me with a hard set to his eyes. "In this county, aggravated murder is a hanging offense. It just goes to show you, Ben. Even a little crime like shaving some money off the top can drag you deeper and deeper, till you wind up where Captain Brigginshaw is now."

I vowed right then to give up stealing watermelons forever.

The sun was high by the time Pop got finished with the story, so I ran to Esau's place where Adam and Cecil were waiting to run the trotline. They hadn't heard about what had happened overnight, so I got to tell them. It was all we could talk about the whole time we were catching our fish and baiting the line.

"You reckon any pearl-hunters will ever come back?" Adam asked. "Now that Captain Brigginshaw's gonna hang?"

"Yeah, they'll come back," I replied. "As soon as the road to Marshall dries up some. Pop said the pearl company will probably send another buyer once they find out Captain Brigginshaw's in jail."

"You're just hoping that Cindy comes back from Longview," Cecil said. "I saw you two on the lakeshore at night."

That changed the subject for a while, but by the time we put the catfish in the holding tank, Cecil and Adam were wanting to sneak down to the jailhouse and look at Captain Brigginshaw through the iron grating. I wanted to go, too, but couldn't. I had invested in a gill net and was catching fish on my own in my bateau. I hadn't invited Cecil or Adam in on this enterprise with me, and they were still mad about it. Once you get started doing business with friends, it's hard to stop without hurting somebody's feelings.

They ran off for the jailhouse as I shoved off alone in my bateau. I didn't feel so left out once I got onto the lake. After all, I had an Ashenback, and they didn't. Cecil and Adam had squandered about all the money they had made over the summer on trinkets and hard candy.

My net was a small one and didn't take long to run. I caught enough to halfway fill the fish box in my bateau and started paddling for Port Caddo, where I could sell them. I had owned my Ashenback about three weeks by that time, and it was still a thrill to me. It was that summer that I learned the joy of paddling the lake alone in a good boat.

When Port Caddo came into view around the last bend in the bayou, my eyes pulled toward the jailhouse. I knew Trevor Brigginshaw was in there. For the first time, I felt sorry for him. Everybody in town liked him, except maybe when he got drunk. He was part of our pearl rush—almost as big a hero as Billy. When I thought of him lying wounded in that cell, or worse, dangling by the neck from a gallows, I got a sudden pang of remorse. I felt as if I had had a hand in it. I was part of that summer of pearls, after all, and now it had gone wrong. A Pinkerton detective and two outlaws were dead, and a fourth man was doomed.

I could feel the gloom settling over the town, though the sky was clear for the first time in days. People were standing on the cobblestone street talking and looking down toward the jailhouse. The bayou ran muddier and faster than usual, owing to all the runoff.

It was an unnatural day—a dark day for my town. I found myself doubting what I had told Adam earlier, what my pop had told me at dawn. They couldn't send anybody to take the captain's place. How could there be another pearl-buyer after Trevor Brigginshaw? It seemed over. I suddenly got the feeling that I would never experience another summer of pearls.

I pulled my bateau up on the bank as usual, and prepared to hike up to town to see who wanted to buy fish. But when I looked toward town, I realized something I hadn't noticed before. The log jailhouse obscured my view of the cobblestone street. The only doorway I could see was that of the Treat Inn, and nobody was standing there. I was hidden.

I don't know exactly why I wanted so badly to look at the Australian in the jailhouse. Maybe I had to see for myself that it wasn't just rumor, even though I had heard it from my pop, who never repeated rumor. Maybe a morbid fascination for the doomed man had fixed a hold on me. I had never seen a murderer before, with the exception of Judd Kelso, and there was no solid proof against him yet.

Whatever the reason, I couldn't overcome it. The tiny window on the bayou side of the log jailhouse drew me like a magnet. I had to have a look.

The mud oozed between my toes as I sneaked silently up the slope to the jailhouse. I felt like as much of a thief as Brigginshaw himself, though all I wanted to steal was a peek. I never got the chance.

When I reached the window, I heard a familiar voice:

". . . but why, Trev? Why did you need to *steal* it?"

"I have no excuses, Billy." The Australian's voice was muted in defeat, and slurred a little by the laudanum, I supposed.

"I'm not asking for excuses. It's too late for excuses, anyway. But you must have had a reason."

There was a brief silence, then the captain's voice rose with a touch of the familiar bravado. "I'm an independent, Billy. These bloody freshwater-pearl rushes are like hell to me. I go to sleep feeling the *Wicked Whistler* under my feet. I see the palm trees, and the island divers. The bare, brown breasts of the women. All the beautiful women. And the waters so clear you can see six fathoms. I dream of them at night, Billy. You probably do, too."

"I used to."

"Yes, well, I'll never make it back now any more than you will."

I heard Billy sigh. "If there's any way," he said, "I'll get you out of this. I'll do everything I can."

The jailhouse bench creaked under Brigginshaw's weight. "Leave it alone, Billy. There's no use."

"I felt the same way that morning the pirates came down on Mangareva. I didn't think I deserved to live after that. But you got me out of there, Trev. And I'll do everything I can to get you out of this."

"Mangareva was different. It was the pirates who should have been punished there, not you. In this case, I'm the guilty one. I killed a man. Didn't bloody mean to, but that does him little good. No, Billy, there's nothing you can do for me now. . . ."

A sudden unexpected image drew my attention away from the jailhouse conversation. I saw my Ashenback drifting slowly down Big Cypress Bayou. It took a second for me to make sense of it. I knew I had pulled the boat up on the bank. It had never dislodged itself before. It didn't seem possible. But I knew my bateau, and there it went.

I sprinted from the jailhouse and dove off the wharf, splashing into the muddy water. When I came up and caught the gunnel, I heard some townspeople laughing at me. Everybody knew how I treasured that boat. As I swam back to the wharf, pulling my bateau, I glanced up at the jailhouse window. The huge bearded face filled it, smiling. Captain Brigginshaw had roused himself from the bench to witness the commotion. Any embarrassment I felt was worth it. I had given a doomed man reason to smile. There was nothing more I could have done for him.

I didn't figure out until later why my bateau had taken off on its own. The bayou was rising and had lifted it from the place I had beached it. It was raining hard somewhere upstream.

I sold my catch and went about my daily routine, which seemed sadly empty since the pearl camps had been struck. There were no water barrels to haul, no dead mussels to feed our hogs. My partners and I had been buying corn to feed them, but we didn't have the cash reserves to do that for long. We were thinking about turning them back out into the woods, or selling them, unless the pearlers came back soon. Anyway, lessons would take up at the Caddo Academy in a couple of weeks, and we wouldn't have time to fool with hogs.

I hid my bateau under some pine branches at Goose Prairie Cove and made the evening trotline run with Cecil and Adam. We had no idea that it would be our last run. When the sun set beyond Port Caddo, we had no way of knowing it was setting on the summer of pearls, and even on the town itself.

22

A BARRAGE OF WIND-WHIPPED RAINDROPS AGAINST MY WINDOW WOKE ME
that night. I could hear gusts roaring in the trees. I slept in the half-
story attic of our house and there was nothing between me and the
storm but a few boards and cypress shingles. The first thing I thought
of was my bateau filling up with rainwater where I had left it down at
Goose Prairie Cove.

I got out of bed and went to the dormer window that looked out
over the street. A flash of lightning gave me a glimpse of pines whipping
in the wind like stalks of grass. The roof was shaking around me. A light
passed below—a lantern that stopped in front of Constable Hayes'
house, just up the street from ours. No one would have been out on a
night like that unless there was trouble. I stepped into my pants, pulled
on my shirt, and scrambled down the narrow stairway to the parlor.
My pop was there, lighting a lantern wick.

"What is it?" I asked.

"I don't know," he said. His eyes shot up the staircase and he almost
told me to go back to my room. But then he looked at me and put his

hand on my shoulder. "Let's go see," he said. "Maybe somebody needs help."

The wind nearly tore our door from the hinges when we went out. The cold rain soaked us to the skin instantly. Water ran down the cobblestones like rapids. I can smell tornado weather now, and that's what I smelled that night, though I didn't realize it at the time. Twister weather charges the air with a fine, rich aroma—almost like the smell of fertile dirt.

The ground was already saturated from the rain we had received in previous days, and the water had nowhere to go but into the bayou. I remembered my bateau lifting mysteriously from the bank that morning. I knew what was happening. The bayou was coming up. It had been coming up all day.

The lantern came back down the street from Rayford Hayes' house. Rayford was in his nightshirt, his gun belt around his hips, his black boots on his pale legs, the key to the jailhouse in his hand. The tinsmith, Robert Timmons, carried the lantern.

"What's wrong?" my father asked as we fell into a trot beside them.

"The bayou's up!" Timmons shouted over the roar of the storm. "The Treat Inn and the jailhouse are flooded! We've got to get Brigginshaw out!"

When we got to the end of the cobblestones, we stopped and stood in shock, along with several other people who had brought lanterns out. The wharf was invisible under the rushing current. I had never seen the bayou go any faster than a crawl, but it was piling up against the cypress trees now. Billy and Carol Anne were helping their guests to high ground. The bayou was into the lower floor of their inn. The jailhouse was already half under. I could see Captain Brigginshaw's fists on the iron grating of the jailhouse door.

"My God!" Timmons shouted to Hayes. "It's come up two feet since I ran to get you!"

Hayes didn't hesitate. He ran upstream about thirty yards and waded in, feeling for footholds.

"Wait, Rayford!" my pop shouted. "You need a rope or something."

"No time!" the constable shouted.

I knew he was right. He had to get the jailhouse door open and help Captain Brigginshaw to the shore before the current grew too swift to cross. Brigginshaw wouldn't be able to swim well with a wounded leg. I made a move toward the water, but my pop held me back.

Constable Hayes was in up to his waist when he slipped. The water had filled his boots like sea anchors and dragged him down. He floundered helplessly, cartwheeling in the water, clawing at the bayou with the fist that held the key. The current carried him twenty feet away from the jailhouse door.

I tried to go in after him, but my pop held me back again. I saw Brigginshaw's arms reach through the iron grating, almost too thick to fit. "The key!" he shouted. "Throw the key, Rayford!"

The constable lobbed the key on the iron ring as he went under. It arched through the rain and hit the side of the jailhouse, about a foot beyond the Australian's reach. The captain drew his arms back into the jailhouse. I knew he was on his stomach, underwater, feeling for the key through the grating. I also knew he would not be able to reach it.

Without the key in his hand, the constable was able to stay afloat a little better. Then I saw Billy dive into the bayou after him. Carol Anne was helping the last of the inn guests up to the cobblestone street. I saw the expression of terror on her face when she saw Billy dive in.

Her eyes sparked something in me. I tore away violently from my father's grasp and plunged in to help. I heard Pop come in after me. The current carried us swiftly down to where Billy had grabbed Constable Hayes. I swam against the torrent as hard as I could, but still slipped quickly downstream. I passed the flooded Treat Inn as I reached Billy and Rayford, and grabbed the constable's arm. Pop was soon there with me, and the four of us drifted into the shadows. We pulled the constable out of the swift current, into shallow water. We finally found our footing behind the Treat Inn.

When we pulled him out, Hayes was coughing and heaving, but we knew he would survive. His boots and the weight of his gun belt would have killed him if not for Billy, my pop, and me.

"Get higher!" Billy shouted. "I'm going after Trevor."

The constable's hand grabbed Billy by the elbow. Hayes couldn't speak yet, but he shook his head, begging Billy not to go in again.

Billy pulled loose and ran through the water toward the Treat Inn, diving in and swimming up to the back porch.

I found more strength than I had ever known. I could have lifted Constable Hayes myself, but with Pop there to help, he felt light as a feather. We carried Hayes to high ground and came through a neck of brush to Widow Humphry's inn, where I dropped the constable and ran back toward the jailhouse.

Pop shouted for me to wait, but I tore on toward the flood. I saw Carol Anne holding onto Billy beside the rushing bayou. He had a crowbar in his hand that he had taken from his flooded store. She was crying, begging him not to go in after the Australian.

The jailhouse was almost flooded now, and the rain was coming down harder than ever. My pop overtook me and grabbed ahold of me with a permanence I knew I wouldn't break. He all but tackled me. Through the lashing rain and the roaring wind, I could hear the long, horrifying cry of Captain Brigginshaw:

"Biiillyyyy!"

I tried to fight my way closer to the rushing bayou. If Billy was going in, I wanted to help him. But my pop wrestled me down with a physical might I had never before felt him use. We slid down the muddy bank together and stopped near Billy and Carol Anne.

"Please, Billy!" she cried, pleading, clinging to him as my father was to me. "You can't help him!"

"Let me go!" he shouted.

"Billy! Billy! He's going to hang, Billy! Don't risk yourself for him! He's going to hang anyway!"

The big prisoner's desperate cry was nearly lost in the maelstrom of wind and water. "Biiillyyyy!" It sounded miles away.

Billy tore free of Carol Anne and sprinted up the bank with his crowbar. The lantern light from high ground illuminated her as she sank to her knees at the edge of the rising bayou and buried her face in her hands. My father would not let me go. I tasted tears of helplessness in the streams that ran down my face.

The hero Billy Treat dove into the water well upstream of the jail-house and let the current carry him to it. The water piling against the upstream side was almost going over the roof. I was wishing the flood would simply lift that roof off or tear it to pieces so Brigginshaw could get out. But I knew the chances of that were slim. The jailhouse had been built to prevent escapes. Iron bars rooted it deep into the ground to keep prisoners from jacking up the logs and crawling under. Trevor's only hope was Billy.

He came against the jailhouse door like an eagle landing on its prey. Brigginshaw had hardly a foot of breathing space left, and the bayou was still rising. I saw Billy's head bobbing, the arms of both men on the pry bar. I could see only the top of the iron door above the water, hoping any second to see it open. But even if it did, the two men would still have to swim to safety, and the Australian with a broken leg.

The current piled higher against the log jailhouse, obliterating hope as it pressed the air out. Maybe it was just my imagination, but the last glimpse I got of the jailhouse door before it went under was by the brief flare of a lightning bolt, and in that fleeting instant, I thought I saw it swinging open, away from the log wall.

A horrible creaking sound came to me from downstream, and I looked in time to see the Treat Inn floating from its foundation blocks. It drifted downstream like a toy and shook as it hit the trees and the abandoned dry dock behind it. The water was inching toward us, so my father pulled me to my feet and forced me up the bank to high ground.

I watched the Treat Inn shake and tilt strangely in the force of the flood, then my eyes turned to Carol Anne. She was backing away from the rising bayou, looking toward the jailhouse, her soaked dress plastered against her like a second skin. When she called his name, it came out as an animal scream:

"Billeee!"

I looked back toward the jail, but the bayou had sucked it completely under. It—like Billy Treat, Trevor Brigginshaw, and the wonderful summer of pearls—was gone.

23

WHEN THE RAIN STOPPED THE NEXT DAY, EVERY BOAT THAT HAD SURVIVED the storm was on the lake looking for traces of Treat and Brigginshaw. My bateau was not among the searchers. The lake had sucked it into some deep hole and buried it. After searching all day, the general feeling was that the bayou had done the same to Billy and the Australian.

The water receded amazingly fast. Less than twenty-four hours after the flood, the jailhouse poked back into view and began rising almost as quickly as it had sunk. Some men in a boat examined it before sundown and found that Billy and Trevor had succeeded in prying the jailhouse door open.

It was a relief to me. In the first place, I hated to think of Captain Brigginshaw drowning in there. I knew how he must have felt waiting for Billy to rescue him from the jail as Billy had rescued me from the *Glory of Caddo Lake*. In the second place, I didn't want to see them pull his body out.

Carol Anne remained down at the bayou from dawn to dusk that first day after the flood, waiting hopefully for a miracle. I felt bad enough about Billy, and I figured it probably hurt her twice as bad as it did me. That's why it surprised me so when she spoke to me. I was watching the men in the boat look over the jailhouse when I heard her steady voice touch my ears.

"He's out there, Ben," she said.

I turned and found her standing at my shoulder. "What?" I said, startled.

"Billy's a strong swimmer. He used to dive for pearls in the South Seas. I'm afraid Trevor's dead. He couldn't swim with that leg wound. But Billy's still out there. He'll turn up."

It was sad to hear her hanging on to a hope so slim. But it was also a little infectious. For a moment, I believed. Billy *was* one heck of a swimmer. "If my boat hadn't got washed away," I said, "I'd be out looking for him right now, myself."

She looked at me and smiled, and briefly I saw the flawless beauty I had once fallen in love with. She put her hand on my shoulder. "I know you would," she said. "Don't worry. He'll come back."

The Treat Inn had settled crookedly, about thirty yards from its original location, and it suddenly occurred to me that Carol Anne's home had been wrecked. "Where are you going to sleep tonight?" I asked.

"I'm staying in my old room above Snyder's store until Billy comes back. Then we're going to leave this town and start over somewhere."

The floodwaters were still subsiding when the town went to bed that night. No one could have guessed that the lake would continue to fall to a level lower than anyone—even Esau—could remember. But when the morning came, Cypress Bayou and Caddo Lake looked as if they had suffered six months of drought.

My pop was the first to figure it out. Those government snag-boat men who had been clearing the Great Raft from the Red River had made a gross error in their calculations. They had predicted that removal of the Raft would provide a better channel into Caddo Lake, opening our town to steamer traffic more of the year. What they had failed to figure out was that the logjam was actually a natural dam that caused Big

Cypress Bayou to back up, deepening Caddo Lake. The flood had washed away the last vestiges of the Great Raft and removed the natural dam, lowering the lake level instead of making it more navigable, leaving tens of thousands of acres of lake bed exposed.

The government, in one ill-planned stroke, had crippled our riverboat trade, drained our mussel beds, and doomed our town. I know it's not a productive thing to hold grudges in life, but I held a dim view of the government for decades because of what happened to Caddo Lake in '74.

The second day after the flood, Cecil and Adam and I walked over to Esau's place to find Goose Prairie Cove nothing more than a mudflat. Esau's shack had been flooded, but it was out of the way of currents and didn't get washed away. Esau was taking things out and setting them in the sun to dry.

"Good mornin', boys," he said, as if it were just another day. "Come to check the trotline? Sorry, but my boats all floated away or sank."

"What trotline?" Cecil said with no small tinge of disgust in his voice. "It probably got torn off into the lake somewhere."

"Probably so," Esau said. "Too bad, ain't it?"

"We just came down to let the hogs loose," I said. "Unless you want them."

The old Choctaw reached for the ever-present flask of whiskey in his hip pocket. He took a small swig, same as always.

It struck me that I had never seen him empty that flask. I had never even seen it near empty. I wondered if he ever really drank any whiskey at all. He shook his head as he put the flask away. "No," he said, "I don't want them hogs. Let 'em go back to the woods. You boys breakin' up your partnership?"

I hadn't exactly thought of it that way, but it seemed as if that was what we were doing. Adam looked at me and I looked at Cecil. Cecil looked out across the ugly field of mud that had once felt the toes of a thousand pearl-hunters.

"I guess," Cecil said. "Me and Ben have to go back to the Academy in a couple of weeks. Adam's old man will have his ass out in the fields, if the flood left them anything to harvest. We don't have a trotline. We don't have any mussels to feed the hogs. We don't have a boat to haul water in, or any pearl-hunters to sell water to."

"We ain't got a damn nickel for all the work we done all summer," Adam added. "Ben don't even have his Ashenback no more."

Esau stood and looked at us sadly for a moment. He was trying to think of something to say that would cheer us up. I beat him to it.

"But we're still partners," I said. "Always will be." I started to hike up to the hog pens. "Well, come on," I said, looking back. "Don't y'all want to see them run?"

I saw the eyes of Adam and Cecil brighten, and knew I had said the right thing.

We let the logs down on one side of our pigpen and had a great time chasing the hogs into the hills, yelling like wild Indians until we were too winded to run any farther. Then we collapsed in the pine needles and talked for hours about everything that had happened that summer. We had survived fights over girls and money. We had gotten rich and gone broke together. We were better friends than ever.

We made a promise to one another that morning under the pines, and we never forgot that promise. We vowed to remain friends and partners until we died. The three of us turned out different when we grew up, but we never lost our friendship. The last time all three of us were together, we were old men, fishing on Caddo Lake. Now I'm the only partner left.

I wish the summer of pearls had ended right there. In fact, as my partners and I walked back to Esau's shack about noon, with the intention of helping him clean his place up, I was sure it was over. I knew that none of the good things about that summer would ever come back, but I didn't think anything else bad could happen. That's when I looked out over what had once been Goose Prairie Cove and saw a familiar figure slogging through the mudflats.

At the time, nobody had connected Judd Kelso with the Christmas Nelson gang or the attempted pearl robbery. The only two witnesses to the crime—Brigginshaw and Colton—were gone. With Captain Brig-ginshaw wounded, Constable Hayes hadn't interrogated him thor-oughly on the subject. Trevor may have told Billy about Kelso's involvement in the robbery attempt, but Billy was missing, too, and presumed by almost everybody but Carol Anne to be dead. In fact, it wasn't until years later that I was able to prove Kelso had taken part in the crime.

"What the hell is he doing?" Cecil asked the old Choctaw.

Esau sneered as his black eyes angled toward the drained cove. "Lookin' for mussels."

"Pearl-hunting?" I asked.

Esau nodded.

"What for?" I asked.

"He's a fool," the old man said. It was the first time I had ever heard him speak ill of anybody. "You boys come to help me clean up?"

"Yep," Adam said. "What do you want us to do?"

"Just take everything out to dry. Then we'll shovel the mud."

I worked around Esau's place for a couple of hours, until I looked up and saw Kelso sitting in one of Esau's chairs, covered with mud. He was holding a keg of whiskey over his head, letting the liquor trickle into his mouth from the open spigot. He cut his malicious little eyes toward me and caught me staring at him. I was afraid of him. I had seen him rough up the rousters on the old *Glory of Caddo Lake*. It worried me to have him there with no Billy Treat or Trevor Brigginshaw around to handle him.

Cecil, on the other hand, threw a shovelful of mud right past him and went to talking business with him as if he were any other citizen. "Find any pearls?" he asked.

Kelso put the keg on his knee. "Hell, no. Ain't like it's your business anyway, boy."

Cecil leaned on the shovel handle, as he had been doing most of the afternoon. "What are you going to do with one if you do find it? We don't have a pearl-buyer anymore."

The gator eyes squinted as Kelso smiled. "Don't you know?"

"Know what?"

"Boy, how old are you?"

"Fourteen."

"Haven't you ever got your peter wet?"

Cecil straightened. "Maybe I have."

"Maybe!" Kelso put the keg in the mud and laughed. "That's a sure sign you never have if you have to say maybe. Boy, when I was you age, I had me my own nigger gal. Got her three times a day if I wanted."

Cecil turned red out of anger and embarrassment. "What's that got to do with pearls?"

"Things is back to usual around here, ain't they? That goddam Billy Treat and that big Australian son of a bitch are gator bait. The town's back to what it was before summer. I'm gonna find me a shell slug and go get me a piece of that whore."

I felt a sickness rise in my stomach. "What whore?" I asked.

Kelso picked up the whiskey keg. "Pearl Cobb," he said, pouring the liquor down his throat again.

My fear of him gave way to worry and anger. "Her name's Carol Anne, and she's not a whore."

He spewed whiskey from his mouth as the keg came down to his knee. He coughed and laughed as the cruel gator eyes locked onto me. "She was Treat's whore, wasn't she? Soon as I find me a shell slug, she'll be mine." He put the keg back on the ground. "I'll owe you for the whiskey," he yelled to Esau as he trudged back toward the muddy cove.

I watched him dig for mussels and open them all afternoon, hoping he wouldn't find so much as a dust pearl. If he did, I planned to run ahead of him to warn Carol Anne, and maybe alert Rayford Hayes. I felt as if Billy were counting on me to look after Carol Anne now that he was gone—or until he got back. I was still holding on to the hope I had caught from Carol Anne. The hope that said Billy was still alive and just lost in a cypress brake somewhere, trying to find his way home.

Finally, though, Kelso came up from the cove about sundown without anything to show for his day of hunting. My partners and I left when we saw him coming. He looked to be in a sour mood and we didn't want to hang around if he was going to get drunk.

When we got to town, I said so long to Cecil and Adam and went home for supper. I didn't have much of an appetite. All the way through the meal, I worried about Kelso finding a pearl. Maybe the next day, or the day after. I couldn't talk to my folks about it. Especially not to my mother. They were awful quiet over supper, too. The only thing Pop said was that he was going to have to drop four pages from the paper and go back to a weekly format.

After we ate, I helped clear the table, then started to slip out through the front door.

"Where are you going, Ben?" my father asked.

He caught me off guard. We had a deal that I could go out and prowl at night, as long as I didn't get into any trouble and came home by nine-thirty. I usually ended up looking through a knothole at Esau's, or spying on some girl who had a habit of leaving her curtains open. Now I knew, however, that those ungentlemanly pursuits were behind me.

"I don't know. I guess I'll go over to Cecil's." That was a lie. I knew exactly where I was going, but I didn't feel comfortable telling my pop about it. He would probably have tried to stop me. I was going to tell Constable Hayes that Kelso had been making noise about bothering Carol Anne. Then I was going to watch her room. But this time I wouldn't be trying to peep at her through the curtains. I would be guarding her, in case Kelso showed up.

"All right," Pop said. "Just be back by ten."

I smiled. "Yes, sir." Some kids' folks never let them grow up. When I became a father, years later, I learned how difficult it was to let my kids go out on their own. My pop let me do a lot of growing-up that summer.

Rayford Hayes' wife, Hattie, greeted me at the front door. "Well, hello, Ben. Come in." She shouted at her husband, in another room: "Rayford, your little hero is here to see you."

Constable Hayes came out of the back room, bootless. "Howdy,

Ben," he said. "If you've come to check on me, you might as well go home. I'm sound as a horse, thanks to you and your old man. And Billy Treat, God rest his soul."

"I didn't come to check on you, sir," I said. "I wanted to talk to you about something."

Hayes motioned to a chair near the dark fireplace. "Have a seat," he said, "and tell me what's on you mind."

I looked nervously at Hattie. "Well, it's kind of . . . I don't think Mrs. Hayes wants to hear about it."

The constable wrinkled his brow at me for a second, then held back a smile. "Well, you heard the boy, Hattie," he said to his wife. "Excuse yourself."

"Oh, all right," she said.

When she left, I told the constable about what Judd Kelso had said that afternoon at Esau's saloon. I could tell by the expression on Hayes' face that he took me seriously. "So, Kelso's back at Goose Prairie," he said, rubbing his head. "I was hoping he would stay at his place over on Long Point." He leaned back in a creaking wooden chair and asked me a lot of questions, several times making me repeat exactly what Kelso had said about Carol Anne.

"I could keep an eye on her place," I suggested.

"No, Ben, don't do that. That's not your worry. I'll have a talk with her tomorrow and warn her. Delicate subject, though. Maybe I'll send Mrs. Hayes to do it—woman to woman. Anyway, I wouldn't worry about it. Kelso's not likely to bother her unless he finds a pearl, and that's not likely, either. I bet he'll give up and quit town in a day or two, go on back to Long Point, or head to Shreveport to find work on another steamer. Sure won't find any steamers to work on around here." He got up. "Thank you for bringing it to my attention, though. I'll keep an eye out for him."

I rose and shook the constable's hand. Just as I was leaving, Hattie burst into the parlor from the back room, pale as a sheet and out of breath.

"My God, woman!" Rayford said. "What's gotten into you?"

"It's gone!" she said, gasping.

"What's gone?"

She pointed into the back room. "The leather case with the pearls and the money in it!"

"What do you mean, 'gone'?" her husband demanded.

"I just went to check on it again, and it's not there!"

"Are you sure?"

"Yes!"

"When was the last time you saw it?"

"I took it out to look at the pearls just before supper. Then I put it back. Now it's gone!"

"Gone where, woman?"

"The window was open," she said, almost crying. "I think somebody reached in and stole it!"

A terrible notion struck me. "Mr. Hayes," I said, "what if Kelso took it?"

"Now, calm down, everybody," he said. "Just stay put. Let me get my pistol and I'll look into this."

But I could not stay put or wait for Hayes to find his pistol. Kelso could have stolen the pearls an hour ago. He could have been in Carol Anne's room long enough to . . .

I tore out through the front door and barely heard the constable shouting at me to wait. I wondered what I would do if I found Kelso in Carol Anne's room. I didn't have a clue. I just knew I had to get to her room fast.

I knew the hidden passageways of Port Caddo better than anybody. I cut behind houses and leaped picket fences like a deer. I sprinted like a boy with a mean dog on his heels, but felt twice as terrified.

I had seen too many things go wrong already. The *Glory of Caddo Lake* had sunk, almost taking me with it. The pearl beds had been drained. The riverboat channels had run shallow. Billy and Trevor had been swept away by the flood. I could not stand to think of Judd Kelso forcing himself on Carol Anne now. That would be the worst thing of all. Port Caddo had seen enough ruin for one summer.

When I turned the back corner of Jim Snyder's store, I saw no light in Carol Anne's room. I sprinted up the stairs, taking three steps at a time. I have never run faster in my life, but I felt as if I were wading chest-deep in molasses. A thousand thoughts went through my mind before I reached the top of the flight.

I pounded on the door. I heard someone call my name from back toward Hayes' house. I probably didn't wait half a second before bursting into Carol Anne's room.

I spoke to her as I entered, took two steps, and tripped over a bulk on the floor that I knew in an instant was human. I landed on the leather satchel and heard pearls rolling across the wooden flooring. I bounced once, scrambled to the back of the room, and turned to see the vague form of a human torso against the faint moonlight streaming through the door. One pale moonbeam glinted against the metal handle of a knife, jutting straight up from the dead body.

I couldn't tell if it was a man or a woman. The clothes were wadded and wrinkled in such a way that I couldn't even tell if the dead person was lying face-down or face-up. But I could clearly make out the severe lines of the knife handle, its blade buried deep in the corpse.

I heard people coming, but could not move. I thought of every possibility. At best, the body belonged to Judd Kelso. At worst, it was Carol Anne. I might as well have been dead myself for all the good I did huddled on the floor. I suddenly wondered if I was the only living person in the room. Maybe a knife would find my chest next.

I heard footsteps on the stairs and heard my father call my name. The light from a swinging lantern cast strange shadows up the staircase. When it filled the doorway, the light blinded me for a second. Then I identified Judd Kelso, lying dead on the floor between my father and me, and felt a surge of relief. At my feet was the leather satchel, money and pearls spilling from its open mouth.

Pop looked at the dead man as Constable Hayes came to his side, gasping for breath, holding his pistol in his hand.

"Ben," Pop said. "Are you all right?" He hurdled the dead man and helped me up.

"Yes, sir," I said.

"Who?" He pointed at the body and looked at me as if I might have stabbed Kelso myself.

"I don't know. I tripped over him coming in."

Hayes put his hand on Kelso's throat. "Still warm," he said. "Hasn't been long." He looked at me. "What about the woman? Where is she?"

"She wasn't here," I said. "She's gone."

24

CAROL ANNE COBB VANISHED FROM PORT CADDO LIKE A FOG, AND THE mystery over who killed Judd Kelso began. I have heard all sorts of theories. Most people believe Carol Anne killed Kelso, then fled town, fearing Kelso's people over at Long Point would seek revenge.

I never did believe that. If the knife had been in Kelso's back, I could have considered it. But I never saw how Carol Anne, a healthy young woman though she was, could have overpowered Kelso face-to-face.

Some wild imaginations have come to the conclusion that I killed Judd Kelso. They say I caught him trying to force himself on Carol Anne and plunged the kitchen knife into his chest. They say Carol Anne agreed to disappear then, to make everyone think she had killed him, so the Kelso clan wouldn't come after me.

Take my word for it, that theory is hogwash. Even if you won't take my word, consider this: at fourteen, I wasn't strong enough to take on Judd Kelso, either. And as long as they lived, my Pop and Rayford Hayes swore I couldn't have killed Kelso. They had entered Carol Anne's room only a minute behind me. They knew I didn't have time to kill Kelso and help Carol Anne disappear.

Besides, if I had killed Kelso, I would still be bragging about it today instead of denying it.

A third theory says the Christmas Nelson gang killed Kelso for trying to take all the pearls and money for himself. That doesn't make a lick of sense, of course. Trevor Brigginshaw's satchel was left in Carol Anne's room. Those outlaws would have taken it with them if they had killed Kelso. Kelso was killed for reasons other than greed.

The wildest explanation of all says that Billy Treat rose from the swamps and killed Judd Kelso to rescue his true love. I liked this theory, of course, but where was the proof? For four decades, I tried to think of a way Billy could have come out of the flood alive. It wasn't really all that difficult to imagine. Billy could swim like an alligator and hold his breath almost as long. He could have survived the flood that washed him and the Australian out of the Port Caddo jailhouse.

But why did it take him two days to get back to town? Over the years, I came up with a lot of possible reasons. Maybe Brigginshaw survived the flood, too, and Billy had to help him escape to Louisiana before returning to Port Caddo.

Or, if Brigginshaw drowned, which seemed more likely, Billy could have been trapped in a cypress tree anywhere between Carter's Chute and Whangdoodle Pass for a full day before the water went down. A stranger to Caddo Lake, Billy could have wandered another day in the swamps trying to find his way back to town.

Then what? Perhaps Billy got to Carol Anne's room shortly after Judd Kelso did, or shortly before. Either way, once both men were there, the fight started, and Kelso grabbed a kitchen knife. Billy took it from him and killed him with it. He would have been strong enough, even after spending two exhausting days in the bayous. He had plenty of motive.

And Carol Anne's disappearance? How did I explain that one to myself? She and Billy were wise to quit town after Kelso was killed. The Kelso clan had been thick in the old Regulator-Moderator feud. Violence didn't spook them. They would have sought revenge.

Eventually I found out what happened, but you'll have to take my word for it. There is no solid proof. Only my word. You have to understand that the summer of pearls became a lifelong obsession for me. A few years after it was over, I started investigating all its angles and facets, and continued searching for clues for forty years. I repeatedly questioned everybody involved, from Giff Newton to Emil Pipes. I searched old records and newspaper reports. I turned up a lot of evidence, but the final proof found its own way to me.

After the government accidentally drained Caddo Lake, a few riverboats continued to steam all the way up to Jefferson, but only during the wettest of times. Port Caddo declined steadily.

In just five years, there was not enough of a town left there to support my pop's newspaper, so my folks moved to Mount Pleasant, where they died as honored and respected citizens of that town, after forty-seven years of good news coverage. I was nineteen and mature enough to make my own decisions when the *Steam Whistle* went under. I didn't follow my folks to Mount Pleasant. I stayed in the old family place at Port Caddo. I also talked my pop out of any of his old notes that in any way related to the summer of pearls.

To my surprise, I found Billy Treat's diary among Pop's notes. Pop said he found the diary in the Treat Inn the day after the flood. I'm sure Billy had always kept a diary, but his old one would have been destroyed when the *Glory* went under. The diary Pop found began the day after the boiler explosion, and ended with the night of the flood. Billy made amazingly detailed entries, sometimes even recording conversations he had had with Carol Anne or Brigginshaw. That diary, more than anything, sparked my need to know everything about the summer of pearls.

The year my folks left Port Caddo, I finally took my trip down to New Orleans—by rail—and hunted up Joshua Lagarde, the insurance investigator who had looked into the sinking of the *Glory of Caddo Lake*. He told me that the owners of the *Glory* had been convicted in a number of insurance-fraud cases and multiple claims. One of the owners had confessed after a two-day police interrogation and named Judd Kelso as the man hired to blow up the *Glory*.

When I got back to Port Caddo, I learned that Charlie Ashenback had died while I was gone. I spent my last pennies buying his tools from his heirs, who lived in Dallas. I started building my own boats, but it took me thirty years to learn how to make a bateau that would stand up against an Ashenback.

Cecil Peavy moved down to Nacogdoches shortly after that and went into business. I went down there to see him every winter until he died a few years ago. And he came back to Caddo Lake every summer to go fishing with me and Adam. When it was all over for Cecil, he owned four stores, two cafés, and a hotel—and didn't have to do a lick of manual labor in one of them. He created a lot of jobs in Nacogdoches. His employees hated him, though.

Some time in the eighties, things got hot around here for the Christmas Nelson gang. They went west and tried to rob a bank in Waco. The Texas Rangers were waiting for them. Every member of the gang was killed, except for Christmas himself, and he was shot eight times and captured.

When I heard about the arrest, I spent my entire bankroll getting to Waco. It had occurred to me that if Judd Kelso had stolen the pearl satchel the night of his death, maybe he had been in on the attempted robbery aboard the *Slough Hopper* three nights earlier. I was the first person to even think about linking Kelso to the Christmas Nelson gang.

Posing as a New Orleans newspaper reporter, I wangled an interview with Christmas Nelson in jail. He was the most pleasant and well-mannered man I have ever met, but he was also a cold-blooded killer and didn't mind telling you about it. Among other things, he told me that he and four of his men were in Port Caddo the morning the boilers blew on the *Glory of Caddo Lake*. They were the horsemen who had rescued so many passengers.

I grilled him thoroughly on the attempted pearl robbery, of course. He told me that the Kelso clan over on Long Point often let his gang hide out on their place. He said Judd Kelso had come up with the idea of robbing Trevor Brigginshaw. He also said he kicked Kelso out of the gang for jumping off of the *Slough Hopper* like a coward when the shooting started. He claimed he would have come to Port Caddo to steal the pearls if he had known Captain Brigginshaw was in jail, or presumed drowned. But he didn't know. He also said he would have gladly killed Judd Kelso, but didn't.

When I returned broke to Port Caddo, Adam Owens told me he had fallen in love with a girl from Buzzard's Bay, across the Louisiana line. Eventually he tried to marry her, but she jilted him—actually left him standing at the altar in front of all the wedding guests. It almost destroyed him. He started drinking and lived like a hermit in a filthy shack up Kitchen's Creek, across the lake. He used to shoot at people who came up the creek. He even shot at me once.

I finally got him to give up drinking, but I had to move in with him for a year to do it. We fixed up his house and he stayed there until he died. Never married. I don't think he ever knew the pleasure of having a woman in bed. He was my friend for life, and a wonderfully innocent kind of fellow. He knew things about animals and nature that God shares with only a few chosen mortals.

I went to find that girl Cindy from Longview once, and found out she had gotten married and fat. I went through a lot of girlfriends and finally fell in love with a beautiful thing from Marshall. I married her and moved her to the house in Port Caddo. She became my best friend, most horrific critic, constant debating partner, and the love of my life. We had a wonderfully successful marriage and I have five kids and twelve grandkids to prove it. I lose count of the great-grandkids.

By the turn of the century, the riverboat trade and Port Caddo were dead. My family was the only one living in the deserted city that had once been a port of entry to the Republic of Texas. Our house stood like an oasis of life in the ghost town.

About that time, I got the notion to go to Chicago and look in the Pinkerton Detective Agency records to see what Henry Colton had written in his reports. I had to sneak out in the middle of the night, because my wife didn't want me spending the money on my silly obsession with that summer of '74.

Those Pinkertons were a peculiar bunch, and wouldn't hear of any old bayou rat snooping around in their files. I had to bribe one of the office workers to get Colton's reports for me. They made up some of the most humorous writing I have ever enjoyed.

Colton had led an unbelievably reckless life as a Pinkerton, and was a pretty successful detective, except that he had a habit of shooting people the Pinkertons wanted him to take alive for questioning. He also drank too much, fought too often, and treated all good-looking women like prostitutes. The International Gemstones case was his last chance as a Pinkerton, and he failed in the most permanent kind of way.

His final report was written aboard the *Slough Hopper*, just after his shoot-out with the Christmas Nelson gang. He was sure proud of himself in that report. I guess he died happy.

To keep my wife from divorcing me on grounds of abandonment, I had to swear on the family Bible that I wouldn't go off on any more wild-goose chases. I was out of leads, anyway. I had spent a fortune sending letters of inquiry to every postmaster and newspaper editor in the states of New York and New Jersey, trying to track down Billy Treat's family. The only leads I got turned out to be false ones.

I finally resigned myself to the fact that I would never know who had killed Judd Kelso. I would never find out what had happened to Carol Anne that night. I would never know for sure if Billy was alive or dead. The summer of pearls would have to remain an enigma to me. It had become sort of a tragic legend around Caddo Lake by that time. As I reached my fiftieth year, I became known as the unofficial historian for the Great Caddo Lake Pearl Rush. People would come around to ask me about the stabbing death of Kelso, and we would talk about all the theories. To most folks, it was just a story. To me, it was real—an image I carried with me all day long, every day, then even into sleep. It was only then—when I resigned myself to search no longer—that the proof found its own way to me.

The summer of pearls prepared me for life. It was like a lifetime in itself. It was that summer when I made and lost my first fortune. I have made and lost many more since then. It was that summer when I first got my heart broke. It got broke many more times before I finally found my wife. And it's even been broke a few times *because* of my wife. That summer I forged the friendships that sustained me through life. Friendships that even death cannot end, but only interrupt. Friendships that will resume in the afterlife. It was that summer that I learned life would not always be simple, or fun, or easy. Neither would it always be complicated, or painful, or hard.

It was the summer I learned nothing would stay the same. Change would come, and come again, and destroy things, and strengthen things, and shock, and soothe, and sadden, and fill with rapture. That is why I should not have been surprised by the most astounding change of all, but I was.

The government, after thirty-seven years, finally decided to repair the damage it had done to Caddo Lake in '74. It built a new dam down at Mooringsport, Louisiana, that raised the level of the lake to what it had been in the days of the Great Raft.

As soon as I heard about them building the dam, I bought the piece of land where old Esau had once run his saloon. My wife thought I was crazy, but I knew the lake would fill Goose Prairie Cove again, and make a fine location for a fishing camp, hunting lodge, and boat-building yard.

The lake came up just as the government said it would, believe it or not, and I began to make a pretty tolerable living. My wife and I built a new house where the pearl camps had once stood. If I had told her that I had situated it to overlook the spot where I had once kissed a girl named Cindy who hailed from Longview, she would have done me in like Judd Kelso was done in.

Then it happened. The thing that ended all my torturous questions about Kelso, Carol Anne, Billy, and Trevor Brigginshaw. Proof came to my fishing camp, for only my eyes to see, and my ears to hear.

EPILOGUE

Goose Prairie Cove, 1944

I AM AN OLD MAN NOW. I ALONE REMEMBER THE SUMMER OF PEARLS. I HAVE told everything I saw with my own eyes as it happened to me. The parts I didn't witness personally, I have told as a story, but I know those parts as if I *had* been there, and I can prove them through documents, statements, and interviews.

This last part I cannot prove, however, because the proof came to visit only me. And it is the final, clinching evidence. This incident I am about to tell you happened thirty years ago. I never told it to anyone else, because I was protecting someone. But those I sought to protect were older than I was, and so must have died years ago. There is no longer anyone to protect. You wanted to know about the summer of pearls, and here is the final chapter.

It happened a couple of years after the government dam raised the lake level, and exactly forty years after the summer of pearls. It was 1914. One day, a Cadillac automobile drove down to my fishing camp. The sun was just rising on a summer morning, warm and humid. There was a thunderhead in the west, and I was hoping we might get some rain, but the dark cloud didn't take up much of the sky.

I was trying to decide whether or not I should water the vegetable garden when I heard the Cadillac coming down the old Port Caddo Road to my fishing camp.

Thinking a rich sportsman had come to hire me to guide him at hunting and fishing, I walked to the front gate to greet the automobile. The driver's door opened and an old man stepped out. He was a good seventy years at least, but he stood straight as a pine. Instantly, I felt that I recognized him, yet couldn't quite place him.

"Mornin'," I said. "Can I help you?"

He looked me up and down. "Mind if we look around?"

"Not at all. Can I show you a cabin?"

"No, thanks. We just want to look around."

"Feel free," I said.

The moment I saw him walk, I remembered Billy Treat. Some things about people don't change, even with age. It could be him, I thought. But I had made that mistake before. I was always looking for Billy wherever I went, and never finding him.

The door on the passenger side opened, and an old woman got out. The old man met her at the front of the car and they came through the gate. As she walked by me, she looked at me, smiled, and pulled her collar together at her throat, as if against some kind of chill.

I had to wonder if it was Carol Anne. Of course there was no way I could have recognized her, even if it was her. The Carol Anne I remembered was the peerless beauty of my fourteenth year who would never grow old, never wrinkle, never die.

I watched them walk to the lakeshore. They seemed like something from a dream to me. The old man found the place where Esau's shack had once stood. He took the woman's hand and they walked along the shore, pointing at landmarks, talking, even laughing. They spent about fifteen minutes on the shore. Then they walked back to the gate.

I intercepted them at the car. "Sure you don't want to stay?" I asked.

"No, thanks," the old man said. "But we appreciate you letting us look around."

I caught the old woman's eyes and raced to her side of the car to

open the door for her. "Come back any time," I told her. "Fishing's been good."

"Thank you," she said. When she bent forward to crouch into the car, a gold chain swung like a pendulum from under her collar. I only got a glimpse of it before she grabbed it and tucked it back in at her throat, but I swore I recognized it. The Treat Pearl. The perfect orb that had launched that wonderful summer, long ago.

Two doors shut me out and the car started. That Cadillac was the first automobile I ever saw that had an electric starter, and it caught me by surprise when it cranked itself up.

"Wait!" I shouted, over the engine noise. The car backed away. "Wait!" I waved like a madman and ran to the driver's side. I banged on the window until the old man stopped. "Let the glass down!" I yelled, making motions with my hand.

The old man lowered the window and looked at me. "Well?" he said, in a demanding tone of voice.

No, I wasn't absolutely sure. It could have been another pearl. But I had to know, even if it meant making a fool out of myself. "I was wondering . . ." I began. "Whatever happened . . ."

The old man swallowed and gripped the steering wheel tighter.

"Whatever happened to Captain Trevor Brigginshaw?"

He tensed in the driver's seat and faked a look of ignorance. "Sir, I don't know what you're talking about."

Then the handsome old woman put her hand on his arm and leaned over him to look at me through the car window. "He died, Ben," she said. "About ten years ago on the island of Mangareva. He went there to live after he sent back all the money he had taken from that gemstone company. He sent us a photograph once of his wife and three beautiful little dark-skinned children. He was dressed like an island native. Can you believe that?"

I stared at her in awe and felt years of sorrow wash away from me. "Yes," I said. "I believe it."

The old man was still staring. "Ben?" he said. "Ben . . . Crowell! My goodness, boy, you're an old man!"

I laughed, and felt tears of gratitude filling my eyes, but I held them back.

"We had to leave, Ben," Carol Anne said. "If they ever found out we helped Trevor escape. . . . Then there was the Kelso clan. . . . We *had* to leave."

I nodded. "I know. I've missed you both, but I understand."

Billy Treat flashed the biggest smile I had ever seen him wear. "I'm glad it's you, Ben. I'm glad you're here."

I smiled back at them until I could no longer keep the tears from coming down my old weathered cheeks.

Carol Anne stroked a few tears away from her eyes as well. "We have to go now, Ben."

I nodded and stepped away from the car. Billy put it in gear. He smiled at me and drove away. I didn't wave as they left. I just watched until the Cadillac disappeared over the hill toward the ghost town of Port Caddo.

I stood in the road for a while, then walked down to the lake. My wife came to the back door of the house. "Who was that, Ben?" she shouted. I waved her off. She wouldn't understand. Nobody would.

I took off my shoes and waded in, feeling for mussels with my toes. I had suffered bouts of nostalgia before, but never one like this. As I found the mussels, I opened them with my pocket knife and probed carefully at the unfortunate little animals. I heard the rumble of thunder again to the west, but didn't even look at the sky.

A couple of my cabin guests rowed out to the lake in one of my boats to do some fishing. "Going to bait a trotline, Ben?" one of them asked.

"Nope," I replied. "I'm pearl-hunting."

They laughed and floated over the stumps of cypress trees that had been cut down during the years of low water.

I had left my hat in the garden, and when the morning sun rose over the treetops, I felt it beating down on the bald spot on the back of my head, so I waded out. The summer of pearls was long ago.

About that time, my son, Ben, Jr., drove up in his Model T and

dropped his three kids off at the gate. I was expecting them. Junior waved at me, and drove on.

The thunder spoke to me again—a long grumble. This time, I looked. The dark cloud had come closer, but was drifting north. It would not rain on me today. I should water the garden. A light-gray curtain of rain was slanting from the cloud, and the morning sun was striking it. A rainbow was beginning to form.

Just as I looked down for the garden hose on the ground, something white bulged from the side of the dark, drifting thunderhead. I glanced back up to the west and saw a chalky moon, almost perfectly round, peeking out from behind the cloud as it moved north. The moon was falling fast, nothing between it and the horizon but a rainbow. It would be gone in a minute.

"Hi, Pop," Ben the Third yelled. He was seven, and his little sisters were five and four.

"Come here, kids!" I called, waving them toward the garden. They met me at the garden gate. "You kids remember me telling you about the summer of pearls?"

"Yeah, all the time, Pop," Ben the Third said. "You're not gonna tell us again, are you?"

"No, but remember how I told you that someday I'd show you a pearl?"

The girls got more excited than their brother. "You found a pearl?" Vickie shrieked. "Where is it? Let me see!"

"Let me see!" Connie said, hopping like her older sister.

I glanced to the west. The moon was diving like a kingfisher. And the rainbow—why, it was waiting there, its colors growing deeper and richer. The moon and the rainbow were just about to touch. "I don't have a real pearl," I said, "but I'm going to show you exactly what one looks like."

I lined them up and turned them westward. "See the moon?" I said.

"I see it," Ben the Third answered.

"And a rainbow!" Connie squealed.

"Watch!"

The moon slipped behind that rainbow as a little wind came from somewhere and whipped the shower into a light mist, heightening the hues in the arching bands of color. The moon seemed to slide along inside the curve of that rainbow, all the way to the horizon, like a South Seas god riding to Earth.

The girls clutched at my arms, and Ben the Third bear-hugged my waist. Their little gasps told me they knew how rare a moment it was.

Billy Treat was right. It was one in ten thousand. It was just like a pearl.